Self
Realization

The est and Forum Phenomena

in American Society

ESPY M. NAVARRO &

ROBERT NAVARRO

This book was printed in the United States of America.

To order additional copies of this book, contact:
Xlibris Corporation
1-888-7-XLIBRIS
www.Xlibris.com
Orders@Xlibris.com
14026

CONTENTS

PART 3 –

The Effect of est on Our Society

APPENDIX

DEDICATION

This book is dedicated to Werner Erhard and to all of the est and Forum graduates who created a new possibility in life.

Preface

"There is no such thing as attainment when it comes to being spiritual."

In these days of ever increasing violence, confusion, despair and mistrust, it is useful to revisit the est training and the Forum series. Spun from the mind of Werner Erhard in his quest to make a difference in the world, the perspectives from est and the Forum offer many profound insights into our own self-realization of who we really are as human beings. While we have made numerous technological advances, and have even sent space interplanetary probes into the farthest reaches of our solar system and beyond, in terms of the exploration of our own consciousness we are but "babes in the woods." In spite of everything that we have done, the persistence of the major problems of the world such as hunger, disease, environmental degradation, violence and poverty points to the undeniable fact that our world does not work for everyone.

Inevitably, religion gets invoked in any discussion on these matters. While almost all religions center upon God as the great prime mover, what gets lost in the religious process is the true spirit of what it means to be a human being. Probably Werner Erhard said it best when he stated that, "Belief in God is the greatest single barrier to God in the Universe. Experiencing God is experiencing God, and that is true religion." The true spirituality is perception—*to see things thoroughly all the way through to the end*. Again, to quote Werner Erhard, "The point is to be de-hypnotized, to go beyond the mind, to what I call

---

11

the Self." The problem is that religion has and is being used to promote courses of action that are detrimental to our existence—even to the point of justifying suicidal events. How does one begin to deal with the dangers of terrorism, war, sabotage and other violent acts that are rooted in centuries of cultural traditions that justify such actions as being "righteous" and which are done in the name of God? Where is the dignity and integrity in the behaviors that perpetrate such repressive, hateful, barbaric, evil and destructive acts?

We owe each other the respect that will enable us to thrive as a benevolent civilization. All that we can state is that we should be "star-trekking" by now instead of being stuck in problems that we could easily solve if only each of us acted with total responsibility and freedom. What point is there to fighting endless wars, to constantly having to deal with epidemics caused by our own carelessness, and to perpetually deal with famines that arise out of our arbitrarily assigned economic, political and social demarcations? All of the rules that we have set up have only served to create chaos in the world. As Werner Erhard summed it up once, "They want rules for life and not the truth about life." As long as we persist in a state of denial about what is going on in the world, we will continue to suffer and struggle in the futile attempt to straighten things out. While no one has "the answer" to our predicament, we must certainly move away from everything that we have attempted and which has not worked. Our viability and our mutual survival as a species are what are at stake in this matter. It behooves us to think profoundly in a realm that transcends our normal everyday set of circumstances—to take the next step forward in our interrelated and interdependent journey as human beings on a path of harmony and enrichment.

Espy M. and Robert Navarro

PART 1 –

What est Was All About

"A lot of disciplines feel that they are spiritual so they can let it all hang out. If they let it all hang out, they will never make it in this world, and this is the world that can use it, not the other one. The other world is already spiritual."

Introduction

"You have got to figure out for yourself whether you are on a total ego trip or whether you are telling the truth[1]."

The est Phenomenon

The Beginnings

Werner Erhard (aka John Paul "Jack" Rosenberg) is the founder of est[2], an organization that began in California in October 1971, and that later became known as the Forum in the mid-1980's after Erhard closed down the original form of the training. The name that he pegged for himself was derived from an article that Rosenberg had read entitled "The New Germany." He took his first name from the German physicist Werner Heisenberg and his last name from the German economist Ludwig Erhard. This was done to avoid being traced by the members of the Philadelphia police department who were looking for him in connection with the abandonment of his family in 1960.

Erhard started this series of trainings as a result of his direct experience of "enlightenment" that occurred while driving his black Ford Mustang on a freeway in 1971 while en route to crossing the San Francisco Golden Gate Bridge in California. Before this time, Erhard had been an instructor for Mind Dynamics, a four-day training course that had been started by Alexander Everett. Everett had in turn been influenced by the works of Edgar Cayce, Jose Silva, Rudolph Steiner and the Rosicrucians. Erhard had also been a salesman for Grolier, and had previously taken a variety of trainings in several disciplines—including Zen, Subud, Transcendental Meditation and Scientology. He had immersed himself in all of these disciplines with a purpose of finding out the basic underpinnings of human behavior, or in his own words, for the purpose of "getting it." After his insight of self-realization and actualization on that day in California, he decided to share this experience with others, to take responsibility for his own transformation as a result of this experience, and to confront all of his past deeds and misbehaviors for the purpose of "cleaning them up."

Some Marker Events

In October 1971, Werner Erhard incorporated as est—Erhard Seminars Training and opened his first office in San Francisco, California with Laurel Scheaf as President of est. This was the beginning of the seminars for both adults—led by Werner Erhard—and for children—led by Phyllis Allen. In November 1971, the first college training occurred. By May 1972, a total of 1000 graduates had been achieved. In January 1973, Stewart Emery became Erhard's first male trainer (other than himself). The boom continued so that by November 1973, a total of 10,000 graduates had been through the est training. In July 1974, the first prison training was conducted at Lompoc, California. By October 1974, 25,000 graduates had emerged from the est training—a remarkable figure for the first two years of operation. Don Cox, a Doctorate in Business from Harvard University and a former Vice-President of the Coca-Cola Company, joined the est staff, becoming its President in January 1975 and Chairman of the Board of Directors in November 1975.

In 1975, est hit the big time and was highlighted in several magazine articles. Among these articles were the following:

- "Getting it" by L.R. Francke in *Newsweek*, February 1975
- "I am the cause of my world: Erhard Seminars Training" by R.P. March in *Psychology Today*, August 1975

- "We're gonna tear you down and put you back together" by M. Brewer in *Psychology Today*, August 1975
- "Est! Est! Est! Erhard Seminars Training" by I. Schwarzbaum in *Mademoiselle*, October 1975
- "Power of Positive Eyewash" in *Forbes*, December 1975

By August 1975, 50,000 est graduates had now been trained. In 1976, many full-length books on est were published as the phenomenon spread. Among these were the following:

- *est: 60 hours that transform your life* by Adelaide Bry
- *Getting It—The Psychology of est* by Dr. Sheridan Fenwick
- *est—Playing the Game the New Way* by Carl Frederick
- *est—Four Days to Make Your Life Work* by William Green
- *est—Making Life Work* by Robert Hargrove
- *The est Experience* by James Kettle
- *est: The Movement and the Man* by Pat R. Marks
- *The est Experience* by Donald Porter and Diane Taxson
- *The Book of est* by Luke Rhinehart

In 1976, the est training was conducted for the inmates at San Quentin State prison in California by Erhard himself with Ted Long and Stewart Esposito assisting him. This free training was provided by the est organization in conjunction with California State government officials. In this same year, the great American singer, John Denver, featured the est mindset in a beautiful and very poetic musical album entitled "Looking for Space." The first monthly issue of the *Graduate Review* also appeared in June 1976, a publication that was meant to convey the positive aspects of the est training and to provide some information about the organization. As it matured the magazine featured some very powerful articles that gave insights by other "mind practitioners" such as George Leonard, Michael Murphy, Alan Watts, Moshe Feldenkrais and Dr. Joe P. Tupin. Of course, the magazine's intent was primarily one of marketing since much of the material was always devoted to the promotion of the various est seminars.

In 1976, as a result of Jaime Snyder taking the est training, Werner Erhard was introduced to R. Buckminister Fuller, the American genius inventor and designer who was known for the construction of the geodesic dome. Jaime Snyder was Buckminister Fuller's grandson and it was through him that a meeting occurred to introduce his grandfather to Werner Erhard. This led to a series of events entitled "Conversations with Buckminster Fuller" that were held across the United States in which Fuller demonstrated the concepts of synergetic mathematics to the est graduates in attendance. Fuller—who was also renown as a great humanitarian—admonished the audiences that it was earth's critical moment and that it would be up to the integrity of individuals that would determine whether humanity would survive.

In 1976, The United States Government charged Harry Margolis, an attorney for the est organization, with conspiring to report fictitious, tax-reducing transactions. The est organization had been founded as a profit-making educational corporation that was owned by a non-profit, charitable educational trust called The Werner Erhard Charitable Settlement. The est Corporation was not charged with any wrongdoing, and eventually, in October 1977, Margolis was acquitted on all 24 charges that had been brought against him by the Federal Government.

The year 1977 was the pinnacle year for the est organization as 100,000 est graduates were now in existence. Many est centers were located in several major cities in the United States. Several post-graduate seminars were being offered, including "Be Here Now," What's So," "About Sex," The Body," "Self-Expression," "est and Life" and the "Graduate Review." The est training had also spread to London, England. By this time many prominent actors and artists had taken the est training. These notables included Diana Ross, Cher, John Denver, Valerie Harper, Cloris Leachman, Raul Julia and Roy Scheider.

In the spring of 1977, Werner introduced the Sixteenth Karmapa of Tibetan Buddhism, Gyala Karmapa, in a series of events in which traditional Buddhist Black Crown ceremonies were held for the purpose of "getting off the wheel of life and death in this lifetime." The Sixteenth Karmapa was a holy man of lineage that Erhard had met during his visit to the province of Sikkim in the Himilayas during the latter part of 1976. During this time Erhard had traveled to Europe where he addressed the members of UNESCO in Geneva, Switzerland and the Sixth World Congress of Social Psychiatry that was held in Yugoslavia. He also traveled to Asia where he met Swami Baba Muktananda and Satya Sai Baba in Bombay, India and Bhagwan Shree Rajneesh in Poona, India.

Earl Babbie, a member of the est Advisory Board, published a landmark book entitled *Society by Agreement: An Introduction to Sociology* in which he expounded on the "system of agreements" and how these would eventually move into a "system of alignment." During this year the est training was provided *pro bono* for the staff of the city government of the economically disadvantaged city of Compton, California.

In late summer of 1977, Werner Erhard introduced the Hunger Project. This was to be the beginning of the end of starvation in the world, a project whose purpose was to "create the context of responsibility and sufficiency." In a series of presentations that were given across the country, world hunger was explored from a viewpoint of the underlying conditions that held it in place. Among these reasons given for the existence of world hunger were the inevitability of its existence, the concept of scarcity that people held in their minds that prevented any different line of thinking about the problem, and that no solution was possible. Erhard stated (from a line in Victor Hugo's book *Les Miserables*) that it was " an idea whose time has come" and he committed himself to ending world hunger within twenty years (an awesome task indeed!). Initially, the enthusiasm of the Hunger Project enlisted the help of people like John Denver and Valerie Harper—as well as President Jimmy Carter who appointed John Denver to a blue-ribbon commission that would be entrusted with studying the issue.

Later, Werner Erhard appeared on NBC Television on the *Today* show with Tom Brokaw in an interview in which Erhard put forth his position in the matter. Brokaw was quite the hardline interviewer and dispatched him in a few minutes. Werner Erhard had mentioned that it had only taken ten years to put a man on the moon—to which Brokaw had replied, "Yes, but that project had the financial backing of the United States Government and it had thousands of people in industry working on it." Brokaw also stated that many people had espoused the same idea of ending world hunger dating back to the times of Jesus Christ and that nothing of significance had ever resulted.

In May 1978, the est training was provided to the mostly Hispanic town of Parlier near Fresno, California. In October 1978, a biography of Werner Erhard was also published by William Warren Bartley III entitled *Werner Erhard: The Transformation of a Man, the Founding of est*. This book revealed some of the personal details of Erhard's life as part of his search to "find himself"—his identity and true self in the world. In November 1978, the first training in India was conducted in the city of Bombay and in January 1979, another one was held in the city of New Delhi. In March 1979, the first training in Canada was held at the city of Vancouver in British Columbia. By September 1979, 200,000 graduates had now taken the est training. The first training in France was also held in the city of Paris. In October 1979, Werner Erhard met with the Fourteenth Dalai Lama, the exiled spiritual leader of Tibet.

In 1980, the organizational problems began to manifest themselves as the number of est graduates passed the 250,000 mark in summer. The loss of trainer Stewart Emery in 1975 had affected the est organization, but with the departure of trainer

Landon Carter in 1980, the organizational problems became even more significant. Werner Erhard tried in vain to recreate the est organization, but something (maybe the "freshness" of it) had been lost by this time. Probably the election of Ronald Reagan as President and the swing toward more conservative values in America were part of the defocusing of attention on the est movement. Nevertheless, in December1980, the first est training in Israel was held in the city of Tel Aviv—an accomplishment of sorts considering the tinderbox nature of the Middle East. Also, more than 1,000,000 people had now enrolled in the Hunger Project. In that effort, an event labeled as "A Shot Heard 'Round the World: A World That Works for Everyone" became part of the Hunger Project. In particular, it focused on the problem of famine in Cambodia—which because of the holocaust caused by the regime of Pol Pot—created a tragedy of immense and unprecedented proportions.

The January-February 1981 issue of the *Graduate Review* carried an interview with Werner Erhard's mother, Dorothy Rosenberg. As is true of almost all mothers, Mrs. Rosenberg extended her love to her son in support of him and did not seem vindictive—in spite of the fact that her son had literally disappeared for a number of years without a word or a trace of his whereabouts. In the March-April 1981 issue of the *Graduate Review*, the topic that was highlighted was the nuclear weapons reality. It was out of this discussion that the group Physicians for Social Responsibility was created. The first colloquium of the International Physicians for the Prevention of Nuclear War was also held in March 1981.

After August 1981, the publication the *Graduate Review* ceased to exist. It became known simply as *The Review* with the September-October 1981 issue. This new publication continued until the November-December 1982 issue and then it too ceased to exist. A total of 300,000 people had now taken the est training, and 2,000,000 people had signed up with the Hunger Project by June 1982. In January 1983, a new publication entitled *The Network Review* began to be published. In January 1985, the last issue of *The Network Review* was published, indicating that the est training had been "retired" as of December 1984, and that a new organization, The Forum, would be taking its place. A total of 500,000 people had taken the est training by then, some of them in Stockholm, Sweden; Dublin, Ireland; Amsterdam, Netherlands; Munich, West Germany; Mexico City, Mexico; Auckland, New Zealand and Sydney, Australia. By 1991, when Werner Erhard sold his interest in the est Corporation to the Landmark Education Corporation, a total of 750,000 people had taken the est training in its original and modified format. At present (2002), over 650,000 people have taken the Forum seminar, thus putting the number of people who have taken either the est training or the Forum series to approximately 1,400,000.

Endnotes

1   Unless otherwise specified, all quotations at the beginning of each chapter are from Werner Erhard.

2   The word "est" in Latin means "it is." It is also part of the title of a work published in 1970 by L. Clark Stevens called *EST: The Steersman Handbook: Charts of the Coming Decade of Conflict*. This book—which Erhard was very familiar with—was about electronic social transformation (est). The series of essays talked about the unfolding of social transformation in America in forms never experienced before. The est people would be technical, eclectic, computer literate individuals who would be capable of handling constructive activities that would be crucial to the earth's survival. They would also be people who would demonstrate love, care for others and who would help create the climate of freedom and peace that would be necessary to enable a social transformation to occur. Among the

thinkers who are quoted are such luminaries as R. Buckminster Fuller, Jiddu Krishnamurti, Ralph Nader, Marshall McLuhan, Malcom X, Albert Einstein, Lewis Mumford and Eric Hoffer. These are considered to be "est people,' or the prime movers of the coming electronic social transformation.

The Experience of est

"This is it. There are no hidden meanings. Here is where
it is. Now is when it is. You are what it is. All that
mystical stuff is just what's so. A Master is someone
who found out."

A Remembrance

The Article

We first learned of the est training by way of a magazine article
entitled "Has Werner Erhard Found the Answer?" by Marcia
Seligson that appeared in the Spring 1975 issue of the magazine *These Are New Times*. The article spoke about the est training
and how it was different from the iconoclastic and nihilistic
teachings of Jiddu Krishnamurti and the esoteric writings of
Gurdjieff. She also wrote that it was unlike the deep philosophical points of Nietsche, the consciousness raising works
of Baba Ram Dass (Richard Alpert) and a whole slew of other
disciplines and mentors. Although reading the article made an
impact, we did not pursue est with any great interest.

The Guest Seminar

We attended an est guest seminar event at the Santa Monica,
California civic center in summer 1975 (No one invited us; we
went on our own volition). The lecturer was Stewart Esposito,
one of the people who conducted the trainings for est. I (Robert) don't remember much of what he said, but on the
one-on-one personal sharing by the est graduates after the pre-

sentation, there was something that got my attention. It wasn't so much of what this person said to me, or how he answered my questions—which were very pointed, direct, confrontational and somewhat skeptical—but how this person conveyed what his experience had been. He also convinced me that there was something of value for me if I were to undertake the training.

The price of the est training was $250 per person. We signed up for it by putting down a deposit. Although Espy was reluctant to take the training, she decided to do it just in case she might be missing out on something valuable. Besides, Espy had just graduated from UCLA in May 1975, with a Bachelor's Degree in Psychology and therefore her interest was definitely in this area.

The Training

We took the est training in August 1975 at an hotel ballroom located in Los Angeles, California. The training was conducted in four weekday nights during the first week, and then was concluded by a weekend marathon on the following week. Visceral effects of the emotional confrontation were quite evident. Physical reactions such as vomiting, crying, anger, fainting and disgust became common.

The stated intent of the training was expressed as follows: "The purpose of est is to transform your ability to experience living, so that the situations you have been putting up with or trying to change clear up just in the process of life itself." The training was long and exhausting, and sometimes was boring and dull. The training format seemed to be geared towards unearthing all of the hidden "stuff" that lay lurking in one's mind. During the second day of the training, I (Robert) do explicitly remember having a shift in my head during the first exercise of "going into one's space." When I came out of the session, the colors were extremely vivid, and the lights were as bright as I had ever seen them. At the time I didn't know quite what had happened, but in retrospect it was the beginning of a "breakthrough" in my consciousness to a different level of awareness.

Another mental exercise that was conducted by the est trainer was the "Truth Process." This was a guided meditation whose intent was to work on a significant problem that was desired to be solved. The instructions given by the est trainer were to search for all of the emotions and physical reactions that were associated with this problem—and to see the emotional consequences of holding this problem "in place" through one's memories. Much crying, screaming and moaning ensued as various people suffered "breakdowns," and in some cases persons even vomited as a result of this intense process that lasted for a very long time. The end goal of the "Truth Process" was to discover the ultimate cause of this problem—to tell "the truth" about the matter—after which the problem was supposed to disappear through the re-experiencing of the source of the problem.

The most intense process was the "Danger Process." The est trainer instructed each row of participants to stand at attention on the stage with the rest of the audience staring at them. Each participant was individually confronted by members of the est staff who stood very closely to each person, staring eyeball-to-eyeball, to elicit any fears that a person may have. Some of the participants reacted with nervousness, others cried, and some even fainted (these were caught by est volunteers). During all of this process, the est trainer shouted insults at those standing on the stage to further traumatize those who were seized by fear.

There was always some interaction going on between the est trainer and the trainees in the form of "sharing" by speaking into a microphone about anything that was going on. There were also plenty of exercises to participate in, some being of a physical nature and the others being purely mental. Several confrontations occurred at the entry doors by people who were wanting to leave; all of them were admonished about the "agreement" that they had made and about their responsibility for keeping this agreement. In spite of this confrontational "barrier," some of them never returned to finish the training; they simply dropped out. Of course, midway through the training there was an opportunity to leave on one's own volition. The est trainer stated that anyone was free to leave, that their money would be returned, and that not to let people's thoughts about leaving "be a consideration" against a choice of leaving. The est trainer said not to be concerned about what others would think since the people in the audience would only hold it in their minds for very brief moments after they were gone. There was a handful of them that took up the offer, but the great majority of the people that were in attendance decided to remain.

During the second half of the training we were exposed to the construct of the mind. In its totality the mind is a linear arrangement of multi-sensory records of successive moments of now. In this arrangement the mind records three types of incidents in memory that it thinks are important to its psychological survival—but not necessarily for the well being or physical survival of the being. The first, or "number one incident," is a threat to its survival. This can be in the form of pain, unconsciousness or even relative unconsciousness (such as a concussion). These incidents can be brought about through accidents, through exposure of something deep or shameful in one's past, from a traumatic event such as rape, or by some other catastrophic type of occurrence that affects the mind in an intense and powerful manner. The second, or "number two incident," is represented by the death of a friend or a relative, a shocking loss, a wrong reaction to some event, or by an emotion that was not fully experienced. It is not as severe as a "number one incident" but it can have a prolonged and deeply ingrained effect on the mind. The third, or "number three incident," is an unwitting reminder of an earlier recorded "number one" or "number two" incident. This <u>third type of event is called an upset and can take the form of anger, sadness, depression, violence, neurotic or irrational behavior, or other disruptive activity</u>. Thus anything that resembles the situation in which a "number one" or "number two" incident occurred will trigger the mind into a reaction by which it survived in a psychological—and physical—sense.

This analysis of the mind taken to the extreme serves to explain how a suicide might take place. For it is in this fashion that the mind—in order to be right about something and to do whatever it needs to survive mentally—will take an action that will be contrary to preserving the life of the self. Thus, the mind will cause the being to jump off a tall building, shoot a bullet through the brain, drive a car off a precipice, crash an airplane deliberately, blow himself up for a cause, or do some other act of suicide because of some reason that is more important than anything else—including the survival of the being. The mind will literally do away with the physical being if the reason for doing so fits into what is necessary for its psychological survival—even if it causes harm to the physical being.

On a lesser scale, if the mind of someone survived the death of a mate by eliciting sympathy from others, then anything that reminds that someone of that experience in a similar circumstance will cause that same behavior of eliciting sympathy to happen once again. This is the crux of the matter: that all upsets are a result of a previous incident that got associated with certain events, emotions, behaviors, sounds, smells, visions, tastes or other events—and which are therefore repeated whenever similar circumstances arise in a new context.

The processes of the est training were all geared towards discovering and "experiencing out" these previous incidents so that their persistence would cease to exist—or at least lessen in intensity. This was the "lightening up" of the "heavy stuff" to get at the truth of things. In the end, the message was that enlightenment was to recognize that we were all machines acting like puppets on a string as a result of being conditioned by effects. The way around all of this was to be responsible for causing your own experience in the matter—to be at cause with whatever happened by being responsible for your own experience of it. This was to be in a position of being "at source" with things so that you were the creator of your own experience—and of everything else in your life. It was a matter of "seeing where you are and seeing who put themselves there." Of course, it was stated that no matter what you did, that you would always have uncertainty facing you in every situation in life. This was the big "what's so" in life. On the other hand, it was also a perspective of having a "so what?" attitude about it. It was simply a matter of looking at life through these "two sides of the same coin." Constantly throughout the training it was stated that, "At all times, and in all places, and in any situation, you have the power to transform the quality of your life. Stop waiting for it to 'turn out,' because this is how it turned out. This is it, and it is all as it is, and it is all as it isn't, and it is as only it can be. Therefore it is perfect."

Towards the end of the training we were given lectures as to how everything in our lives is based on agreement. The "agreement reality" is based upon contracts that we make with others—whether we recognize them or not, and whether we are even aware of them at all—and which we share with others in our particular environment. From the simplest things like stopping for a red light to more complex situations such as our political organization, we have chosen in some way or another to abide by these compacts of our society. Most of these agreements have been inherited by us as a consequence of living in society and abiding by the rules that have been created by previous agreements. But, even though the "agreement reality" feels very real to us, it is markedly different from our "experiential reality" which is based upon our direct experience of events and things. Thus, we can agree to change something by sharing this with others and getting their agreements, but each of us is still solely responsible for our own direct experience in matters.

Finally, at the very end of the training we were immersed in a communication by the est trainer about what love really means. The perspective that was shared was that many of the so-called relationships that exist in the world between two people are primarily involvements based on some fantasy or romantic ideals rather than being based on commitment and a true understanding of the other person. Many of these relationships are "based on their own survival" and thus leave very little room to experience anything else. These relationships wind up being more about image rather than substance—with the accompanying disastrous results such as separation, abuse, alcoholism, drug-taking, violence and all other sorts of problems.

The crux of the matter was that each of us had to discover that love was really a function of communication. This experience of love is the basis from which all of our relationships are created. At the core of this experience is the acceptance of "what is"—and more important, of "what is not." For if you can accept another person totally as he or she is, and also accept them for what they are not, then all resistance to the relationship will end. Otherwise, it would be a matter of "whatever you resist will persist."

Post Training Activities

After the initial training we enrolled in the advanced est seminar series until 1979, including the first 6-day training for adults in 1977 with Werner Erhard himself. Robert continued his career in information technology with the aerospace industry. Espy was employed as a rehabilitation counselor for the state of California, and continued in this position for the next four years. In 1980, she left to devote full time to her own personal pursuit of the study of the mind—in particular, to study the complete works of Jiddu Krishnamurti[1], the famous World Teacher. In 1985, we moved to the Seattle, Washington area where we have lived ever since.

Endnotes

1   Jiddu Krishnamurti was born on May 11, 1895, at Madanapalle, India where he was raised by Brahmin parents. When his mother died in 1905, his father assumed the total role of raising the family and eventually moved to Adyar, India to be near the Theosophical headquarters. There Krishnamurti was "discovered" by the Theosophist Charles Leadbetter, and from that point on he was brought up in an organization that nurtured him and proclaimed him to be the coming Messiah and World Teacher. The Order of the Star of the East became his personal organization for his talks and eventually reached a peak of 45,000 members by 1928. However, he became increasingly disenchanted with all of the ritual and tradition that was associated with the Theosophical Society, and on August 2, 1929, Krishnamurti disbanded the organization, broke away from Theosophy and proclaimed that "truth was a pathless land" that could not be reached through any organization or doctrine. In the 1930's he underwent a "process" that altered his consciousness in very profound ways. These processes continued intermittently throughout the 1940's and 1950's although he seemed to recover after each of the episodes. He continued in his mission to spread his message, and was interrupted only by World War II, a period during which the United States government put great pressure on him not to give public talks. The "persuasion" was done under the threat of sedition and treason for what he was saying,

and with subsequent expulsion from the United States if he continued to speak publicly. After the war, he gave talks all over the world for the rest of his life with the purpose of setting humanity completely free from the constraints of all religions and beliefs, as well as from the accumulated knowledge of social, economic and political institutions. His talks were documented into over 100 books and those that were recorded were made into hundreds of audio tapes and videos. He left behind a legacy of schools and education centers, primarily in India, the United States and England. He died at Ojai, California on February 17, 1986, at the age of 90.

The Man Behind the Organization

"Create your future from your future—not from your past."

The Remarkable Person Called Werner Erhard

The Early Years   *2006   7 / Y·ᵒ·*

Werner Erhard was born in Philadelphia, Pennsylvania on September 5, 1935. Born to a Jewish father (Joe) and an Episcopalian mother (Dorothy), he was actually baptized as an Episcopalian under his real name, John Paul (Jack) Rosenberg. He was very religious as a child. Before he was a teenager he began to take up the study of Yoga. His teenage years were mostly uneventful, and he eventually graduated from Norristown High School in June 1953. Although he had a variety of interests, what motivated him the most were the subjects of English and physics.

After high school, Werner began to spend more time with his high school sweetheart, Pat Fry. After Pat became pregnant, she and Werner—who was only 18 years old—were married on September 26, 1953. He found a job with an employment agency, then became a meat packer, and then took jobs at a restaurant and a health club. He then held a job as a salesman for a heating and plumbing company. In the meantime, he had two daughters, Clare and Lynn. Moving to Germantown, Werner worked for a construction firm, and then moved to Norristown where he worked for an industrial equipment firm.

Eventually, he became a Ford automobile salesman under a dealership managed by Lee Iacocca, and later worked for both a Mercury and then a Chevrolet dealership. In 1958, Werner began to work for a Lincoln-Mercury dealership. Werner was very successful in selling cars and making money became very important to him. He also started to charm his way into other women's lives, and as a result grew distant from his relationship with Pat. Being married to a housewife and mother was simply too conventional for Werner, but he continued in that role. The family moved again to Riverton, New Jersey where a third child, John, was born in 1958.

Years of Searching

In January 1959, Werner met June Bryde, a friend with whom he began having an affair. Werner and his family moved to Hatboro, Pennsylvania—a place where he would be in close proximity to Philadelphia where June resided. When marital troubles mounted for Werner, he personally moved to work in Allentown, Pennsylvania where he stayed in motels to enjoy his relationship with June during the weekends. Confronted by Pat and his mother, Dorothy, about his affair with June, Werner decided to leave the marriage upon the birth of his fourth child. When Debbie, his fourth child, was born in late 1959, Werner was under the deep strain of leading a double life. In May 1960, he was also again confronted by his entire family for planning to leave his wife and kids.

Finally, on May 25, 1960, Werner eloped to California with June, leaving behind his first wife Pat and his four children—a family whom he abandoned and did not see again for twelve years. They flew from Newark, New Jersey to Indianapolis, Indiana. From an *Esquire* magazine article that he read aboard the airplane on the New Germany, he changed his name to

Werner Hans Erhard, a name that was derived from three prominent Germans: Werner Heisenberg, Bishop Hanns Lilje, and Ludwig Erhard. June also changed her name to Ellen Virginia. From there, they traveled to St. Louis, Missouri by train. They settled there living on the cheap because of lack of credentials, credit, work references or family to draw on.

With fabricated pasts, Werner and Ellen stayed in that city for a year where he again sold cars for a living. He also continued his self-study by reading all of the books on career and success which he borrowed from the St. Louis Public Library. Erhard was profoundly affected by the book *Think and Grow Rich* by Napoleon Hill. This altered his perception of life—which up to this point was one in which he was profoundly dissatisfied with the competitive and meaningless status quo—into one of a positive view of ideas, plans and intentions. Another book that altered him deeply was *Psycho-cybernetics* by Maxwell Maltz. Werner Erhard apparently had a lot of negatives in his self-image and he was deeply affected by Maltz who emphasized self-hypnosis and its focus on "reprogramming" the self to counter these perceived negatives in one's life. This process would lead to the eradication of the bad habits that have been programmed into us through an unconscious process of being "hypnotized" during normal awareness by events, thoughts and experiences. Instead one would replace these bad habits—the source of many problems—with positive and life-enhancing beliefs and habits.

In the spring of 1961, Werner and Ellen left St. Louis, Missouri and began traveling. Werner worked as a traveling salesman for a construction equipment correspondence school, covering a territory throughout the Midwest. They finally left St. Louis for good, and wound up at the school's headquarters in Upland, California. However, Werner was assigned to the Spokane, Washington territory where he and Ellen stayed for about a year. He then switched jobs to work as a salesman for Great

Books, a division of the *Encyclopaedia Britannica* that was managed by Mortimer Adler. Soon after he became a training manager for the program. However, he became involved in a dispute and wound up briefly in Montana.

Then, Werner got a job with *Parents' Magazine*, a division of Parents' Magazine Cultural Institute located in Spokane, Washington. He was very successful, and he also enjoyed activities on Coeur d' Alene Lake in Idaho. Werner became Territorial Director in the summer of 1962, and covered an area that ranged from Seattle, Washington to San Diego, California, to Denver, Colorado. He then moved in late 1962 to live in San Francisco, California where he immersed himself in the human potential movement that grew out of the work of Fritz Perl and the Esalen Institute. This was work that was based on the ideas of Abraham Maslow and Carl Rogers, and which embodied optimism, growth and determinism. Werner then relocated his office to Beverly Hills, California in the fall of 1963, where a daughter, Celeste, was born in August of that year. In October 1963, Werner underwent a mystical and peak experience in which he felt and knew "the Self" at a profound and intimate level. At this time he also met a lady with whom he had an affair—albeit to explore his "rebirth" into a different kind of clarity about his life.

In January 1964, Werner was transferred by *Parents Magazine* to Arlington, Virginia. Although he was very successful at his job, he resigned over a dispute concerning another employee. Again, Werner returned to California in August 1964, where he experienced the culture of the 1960's in all of its height and glory. He made his home in Sausalito, California, a small city that is across the bay from San Francisco. In December 1964, another daughter, Adair, was born.

California Living

Once again, Werner immersed himself in a number of human potential disciplines and Eastern religions. In particular, Alan Watts was instrumental in exposing him to the Oriental philosophies—especially Zen and Buddhism. In 1967, Werner took the Dale Carnegie course. Werner delved into Subud, the martial arts and other disciplines. Since the psychological climate in California was one of searching by whatever means, Erhard undoubtedly experimented with drugs during this period, probably with hallucinogenic substances. He also continued with his unabated love for women and had a series of affairs during this time. In June 1968, a son, St. John, was born.

When Time-Life acquired the Parents organization in 1968, the acquired business underwent a dramatic downsizing. In 1969, Werner resigned from Time-Life to work for the Grolier Corporation. Early in 1970, he became very involved with Scientology and read through the works of L. Ron Hubbard— as well as immersing himself in many of the courses that were offered by the organization. Later in 1970, he got interested in Mind Dynamics—an approach to things in terms of "living life from the inside" that had been created by Alexander Everett. ✓ Everett himself had drawn from the works of Edgar Cayce, Jose Silva, the Rosicrucians and the Theosophical Society.

In February 1971, Werner became a trainer for Mind Dynamics, giving his first course in San Francisco, California. By June 1971, Werner had expanded his training territory to the Southern California region. By now he knew that these endeavors were absolutely what he wanted to do, having turned down a $100,000-a-year offer from Parents Home Service Institute in New York. However, the inspiration for his own theory of en- ✓ lightenment occurred to him while he was driving across the Golden Gate Bridge in his black Ford Mustang sometime in March 1971. In an instant of very powerful insight, Erhard was "transformed," a state that he later described as one of "knowing everything and knowing nothing." He stopped smoking (he consumed between 3 to 5 packs of cigarettes per day!), he gave up coffee and sugar (a habit through which he consumed 20 to 30 cups per day—each with double sugar!), and he stopped using alcohol. He also lost 20 pounds in two weeks, and most important, he decided to share this transformational experience. His set of values also shifted from a path of attaining success and satisfaction by climbing to the top of a bunch of "dead" bodies (casualties in the climbing of the "ladder of success") to that of experiencing real fulfillment, joy and aliveness in his life.

Fame and Fortune

After Werner Erhard resigned from Mind Dynamics in October 1971, the first est training was conducted during this same month by Erhard at the Jack Tar Hotel in San Francisco, California. The training emphasized the need for personal responsibility and for the "possibilities of individual fulfillment" through a strict methodology. Werner Erhard thus became the "guru of gurus" to a self-improvement era that many now believe captured the essence of the "me decade" of the 1970s. In its first year, over 6000 graduates were trained by him, and the region where trainings were held spread from San Francisco to Los Angeles, and then to Aspen, Colorado and Honolulu, Hawaii. In October 1972, Werner returned to his previous family to make amends for his past behavior.

By the end of 1975, it was apparent that the est training was having an effect in America. It was mentioned in television talk shows, endorsed by actors who had taken the training, analyzed by psychologists, warned against by some psychiatrists, and was written about in magazines and newspapers. By 1977, over 100,000 est graduates existed and the training had expanded overseas to London, England. Werner Erhard also created the Hunger Project and placed Joan Holmes in charge of it. In just two short years, in 1979, the number of est graduates doubled to over 200,000. By 1980, 1,000,000 people had registered to support the Hunger project. In this same year, Landon Carter became the second trainer to leave the organization in a dispute with Erhard over Carter's participation in the Iditarod dog sled race held annually in Alaska. Don Cox, the President, Chairman of the Board, and CEO of est also resigned in 1980.

In spite of the resignations of two of his top lieutenants, Erhard was still riding the final crest of the wave of popularity in the human potential movement. He weathered tax problems caused by his corporation lawyer, Harry Margolis, traveled to Asia to meet with other masters of enlightenment, and saw his training program being mentioned in the movies and in the comic strips—a sort of acknowledgement of its permeation into American society. By the beginning of 1981, the est program had centers in thirty cities across the United States, was located in four cities in Canada, and had offices in London, England and Bombay, India. In this same year, est entered the arena of politics by highlighting the potential threat of world destruction by the use of nuclear weapons. It also put the spotlight on the Middle East conflict between the Jews and the Arabs by introducing the est training into Israel.

Expanding the realm of est into other matters, the issue of handgun control was raised. By 1982, over 2,000,000 people had registered to support the Hunger Project. Also, the problem of dealing with the massive difficulties of a country like India was presented in the hopes of creating a breakthrough that would allow such nations to expand their possibilities and empower the major portions of their populations. In 1983, Erhard began making formal contacts of knowledge exchange with leading intellectuals from the Soviet Union by heading delegations that visited the country to have constructive dialogue meetings with these academicians. In 1983, he was divorced from his second wife, Ellen, in a bitter dispute that was to have dire consequences for him in the future. Erhard also fired Charlene Afremow, a trainer and an associate of Erhard for almost thirteen years. This action was also to have its repercussions on Erhard. The firing was based on Afremow's assertions of unreasonably harsh working conditions that had been imposed on her by Werner Erhard.

Still, Erhard continued unabated in his pursuit to make the world a better place for all of humanity. The est phenomena even affected the activities of the Club of Rome, a futurist organization that studied the planet and made predictions about its welfare. By using satellite telecommunications, Erhard expanded the awareness of est by staging various events with participation by est graduates as part of a new program called The Forum. Finally, in 1985, Erhard "retired" the est training, and replaced it with the Forum series. By this time almost 500,000 people had taken the est training.

Erhard also started a group of independent management consulting firms in 1984 under the name "Transformational Technologies Inc." for the purpose of training executives of corporations. Erhard maintained that corporations—like human beings—are primarily committed to "looking good" in the eyes of others. This effect marks the corporate culture and its associated network of conversations. Thus, corporations—that is, the executives—listen through a filter of judgement in deciding what actions to take, and worse, how to manipulate these conversations toward those decisions. Erhard's approach was to train executives in the art of generating the future by altering the conversations and creating breakthroughs in employees' actions. And, actions established by these executive declarations would in turn create possibilities for the future of these corporations rather than just options[1].

The Unraveling of Werner Erhard

In its new format, The Forum did not have the dazzling attraction of the est training. By 1987, the number of participants had dwindled, and various offices were closed (including the Santa Monica branch that had once been our local contact). By 1989, the whole program was in economic trouble with new enrollments barely keeping the organization alive. In 1990, various newspaper and magazine articles were published about Werner Erhard and est that were very unflattering in their portrayal of the man and his organization. By year's end, Erhard began talking about a vast conspiracy that had been launched against him by the Church of Scientology—as a direct result of orders left behind by its founder, L. Ron Hubbard.

The Church of Scientology had been collecting information on Werner Erhard for many years at the direction of its founder, L. Ron Hubbard. Hubbard died in 1986, and in 1989, his organization began a campaign to discredit Erhard because its members felt that he had steered their "customers" away to participate in the est training instead. The Scientologists also felt that Erhard had stolen the precepts, concepts, processes and methods that were utilized in the est training from them. Erhard denied all of these allegations although he did admit to using some of the terminology and materials from Scientology. In particular, est adapted Hubbard's concept of an engram—the encoding in the body of persistent memories—as to the fundamental reason for the prevention of a full self-expression in experience of the self. But, Erhard did not pursue any of the "thetan" being notions of Hubbard which were constructed out of the science fiction realm rather than from reality. Erhard successfully patented all of the est curriculum without any challenge from Scientology since his techniques and knowledge content bear very little resemblance to the guiding book of Scientology that is called *Dianetics*. Erhard also incorporated est as an educational firm for profit in a broad market rather than founding it as a church like Scientology.

At the beginning of 1991, Erhard sold his enterprise to a group of his employees and his brother, Harry Rosenberg, and he relieved Don Cox of all remaining duties. Erhard then moved to Windsor, Massachusetts. Nevertheless, the campaign against Werner Erhard continued digging into his personal affairs and his financial arrangements. Scientology concocted a malicious diatribe against Erhard—an effort that culminated with a hatchet job by CBS in March 1991, with its program "*60 Minutes.*" In the television report Erhard was accused of sexual molestation of one of his daughters, the rape of another daughter, and of physical abuse to both his wife and to his son. Several former est leaders were also interviewed and they accused Erhard of being a tyrant and a cult leader who declared himself to be God at staff meetings. The story also told that Erhard had sold the ownership of his company to a group of his employees, put up his prized possessions for sale (including his yacht), and that he had mysteriously disappeared.

Erhard left the United States at this time and chose to remain "in exile." Years later, Werner was interviewed from Moscow, Russia by Larry King of CNN Television. In that segment, Erhard claimed that the Scientologists had hired "hit men" to kill him—and that this was his reason for having left the country. Currently, Werner Erhard is now part of the social security crowd and is probably carrying an AARP card. He is married to his third wife, a former est trainer. His present whereabouts are unknown to all except for a chosen few whom he still trusts.

Endnotes

1   Erhard maintained that this future exists in the network of conversations of management, such as a collaborative statement of vision, which define the corporate culture. Erhard held that a manager—although he or she was being re-

warded for past performance—was really getting paid to create a future. To change the future course of events, managers require access not only to the predictable future, but also the ability to generate a future that is not predictable. Thus, rather than making choices among options—which are developed out of past experience—a manager is instead focused on creating possibilities that are derived from a commitment to the future of the organization. Thus, the essential part in this transformation of an organization was to alter the conversation in order to shift the operating paradigm from a world of options to the realm of possibilities.

The Roots of est

"Man keeps looking for a truth that fits his reality.
Given our reality, the truth doesn't fit."

The Three Legs of est

Werner Erhard immersed himself in many disciplines and
courses, including Dale Carnegie's "How to Win Friends and
Influence People," the Islamic mysticism teachings of Subud[1],
and martial arts. However, the greatest influences on the development of est were Scientology, Mind Dynamics and Zen. These
three disciplines offered Erhard the necessary pillars upon
which to begin his brand of consciousness expansion.

Scientology

The Man Behind the Church

Lafayette Ronald Hubbard is the founder of The Church of
Scientology (from the Greek origin meaning "knowing how to
know"), and the originator of the mental science of Dianetics
(from the Greek origin meaning "through the soul"). Hubbard
was born on March 13, 1911, in Tilden, Nebraska. As a teenager he traveled to Asia where he encountered the Eastern
philosophies and religions. In 1929, he enrolled at George
Washington University (GWU) in Washington, D.C. where he
studied engineering. He also wrote plays and was a contributor
to the university's literary review magazine, *The Hatchet*. In
1932, he left GWU without getting a degree, was married in
1933 to Polly (Margaret Louise) Grubb, and settled in a career

of writing. He wrote western, horror and science fiction stories. Later, he was a reporter for the newspaper, the *Washington Herald*. In 1938, he wrote a book called *Excalibur* that was never published. In it Hubbard claimed to have written a summation of life based on his observations concerning mankind. During this period he also fathered two children, Nibs (L.Ron Hubbard, Jr.) and Katie.

During World War II, Hubbard served in the United States Navy. After the war he complained that the military service had seriously affected his mind, and that as a result he suffered from suicidal tendencies. Supposedly, Hubbard also claimed that he was blinded with injured optic nerves, and that he was additionally lame with physical injuries to his hip and back. As a result, he spent about eight months recovering from his state of mind and body at the Oak Knoll Naval Hospital located in Oakland, California. Later, after he had "recovered," he claimed that he had cured himself by applying techniques that he had discovered on his own. Thus, in 1947, he began a personal quest for a science of the mind, and his initial work appeared in 1948, in a publication entitled *The Original Thesis*. This manuscript was later published in 1951, under the title *The Dynamics of Life*.

In May 1950, he published his groundbreaking and more formal treatise, *Dianetics: The Modern Science of Mental Health*, a book that became a best seller through its discoveries in the causes and treatment of psychosomatic illnesses (The work was first cited in the May 1950 issue of the magazine *Astounding Science Fiction*). Hubbard continued in his studies to further explore what abilities could be attained through the power of mind and spirit. Thousands of people applied his principles to their lives in the hopes of leading happier existences. Many of these attested to the results that they obtained by claiming to have rehabilitated their abilities and thereby increased their potentialities in the process.

Hubbard's personal life, however, was a series of controversies and various events consisting of controlling actions that stemmed from his own manic-depressive bouts, along with occasional paranoid and schizophrenic states of mind. In 1946, he married Sara Northrup—without apparently getting a divorce from his first wife, Polly, who subsequently filed a divorce in 1947. Through Sara, he had a child, Alexis. In 1950, he started an affair with his public relations assistant (pseudo name, Barbara Kaye), and in 1951, Sara filed for divorce. In 1952, Hubbard married Mary Sue Whipp, a teenage bride who was a "clear" and who subsequently ran the Hubbard College in Wichita, Kansas. Mary Sue bore him four children: Suzette, Quentin (who committed suicide in 1976), Arthur and Diana.

In 1952, Hubbard established his headquarters in Phoenix, Arizona. Here, he moved away from Dianetics' focus on the mind and instead shifted it to a more religious and philosophical approach to the human condition, a body of knowledge which he termed Scientology. In 1953, he incorporated The Church of Scientology in Camden, New Jersey. He then did the same in 1954, founding chapters in Phoenix, Arizona; Los Angeles, California; and Washington, D.C. , the latter becoming his new headquarters during 1955 to further promote the studies of human beings under the guise of a non-profit organization. The stated goal of Hubbard—and thus, of Scientology—was to analyze the mental aberrations of human beings and to offer a means for overcoming them.

In 1958, the Internal Revenue Service revoked the tax-exempt status of individual Scientology churches, and in 1963, agents of the Food and Drug Administration (FDA) raided the church's headquarters in Washington, D.C. and seized more than three tons of literature and equipment, including his patented E-meters. In 1966, the Scientology church created the Guardian's Office and assigned it the task of vigorously defending the church. Hubbard resigned from all offices of the Church of

Scientology in 1967, and raised a private navy—appointing himself as Commodore. He also began to do research into "past lives" and began concentrating on the development of the "post-clear, operating thetan" levels. The research was done aboard the *Apollo*, a seagoing ship (originally, the *Royal Scotsman*) aboard which Hubbard made his home. During this period, he formed a close-knit fraternity of dedicated church members who were to be entrusted with the most advanced teachings of Scientology—an organization termed the Flag Service Organization, with its headquarters in Clearwater, Florida that would be responsible for providing instruction. The highest level of training would be performed by a super elite group, the Flag Ship Service Organization, which was located aboard the ship *Freewinds*.

In the 1970s, the church brought legal actions against those that it deemed were its enemies, and launched a widespread campaign as an intelligence operation to gather information about attacks on the church around the world. It even attempted to infiltrate various government agencies in the United States for this intended purpose. As a consequence of this plan, agents of the Guardian's Office of the Church of Scientology were arrested in 1979. The agents were tried and convicted, events that caused the church to disavow itself from these members. To avoid further problems, the church fired and expelled all of these leaders from the church, and then disbanded the Guardian's office.

In 1985, the CBS television program called *60 Minutes* did an investigation of the Church of Scientology. At the beginning of 1986, Hubbard promoted himself to Admiral in his last com-munication to the members of Scientology. Shortly thereafter, Hubbard died in January 1986 at a ranch near Creston, Cali-fornia. The church continued its fight against the government and in 1993, it finally won its court battle for tax-exempt status in the longest investigation ever conducted by the Internal Revenue Service.

Present Status

At present, the Church of Scientology operates in more than 120 countries and claims thousands in its membership rolls, including the actor, John Travolta. Hubbard's writings have been translated into 32 languages, his works have sold more than 120,000,000 copies, and the claim is that Scientology has helped millions of people throughout the world. Dianetics is now over 50 years old, and yet the influence of Scientology is still very much alive, especially in the United States where it is frequently embroiled in controversy. In particular, the church has taken issue with the American Medical Association and the American Psychiatric Association—both of whom it has opposed. In particular, Scientology's stands against medical procedures such as lobotomies, against psychiatric practices such as shock treatments, and against the administration of drugs like Prozac and Zoloft that are manufactured by the powerful pharmaceutical companies which take in hundreds of billions of dollars every year. However, the church has itself been attacked by some of its ex-members for its vindictive actions against them, by charges of financial fraud, for its practices of illegal medicine, and for its harassment of journalists who have been critical of the church.

The Foundations of Scientology

The concepts of Dianetics—the results of his personal search for the answers to the questions of the mind and life itself—ran counter to the prevailing theories that a human being's abilities and personalities were fixed in nature. The prevailing theories held that these were wired into the cerebral cortex, and thus could not be altered very much. The methodology that Hubbard proposed put forth the ideas that unwanted sensations, fears, psychosomatic illnesses and emotions ("engrams" as he referred to these memory patterns) could be alleviated by focusing on what the soul (the "thetan," or creator of things) was doing to the body through the effects on the mind. Through this form of study, Hubbard believed that it was possible for a human being to truly understand himself or herself.

The quest in this undertaking led him to rediscover the fundamental principle that governs the motivation behind all activities of human life: that of survival—the primary purpose of the mind being to solve all problems relating to that survival. He also discovered that were several levels of survival—all of which were based on the reactions to pain and pleasure. Thus, by increasing the level of survival, a human being would be able to attain a greater source of pleasure, satisfaction and abundance in his or her life. On the other hand, if the level of survival were decreased through certain behaviors and actions, then the results would be those of pain, failure and disappointment. The mind was thus nothing more than a machine that was directing the individual in all of these efforts of survival. The mind used the information that it was receiving and recording—its records—as the basis of all of its operations relating to survival. These moment-to-moment mental images contained all of the sensual, perceptual and observational data that went into formulating the conclusions of the individual as a result of the psychological impact of these mental records. Hubbard's analogy was that these data records could be viewed as a three-dimensional motion-picture film that was fully reacting with the individual to lay down a time track of experience within his or her body. More importantly, by tracing this experience through the methodologies of Dianetics, it was then possible to relieve and sometimes eradicate the source of psychosomatic ills and other aberrant behavior that may have been caused by early traumas in life.

Despite some of the miracles that were achieved by the application of Dianetics and Scientology techniques, Hubbard became the target of a backlash from the psychiatrist community. He was featured in *Time* and *Life* magazines and highlighted in the *New York Times* newspaper in articles that were meant to undermine him. He was attacked from many professional quarters as a practitioner of quackery and disseminator of bunk, especially for his views on past life phenomena. Still, Scientology became one of the fastest growing movements in America as Hubbard attracted thousands with his message of enthusiasm and joy that could be had by uncovering the actual workings of one's unconscious and reactive mind. He even fought and won a legal battle that enabled him to regain the names, copyrights and trademarks of his works. He also remarried (supposedly without legally disengaging himself from his first wife), and he was reportedly involved in a series of affairs with the ladies who were attracted to him by his charismatic influence.

Hubbard believed that the failure of human beings in their lives was due to the attempts to handle the underlying symptoms of their troubles without ever investigating the root causes of their patterned behaviors. He always believed that thought took precedence over the physical—a formulation that he phrased as "function monitors structure." He refined his applied religious philosophy into a framework that he defined as the study and handling of the spirit in relationship to itself, other life and the universe. He partitioned life into eight main divisions of motivation that he termed "the eight dynamics." These ranged from the lowest urge towards existence as a self to that of the highest urge—existence as infinity. He also partitioned the human being into the components of body, mind (the communication and control system) and spirit. He further subdivided the mind into three parts: analytical (perceptions of the past, future and the now), reactive (the stimulus-response mechanism) and somatic (the unconscious).

Hubbard developed many axioms to explain causation and knowledge, the first ten being the fundamental truths of Scientology. These ten ranged from the definition of life (the ability to postulate and to perceive) to that of the highest purpose in the universe (to create an effect). He embodied this knowledge of Scientology as being guided by three principles:

- wisdom is meant for anyone who wishes to reach for it
- this wisdom must be capable of being applied.
- the wisdom is only valuable if it is true or if it works.

To that end he defined the goal of Scientology as one of helping the individual lead a better life, and that of playing better games in life with his or her fellow human beings. He stated that suppression and oppression were the basic causes of depression. Consequently, he felt that if these states of being were relieved, then a person would be better able to live a happier life. Eventually through the process of continual auditing by Scientology studies, a person would gain a renewed awareness of self as a spiritual and immortal being—an ultimate state that he defined as a "clear." According to Scientology, a "clear" could then become an "operating thetan" (a being who as a spirit alone can handle things) within a few months, a state in which he or she would know immortality and freedom from the cycle of birth and death.

Thus, the ultimate aim of Scientology was to elevate the world's civilization where insanity, criminals and war were absent (a lofty goal indeed!)—a society where human beings could prosper, and an environment that was conducive to each person being able to rise to his or her highest level of awareness. In its farthest extensions of explanation into the cause of all things, Scientology postulated several principles. One of these was that each individual is a spirit—a "thetan"—who controls a body via a mind. Another of these is that the "thetan" is capable of making space, energy, mass and time. A third one is that the "thetan" is separable from the body without the phenomenon of death, and thus can handle and control a body from well outside it. Also, the "thetan" does not care to remember the life which he has just lived after he has parted from the body and the mind (the process of death and subsequent reincarnation). Thus, a person who is dying always exteriorizes (from body and mind), and this person, having exteriorized, usually returns to the planet to procure, if possible, another body of the same type of race as before.

Within this framework, Hubbard continued his explorations into the causes of the problems of the human psyche. In particular, he studied the aberrative effects of all traumatic actions upon the mind. Of special interest to him were the conditions of severe injury, major surgery, shock and near-death experiences. He surmised that these events caused the exteriorization from body and mind. This exteriorization was produced under duress, it was often very sudden, and for the most part was inexplicable to the person undergoing the experience of trauma. The important consequence that he noted was that the person would suffer mentally from that experience afterwards if a memory of it was triggered by a similar occurrence or by remembering circumstances that were recorded by the reactive mind when the original trauma had occurred.

He discovered that when the mind was not fully functioning, then the reactive mind would take over and would store images of experiences called engrams. These engrams contained strong and negative emotional content along with unrelated elements of the experience, such as sounds, smells, images, and so forth. A later encounter with these unrelated elements, an unwitting reminder, could then bring forth negative emotional reactions that were derived from the stored engram—reactions that could lead to actions that might be contrary to the survival of the being. Since these engrams were stored at the subconscious level (the somatic mind), Hubbard devised a methodology to help people bring these engrams to their consciousness level. In this manner, they would be able to confront these stored experiences, and thereby eliminate them as a source of recurring problems. The methodology that Hubbard developed was called auditing, a process that consisted of a one-on-one counseling by an auditor—a person who was trained to facilitate the individual's handling of their engrams. Part of this process used an E-meter, an instrument that measured the strength of a small electrical current that was being passed through the body of the person who was undergoing the auditing process. Once the stored engrams were identified, the goal was to then get rid of these engrams to help the mind become clear.

The est Connection

In the book *Dianetics* one can see where Werner Erhard got the characterizations of the mind that he subsequently used in the body of knowledge for the est training. The true self of the individual exists in a world of matter, energy, space and time (MEST). In the MEST universe, the way to happiness is to release the self from the entrapment of this illusion, and to exist instead as an "operating thetan." While accepting the body of knowledge of the causes for individual trauma—for the machinery of "unconsciousness" in a person—Erhard clearly rejected the idea of the "thetan," the god-like force that Hubbard stated was the definer of the universe. Erhard also shifted the emphasis in the purpose of life for an individual from that of survival to that of seeking the truth to enable an individual to achieve wholeness and completion in his or her life. Erhard also made a significant distinction in how the body of knowledge (epistemology) was to be held by an individual. For Erhard the context for an individual was one of experiencing the truth rather than believing in the ideas behind the knowledge.

Mind Dynamics

The Founder

Mind Dynamics, founded by Alexander Everett, was the major forerunner of large group awareness trainings. Although Mind Dynamics was only in existence for a few years, it sparked an entire industry of similar trainings. Alexander Everett was born in England in 1921, and as a young man was inspired by the book *The Perennial Philosophy* by Aldous Huxley. He traveled to Egypt, Greece and India in search of spirituality, and he studied Christian Science, the Unity School of Christianity, and Rosicrucianism. He also got involved with Theosophy—in particular, with Rudolph Steiner—and learned from this discipline the power of imagination and visualization. Everett became a successful teacher and established a preparatory school (Pendragon) in Sussex, England. He also founded Shiplake College.

Driven by a desire to help people understand themselves, he emigrated from England, arriving in America in 1962. Because of his background, he went to Kansas in hopes of becoming a minister. Deciding that the Unity ministry was not his calling, Everett left Kansas in 1963 and went to Fort Worth, Texas, where he had been invited to help establish a private boarding school and where he helped set up the Fort Worth Country Day School. But, more importantly, he came in contact with Jose Silva, a practitioner of self-hypnosis. Through Silva, Everett acquired the methods of mind control, the characteristics of learning and memory, the feats of spontaneous healing, and the creation of states of bliss through meditation. While he was in Texas, Everett was also influenced by the works of Edgar Cayce (America's "sleeping prophet") as a means to reach the psychic subjective level of being. However, it was mostly from the work of Jose Silva's Mind Control that he created the Mind Dynamics course.

In 1968, Everett founded Mind Dynamics, the experiential human potential training organization that was to become the forerunner of est, Lifespring, Actualizations, Insight and several other organizations that flourished in the 1970s. Everett developed the experiential four-day training to deal with the workings of the mind. His methods included lectures on spirituality, chanting, guided but unstructured meditation, self-hypnosis, and relaxation exercises. It was a non-confrontational environment in which Everett avoided direct interaction with his audience, and one in which there was no personal sharing of experience.

Although Everett first offered these courses in Texas, the trainings became popular in California instead. Thus, he moved the headquarters of Mind Dynamics to San Francisco, California in 1970, from where it spread throughout the United States, Europe and Australia. In 1970, William Patrick Penn bought Mind Dynamics. Penn headed a sales organization called Holiday Magic, Inc. that was involved in cosmetics; he also had a training organization known as Leadership Dynamics that was based on a harsh and hard-hitting group encounter format[2]. As the organization grew, Everett hired trainers, one of whom was Werner Erhard—a graduate of a December 1970 training—who gave his first Mind Dynamics training in February 1971. The course became popular not only in the United States but also spread to Europe and Australia. Unfortunately, Patrick's business became further embroiled in pyramid schemes and as a result both Leadership Dynamics and Mind Dynamics came to an end in 1973.

In 1974, Alexander Everett traveled to Russia, and then to India to study Eastern philosophies and religions. In 1977, he created a two-day personal growth seminar called Inward Bound. The training was geared towards personal growth and to discover the genius that lies dormant within each of us. Everett continues to be active in giving trainings.

The Essence of Mind Dynamics

The procedures that were employed in Mind Dynamics were meant to explain how the mind functions. The two key aspects of the training were to teach the trainees how to engage the power of the mind as well as how to apply that mind power in a beneficial manner. The processes consisted of meditation exercises designed to induce alpha states in the participants to allow them to function at a deeper, more creative and enhanced mental level. In turn, these states would promote the improvement of memory functioning such that the persons would be better able to solve problems and deal with other issues in a way that would transform their lives. The results would also enable the trainees to alter their view of themselves—and thus of their world around them. Deeper levels of meditation (theta) were also taught to allow the students to reach a state of very deep relaxation. The theta state would be deeper than that of sleep itself, except that it would be accompanied by a special kind of awareness that would have the effect of altering consciousness.

Basically Mind Dynamics was an autogenic mind training mixed with Edgar Cayce's method of remote viewing and diagnosis of a disease in another person. The exercises that were conducted were meant to create states of deeper levels of the mind. In particular, the creation of an imaginary workshop and a "screen of the mind[3]" within it were intended to gain a greater understanding by tuning into persons or events at the subconscious level. The visualization processes—including the "rainbow process[4]"—were designed to provide a relaxed state where autosuggestions could be made to enable lifelong dreams to come true. Very useful abilities and memory feats could also be worked on such as the enhancement of memory by reliance on word associations.

The whole program was designed for the purpose of cutting

through the self-imposed mental blocks to attain a deeper and more introspective analysis of oneself. The self knowledge that was gained would allow a person to illuminate his or her life in such a way that would free that person to lay the foundations for a better life. This would include a more direct communication with others, the expansion of the senses[5], and an awareness of the self at a deeper level. The final "test" of the training involved the projection of oneself into someone else's body to determine their state of mind, their health (or lack of), and their demeanor. The subject to be "scanned" was always picked by someone else, and only the age and gender of the subject were given out as the identifying information. Fundamentally, the psychic diagnosis and healing process was to illustrate and to accentuate the "open door" nature of the mind and its capability to receive messages that were operating below one's normal awareness levels.

The Processes of est

Werner Erhard adopted mind-expansion processes from Mind Dynamics into his est training. Some of the techniques that he incorporated from Everett's training include self-hypnosis, relaxation exercises, visualization of an inner peaceful place ("creating your space"), and guided meditation ("centering"). In particular, the hypnotic trances that induced alpha brain wave states were designed to touch on powers of clairvoyance, extrasensory perception, precognition and healing. Perhaps the best principle that he acquired from this discipline was that of "completion" since this is the gratification and contentment that each of us seeks in life once we have mastered and achieved something—whatever it may be. Completion of something also provides the impetus to master other situations by moving from completion to completion, each time gaining strength, enjoyment and satisfaction.

Erhard also adopted the business model from Mind Dynamics

of using guest lectures as the sole means of recruiting new members for trainings. But, there was never any harshness associated with the trainings of Alexander Everett, and it is from the discipline of Leadership Dynamics—as well as that of Scientology—that Erhard borrowed the confrontational and abusive group encounter format as a Zen Roshi Master technique for enlightenment.

Zen

The Essence of Zen

Freedom is the essence of Zen, a practice that is dedicated to the liberation of the hidden potential of the human mind. Zen—from the Sanskrit word *dhyana* which means meditation—originated in India and made its way to China in the sixth century, and eventually to Japan in the twelfth century. However, it did not reach Europe until the early 1900s, and it did not become prevalent in the United States until the early 1950s. Zen does not require anything external nor does it require the giving up of anything in order to achieve enlightenment. Zen comes from within and is a liberation that is achieved through special knowledge which allows the perception of an individual to penetrate to the root of his or her experience. The freedom comes from realizing the limitations that are imposed on the mind through conditioning, a continual process that awakens the consciousness of an individual from its normal state of dormancy.

Although it is sometimes referred to as a practice of emotional detachment, Zen is instead a discipline that fosters a balance between independence and openness. It is something that unfolds as a direct result of experience—rather than as a formal effort into the world of ideas and beliefs—to unlock the essence of the human mind. Countless variations and schools of Zen exist, none of which are geared towards any verbal formulations or a set of esoteric secrets that are to be divulged to a practitioner. Zen acts in the realm of intuition and in the mode of rationality to deepen and sharpen thought. Thus, Zen is at the source of ideas, but is definitely not a product of ideas.

Zen in its purest form is supposed to transmit the experience of enlightenment that was achieved by Guatama the Buddha. This comes about through a tranquility of the mind, by not being fearful, and by acting with a total sense of spontaneity in life. This quality of being is inherent in everyone but usually lies dormant because of ignorance and years of conditioning of behavior that denies this fundamental aspect. The awakening to this state is done by a sudden breakthrough of the mind from its boundaries of everyday mental processes and from its confinement to logical and rational modes of thinking. But this enlightenment does not happen as a result of studying scriptures (such as in Judaism, Christianity or the Islamic religion), nor is it achieved through rites, ceremonies, the worship of images or through the practice of good deeds. Instead, the transformation is done through training by methods administered personally from master to disciple. The training methods differ according to the various sects of Zen such as Rinzai, Soto and Obaku. The Rinzai school utilizes sudden shock as well as meditation based on koans. The Soto school uses the method of sitting meditation. The Obaku school relies on meditation based on the continual invocation of the name of Buddha.

The Existential Basis of est

Alan Watts, an English philosopher born in 1915. and an avid Zen practitioner, had a profound influence on Werner Erhard. Watts, who was known as a master of communication, authored many books on Hinduism, Buddhism and Taoism. His mastery is clearly reflected in the several works that he published on Zen, among these in 1948, *Zen*; in 1958, *The Spirit of Zen*; in 1960, *The Way of Zen*; and in 1961, *This Is It*. These were books that brought the discipline of Zen to the attention of millions of people, and in doing so, Alan Watts became one of the most well-known figures at the center of the controversy and counterculture that marked the late 1960's. Watts continued doing seminars and audio tapes concentrating on Zen studies until his death in California in 1973.

Erhard has acknowledged that <u>Zen is the essential discipline that formed the backbone of est</u>. The similarity is that est espoused the distinction between self (the "ground of being") and mind (positions and identifications)—a distinction that is at the heart of this Oriental philosophy. Erhard incorporated some of the abstractions of Zen into the practices and teachings of est. In particular, Erhard adopted as fundamental principles of est the following notions from Zen:

- the harmony of body and mind with the true nature of things
- the realization of perfection as a natural state of being in attaining enlightenment
- the acceptance of everything as it is—without judgments or evaluations
- the emphasis on being in the present, rather than taking action based on past events or in future fantasies
- the reliance on koans, or statements of paradoxes that are designed to break the mind from its ordinary rationality
- mental exercises to enable concentration and mind control to achieve experiential knowingness

Erhard used the discipline of Zen to investigate the labyrinth of the mind. It was through this process that one would get to a state of being that was beyond positions and identifications. He utilized intrusive abstractions to enable people to transcend their circumstances and their past to get to the true nature of things. In working through all of the judgments and evaluations that had been established as patterns in life for each participant, Werner felt that there would be a point of realization in which a person would see that "one is as one is." This realization would result in the acceptance of everything that is—as it is.

Endnotes

1   Subud is a religious movement that was founded in 1933 by an Indonesian called Bapak (Pak Subuh) who was a student of Sufism. The name of Subud is derived from three words: *susila* meaning true character, *budhi* meaning divine life force, and *dharma* meaning surrender to God's will. The movement spread to Europe and America in the 1950's, and in the late 1960's Erhard participated in it for over one year. He practiced the mystical exercise known as *latihan*, a process (training) of sitting in a room to await the spontaneous opening of the mind in a moment of rapture. Thus, *latihan* is a form of meditation that aims at creating an inner stillness to open the mind to divine energies—and ultimate meaning. It involves the absolute submission to God to allow the spiritual nature of the individual to come forth.

2   William Patrick Penn founded the cosmetics company Holiday Magic, Inc. based on pyramid sales in 1964, wrote a booklet entitled *Happiness and Success Through Principle* in 1967, and then formed the Leadership Dynamic Institute (LDI) based on the principles declared within the book. The course used language as a shock tool by haranguing and cajoling the trainees, it had overtones of strict military training techniques, and it was concerned with having every participant "tell the truth" about his or her life—no matter how embarrassing or emotionally wrenching it might be. The purpose of the four-day exhaustive training was to find the "guiding light" of self-honesty that would illuminate you for the rest of your life—as well as to make you a better leader and executive. Punishment and pain were employed to get past the lies, individuality was broken down

to stress obedience by using methods and sadistic techniques that utilized nudity, sexual humiliation, depraved actions, and even outright violence. Participants were held as virtual prisoners in a "living hell" environment inside an hotel ballroom during which beatings, deprivation of food and sleep, and other wearing-down actions such as physical exercises were employed by the leader to break through the resistance of the participants. Extreme acts included being stuffed into coffins, forced into cages, and even being "crucified" by being tied to and suspended from a cross. Token resistance was quickly eliminated by relentless pressure through physical abuse and mental derision from an authoritarian training leader. Also, a "shit list" was encouraged to be kept by all class members to record all of the sordid details of one's life. To emphasize the point and to expose each person's subconscious hangups, all seemingly insurmountable problems were labeled as mere rationalizations that were equally held by all people. Happiness and success were promised as the end results of the training, but the elations of the graduates were accomplished through a process of pure exhaustion, isolation, repetition and public humiliation—techniques known since the Roman legion days. Lawsuits eventually shut down LDI, the Holiday Magic Company was closed down as a pyramid scheme, and the founder, William Patrick Penn, died in the crash of his F-86 Sabre jet while he was flying it at an air show in Sacramento, California.

3   The screen of the mind was used to paint a new picture of the self—of how you felt you should really be like in appearance. With the "assistants" that were created within the workshop of the mind, one could also obtain help in solving any problem or in dealing with any issue of concern.

4   The rainbow process used the seven basic colors of the spectrum to induce different stages of relaxation. Red represented the physical body, orange was associated with

emotions, and yellow stood for the mind. The further colors of the spectrum were represented as follows: green was for inner peace, blue was for love, purple was for the self and violet was for the spirit.

5   This included the projection of one's consciousness into inanimate and animate objects such as wood, metal, stone and fruits. It also entailed the creation of a calendar through which it was possible to travel both forward and backward in time.

Other Influences

"In life, understanding is the booby prize."

Actualizations

Overview

Stewart Emery was one of the est trainers who broke away in 1975 from the organization in a running dispute with Werner Erhard as to the way est trainings were conducted. He subsequently formed his own training organization that he entitled "Actualizations." He incorporated in these seminars his personal style that was derived from his Australian background, and from his many readings of the works of Jiddu Krishnamurti. He also used the knowledge and experience that he acquired from being an est trainer, and from his past associations with other similar organizations such as Mind Dynamics.

As a "gentler and kinder" trainer, Emery was able to elicit a deeper and sometimes more meaningful dialogue with the trainees. Emery's approach was geared towards performing what he called "delicate heart surgery"—something that was diametrically opposed to the harsh and confrontational "head" methodology that was used in the est seminars. At times, Emery's body language displayed a lot of the heaviness and mean-spirited abusive treatment that had been inflicted by Don Cox, the President of est, and probably by Werner Erhard as a result of his leaving the est organization. It was ironic for Emery, who got bullied a lot during his early years, that he certainly got to relive some of his past by being bullied anew by his est

64

bosses. Sometimes, Emery did show some of that brutish est behavior with very short outbursts of anger, especially if he got annoyed by someone's stupid behavior, but for the most part he was a very easygoing, soft and almost non-emotional person. During the seminar he appeared to be functioning straight out of a "Star Trek Spock-like" character, delivering his Australian-accent talks with logic that went directly to the core of things. And always, his primary message was one of "You don't have to rehearse to be yourself."

Because of his reputation, and largely through his previous association with est, Emery was able to attract a huge number of guests who subsequently enrolled in his seminars. The awkward part of the whole matter was that although Emery and Erhard were both conducting seminars that were basically dealing with relationships, they couldn't seem to get along with each other. Emery had a lot of stuff going with his previous employer and he never resisted the opportunity to slam the techniques of est. But people who had attended both Erhard's and Emery's trainings—including myself and my wife—kept pointing out this fact. Eventually, Emery and Erhard reconciled their differences somewhat although the two of them were never really very close. It may be that they just "made up" for the sake of image and appearances in order to keep their respective organizations from being distracted by this issue. Nevertheless, Emery had two distinct criticisms of est:

- He thought it dangerous to tell people that each of us is totally responsible for our experience
- He thought that much of the est training (the processes, the confrontations, the dramatizations, etc.) was irrelevant to its success.

To Emery, mastery, or the process of going beyond our limits, had an effect of producing results—the so-called "miracles"—that were out of the ordinary realm of human consciousness.

Through the state of being accountable for one's actions—rather than being responsible for them—he felt that it was possible to move past the level of mediocrity into excellence by removing those things that were limiting in one's sphere of being. He also considered the necessity of surrounding yourself with the best in life—be it people, things, environment or wealth. But, most important, he thought it very important to have friends who would ask more of you than you would of yourself.

The Actualizations Training

The Actualizations training was conducted over the same two-weekend format although it had a lot more breaks and was not as rigid as the est training. My wife, Espy, and I went through separate trainings (after we had initially dropped out of the original one—in the middle of the sessions—that we had signed up for). Because of his approach, Emery was able to reach Espy at a level that no one had been able to do so before. Using this same technique, he was able to get me to release a lot of the hidden aspects of my personality that were in the way of my "aliveness." His format was more of a personal sharing on stage that everyone had to do in front of everyone else—a non-threatening context where it was impossible to hide the personal feelings and deep-seated emotions from everyone else in the group.

The essence of the Actualizations training was one of making people accountable for their actions—that is, to stand up and be counted as in the days of the Roman Senate. The viewpoint was one of combining communication with responsibility, to look holistically at relationships and interactions, and to include other realities so that an experience of separation was not created in the process. The mastery in one's life simply required that we constantly produce results beyond and out of the ordinary, the key being one of balancing both the comforts and the discomforts in life.

———

Synergy, Geodesics and Much More

The Planet's Friendly Genius

R. Buckminster Fuller became closely associated with Werner Erhard in 1977. Erhard presented Fuller at various events in which the planet's friendly genius explained his perception of the Universe from his experience of the world. Born on July 12, 1895, Fuller was one of the last of the New England Transcendentalists. His philosophy was one that was centered on the human potential to overcome whatever reflex conditioning might have entrapped our humanity in a series of counterproductive scenarios, such as scarcity. His focus was thus on "intuition" as coming from the mind, something that is beyond the realm of brain-based experiences.

A self-educated man—much like Werner—Fuller worked in a Canadian cotton mill, and then later joined the United States Navy. While in the Navy, he married his wife, Anne Hewlett. A natural inventor by heart, Fuller developed a winch for rescuing pilots downed over water—a recognition that led to an appointment at the Annapolis Naval Academy at Annapolis, Maryland in 1918. While there he acquired the naval tradition of "thinking globally, and acting locally."

After his honorable discharge from the Navy, Fuller failed in his attempts to make money in civilian life. Beset by both personal and business failures, he contemplated suicide in 1927, but he instead opted to turn the rest of his life into an experiment about what kind of positive difference a single individual could make on the world stage. Starting from scratch, he decided to be a Guinea pig and he resolved to do his own thinking. Over the years, Fuller published several books including *Operating Manual for Spaceship Earth, Synergetics,* and *Critical Path.* Drawing on themes that were affecting the human predicament, Fuller illustrated the problem of overspecialization

---

and how it could be overcome by explorations in the geometry of thinking. These ideas encompassed the concepts of synergy[1], tensegrity[2], syntropy[3], geodesic domes[4] and the placement of the tetrahedron[5] as the fundamental building block—the unit volume—in the Universe.

Association with est

Werner Erhard through the est Foundation provided a forum for Fuller's ideas through a series of events dubbed "Conversations with Buckminster Fuller." Fuller's collaboration with Werner Erhard, someone who shared his home-grown philosophy of the mind, marked another chapter in est that was somewhat fraught with controversy. Although Fuller proclaimed that the relationship with Erhard's group was in no way funded by est, Fuller still endorsed Erhard with his trust and friendship, and thus he gave Erhard—and est—a welcome boost from an independent source. Erhard, in return, saw many similarities in est with Fuller's conceptual system in providing a common language and accounting for both the physical and the metaphysical in the world. Both of them felt that what ultimately counted was the integrity of every individual on earth.

Fuller had a lot of faith in the young people, a group whom he felt would eventually come to grips with their situation aboard the planet—something that he termed "Spaceship Earth." He saw his role as one of providing the big picture viewpoints with a minimum of misinformation. He foresaw a world working together to make every inhabitant on board a virtual billionaire. He was fond of saying that human beings on earth were in the final stage of their evolution—something which he referred to as "the final examination in Earthians' critical moment." His books, although hard to read and digest, offer a great deal of wisdom and thinking that is light years ahead of where most scientists and philosophers find themselves today. He was a "trim tab[6]" who definitely set in motion various experiments on behalf of his fellow human beings. The planet's "friendly genius" died in Los Angeles, California on July 1, 1983, leaving a legacy that—assuming that we don't blow ourselves up, as he always used to say—will lead to a world that works for everyone.

Tibetan Buddhism

The Roots of Buddhism

Siddharta Gautama, was a Prince who was born almost 2500 years ago in Northern India. His parents were King Suddhodana and Queen Maya. Because his mother died shortly thereafter, Siddharta was raised by an aunt and his father in a very elite, sheltered and noble environment. He was married to Princess Ysodhara and had a baby named Rahula. Saddened by his knowledge of what afflicted human beings—old age, sickness, death and the ever-present sorrow—he decided to leave the Royal Palace in search of the truth. After several years of living an ascetic life, and struggling with the main issues that affected all of humanity, he finally became "awakened" by discovering the truth of how all life was linked together in an ever-flowing cycle of generation, changing, growing, decaying and death—and then regeneration into a new cycle. From then on, he experienced equal love for all and a profound happiness in the context of his enlightenment, and he set out to teach others of the freedom from darkness, misery, sorrow and pain. He lived to be eighty years old, always teaching up to the very last day of his life to those who would listen.

Buddhism represents a very old religious philosophy that has a rich and cultural heritage of teachings that are designed for the purpose of transformation of the individual self. The basic "Four Noble Truths" of Buddhism, as taught by the Buddha, can be stated as follows:

- Existence is unhappiness, that all life is fraught with suffering
- Unhappiness is caused by selfish craving for sensual pleasures, for afterlife and for annihilation
- Selfish craving can be destroyed
- The craving can be destroyed by following the eightfold path

The eightfold path represents a manner of leading one's life with steps that are considered crucial to a person being on the right path. The first two steps are essential for one's morality, the next three steps are a pledge of one's readiness for order and consistency through concentration, and the last three steps are the fundamental conditions to assure systematic progress towards the goal of ethical and moral conduct—the wisdom in life. These eight steps are as follows:

- Right understanding
- Right purpose, or aspiration
- Right speech
- Right conduct
- Right vocation
- Right effort
- Right alertness
- Right concentration

Taken together these eight steps of the path are the tenets of truth, love and of achieving "nirvana." They represent gentleness, serenity and true compassion for life on earth. It is a means to achieve liberation from selfish craving—and from the suffering in human life that is caused by self-centered desires. Buddhism denies that there is a personal world creator although it affirms the individual capacity to achieve vast wisdom and compassion as a superhuman saint, such as is exemplified by the Dalai Lama. Buddhism also incorporates charms, oracles, magical rites, prayer flags, beads and other religious symbols into its ceremonies. The core of Buddhism is one that is based on doubt rather than on faith as in the Western religions. It examines the world from its reality instead of relegating its followers to belief in some enchanted promise of a heavenly existence in an afterlife.

Tibetan Buddhism

The Tibetan Buddhist religion incorporates elements from an indigenous and more primitive religion of Bon (a shamanism with gods and rites of sacrifice). The main feature of Tibetan Buddhism is the belief in Bodhisattvas, Great Beings who choose to be reborn into the world to alleviate the suffering of humanity. Two of these sentient beings are the religious master Marpa and his prize pupil, Mila Repa. Through the lineage of the lamas and the karmapas, the various orders of Tibetan Buddhism have produced a wealth of writings and biographies geared towards presenting the doctrines and teachings of the great masters. All of these have as their central theme the belief in reincarnation—the universal and inevitable process by which a soul comes back to a different life in circumstances that are dictated by the previous being's good or evil acts. There is even a *Tibetan Book of the Dead* which is a volume intended to guide the consciousness of a deceased person to some satisfactory form of rebirth. Ultimately, release from this continual incarnation process is attained only by salvation in Buddhahood. This represents the state of becoming a Bodhisattva, or one who is intent on enlightenment.

Ceremonies for est Graduates

In the Tibetan tradition, the present Karmapa is a Bodhisattva who represents the accumulated spiritual energy of the lineage of the more than eight hundred years of enlightened intelligence. Through the est Foundation, Werner Erhard presented to approximately 10,000 est graduates a spiritual leader, His Holiness the XVI Gyalwa Karmapa, in a series of five special events given in 1977. During these events, the Karmapa performed the 14th century Vajra Crown ceremony, a tradition that holds a promise of a glimpse of "getting off the wheel of life and death in this lifetime." The 16th Karmapa wore a ceremonial meditation hat as he invoked the traditional sevenfold service. The invocation involved devotion, offerings, acknowledgement of imperfection, surrendering to a higher wisdom, and praise for the Buddha activity. At the end of the ceremony, the Karmapa made the teachings manifest, and was then asked to remain in the world and not die.

The ceremony had the accompaniment of chants, cymbals and trumpets to create a mystical environment in which the est participants were offered an opportunity to experience some sort of transcendence that would touch their hearts and lives. At the end of the ceremony, those of us who wished to do so were escorted to the feet of the Karmapa (he was sitting on an elevated throne) for his blessing. Finally, each of us was given a knotted orange string by one of the attendant monks as a symbol of the 16th Karmapa's dedication to our participation in these sacred activities.

Current Incarnation

The 16th Karmapa was reborn in 1922 and died in 1982. The current 17th Karmapa, or the Black Hat Lama of Tibet, is Trinlay Thaye Dorje, the true spiritual head of the Karma Kagyu tradition of Tibetan Buddhism. Some contend that the person named Urgyen Trinlay Dorje was chosen erroneously as the 17th incarnation of the Karmapa by the Chinese Communist Party in an attempt to manipulate the religious order as part of its harsh campaign to take over the Tibetan society. But, even the Chinese-appointed 17th Karmapa has fled China and has lived in Dharamsala, India with the Dalai Lama since January 2000.

An American Poet

John Denver was America's singing poet. Born under the name of Henry John Deutschendorf at Roswell, New Mexico in December 1943, he grew up to be one of America's most popular singing performers. From 1969 until his untimely death in 1997, Denver produced a variety of hit songs through which he achieved a mass popularity. He even starred with George Burns in a comedy film called "*Oh, God.*" Denver was also a very dedicated environmentalist who felt that the earth needed custodians to protect it and sound the alarm wherever they saw it in danger.

Denver took the est training and then wanted very much to be a trainer. However, Erhard would not allow the sacrifice to be made although he did place Denver on the est Advisory Board and invited him to participate in events that helped to promote est and its causes. Denver appeared in est events numerous times, he produced a specific song ("Looking for Space") that reflected the consciousness of est, and he got involved with organizations that were making a difference such as Werner Erhard's Hunger Project, David Brower's Earth Island Institute, and Jacques Cousteau's Calypso Foundation. In addition, he created his own Windstar organization to promote causes that were dear to his heart. Denver also produced many television specials designed to make people aware of the fragile state of the environment as well as to highlight the magnificent beauty of the planet. His tragic death while flying an experimental airplane that crashed on October 12, 1997, in the Pacific Ocean off the Monterey Bay coast of California abruptly ended a career that probably would have continued for many more years. Unfortunately, the crash also silenced a voice for consciousness, especially with regard to the environmental damage that is still being done to the planet.

Endnotes

1   Synergy means combined action or operation.

2   Tensegrity describes the fundamental integrity of the Universe that is held together by tensional forces

3   Syntropy refers to the interplay of matter and energy acting through radiation and gravity.

4   A dome is a building or structure with a large hemispherical roof.

5   A tetrahedron is a geometrical structure in a class of polyhedrons. It contains four faces and six edges.

6   A trim tab is an independently controlled device that is set at the trailing edge of a ship's rudder. The trim tab holds the rudder in a position that will enable the rudder to change the direction of the ship. A small change in the trim tab produces a change in the rudder, and thus, changes the direction of the ship—even if it is as big as an oil tanker. The analogy for Fuller was that he functioned as a trim tab for earth.

PART 2 –

From the Mind of Werner Erhard (and Others)

"The truth puts people to sleep. It goes right to what's unconscious in them, and most people are uncomfortable in their unconsciousness, enough just to chance letting some truth strike the truth in them."

A Plethora of Words

"There are only two things in this world—nothing and semantics."

Language as a Tool

A New Form of Communication

Werner Erhard used the English language in a different way in an attempt to convey the context of the existential nature of our lives. Although he relied on tactics of using the metaphors of meaningless of purpose and emptiness of our existence in iconoclastic and nihilistic ways, he still relied on the richness of experience in an innovative manner to produce an enlivenment in the participants of the est training. Werner Erhard was a leading-edge thinker in the field of human performance and effectiveness and he used language to communicate the essence of what it means to be a human being. However, the thinking and language that he used were difficult for the uninitiated to grasp because the vocabulary was couched in a form that was radically altered from its common usage.

Erhard's stated aim was to change the fundamental nature of organizations—something that he considered to be a network of conversations—in order to create a transformation in society. His approach was to change the perception of human beings so that they might alter their behaviors in ways that would be more beneficial to the planet. This alteration of reality was to be achieved by language—by its use in the techniques of conversation to produce breakthroughs in one's reality, in the

---

77

manner of holding oneself in the world, and thus changing the future course of action to produce a new destiny in life.

Of course, some saw this as so much "thought reform" in a series of processes that were intended to manipulate the environment in order to ensnare the participants in a web of control via the information that was provided. Through the offerings of praise and discouragement, by the deprivation of food and sleep patterns, and by causing a hypnotic disorientation through language control, the effect was deemed to cause people to behave like robots. The confrontational methods used in the structure of the est training were designed to break down the resistance of the way each participant was relating to reality. By attacking the filter in one's head that one is always listening through, the effect was really an attack on how one thinks and perceives the world. The effect was also geared towards revealing the basic truths about people through the sharing of their stories about themselves—the source of peoples' identities.

However, the intention of the est training was one of temporarily letting go of all that one knows in order to experience the world anew. Its aim was for everyone to engage life as it is without filtering it through our personal likes and dislikes, by our preferences and aversions, or through our beliefs and opinions. To accept things the way that they are is a very powerful technique, and unfortunately there are those who could not temporarily suspend all judgements. This situation either caused more resistance—or else a disintegration of the person's mode of coping with reality. In extreme cases, the participants suffered traumatic disturbances in their lives—the result of which were the psychotic episodes and other mental breakdowns by those who could not handle the heavy doses of non-stop inputs to the mind.

The Core of the Training

The main point in est—and now of the Forum—was that we respond to events in life through a filter of interpretations since events by themselves do not inherently mean anything except by the context in which they occur. Fundamentally, all meanings of an event are interpretations of something that happened in the past. Furthermore, all actions, decisions and choices in life are colored by notions of what things should be like— instead of by the way that they really are. The perception is also colored by the assessment of assigning rightness or wrongness to a situation depending on what one holds things should be like. Finally, if things are not the way that they should be like, then obviously there is something wrong with one's interpretation, or something wrong with other people, or ultimately, there is something wrong with the whole environment.

Erhard's primary premise was that although you could not change your past, it was possible to alter your future so that it did not depend upon your past. By accepting total responsibility for your life—including that of all choices and actions—Erhard claimed that it was possible to create an extraordinary future for yourself. By engaging yourself in the games of life, by declaring your stand in life, by risking to venture forth in a new realm of possibility that had no supporting proof, justification or success formula behind it, Erhard maintained that a new existence could be brought forth—simply through the power of communication. Instead of determining what was possible in the future as a function of what had been attained in the past, it was about breaking this barrier of adherence to the past by reclaiming your power to decide what is really possible in the future.

This new way of being entailed giving up the notions of what should or should not be, of right and wrong, and of letting go of the idea that your actions are determined and shaped by the emotional experiences of the past. By going beyond the events of your past—as well as to the interpretations that are attached to these events—a "clearing" would be created in which your future would happen. It is strictly a matter of commitment and courage to make your declared possibility a reality. Of course, success is still not guaranteed, but your life will be different in the process of taking a stand for your future because the context of your life will be altered—as long as you continue to move your possibility forward. Thus, while it may not alter how your life will turn out, it will alter who you are being in life. The shift in your context will happen, even if the new requests and promises from the commitment to something new are fulfilled or not. As long as you are not "fixed in concrete" on the outcomes of the possibilities, you will still move forward in a different direction—instead of being stuck with options that are based on the past. And, as always, you are still responsible for the consequences of your actions.

The Truth of the Matter

Werner Erhard supposedly began telling the absolute truth after his transformation. As you read the following words of the fundamental aspects of the phrases that constitute the est training, it is important to reflect on the behavior of Werner Erhard. Admittedly, he included himself as being a liar. Thus, you have to question whether he truly lives by his words or if he is just paying tacit agreement to them (or in the words of the famous adage: "Do as I say—not as I do"). It is important to determine if Erhard has real integrity in his life and whether the legacy of trainers who have followed him are genuine. Some may be merely modeling Werner Erhard, saying something that reflects "referential" integrity—the kind that is accepted in a relationship of consensus, such as in the hierarchy of a corporation. It may also be something akin to the guiding governmental leadership and policies that implemented the principle of "Manifest

Destiny" that was used to overrun the Native Americans in this country. It is very important to decide if these words are the truth about what matters to human beings in their most fundamental selves, and if so, whether it is possible for human beings to adhere to their full intent and meaning by transcending their normal states of operation.

The person who probably knows Werner Erhard in the most profound manner is Ellen Erhard, his second wife whom he divorced in 1983 (although the final agreement was not reached until 1988). She is probably the best judge of the intent and context of his true communication based on her experience and perception of his actions and behavior, both before and after his "transformation." From her point of view, what drives Werner Erhard and motivates him are fundamentally his ego and his view of himself as a public image. Whether it is a statement coming from a woman's wrath that emanates from an ugly separation, or if it is from her clear perception of the man, she has stated (through third parties) that these are the most important things in the world to him. In any case, if the words that comprise the est training—and its present incarnation, the Forum—are truly significant, then they will stand on their own in an eternal fashion. Otherwise, they will fade into oblivion and will only be a remembrance of a past era.

Love

"You don't have to go looking for love when it is where you come from."

The Experience of Love

The Normal State of Affairs

In general, love is defined as a concept that exists some time in the past, or in the future, but never in the present. Love is thus mostly a situation where a relationship is used as a project—one of getting the "loved one" to whom we are related to be exactly like our mental image of the romantic ideal. As soon as that person doesn't conform to the mental images that we have associated with this ideal, then they become inadequate and are no longer the perfect partner. Moreover, if we are with someone whom we can't love for some reason—then it is almost impossible because we know from experience that love happens for everybody else. We become convinced that love is never going to happen for us—not in the past, present or future. And, if we are not in a relationship, then it is almost hopeless to have love exist in our life.

Loving Beyond Survival

If you explore the various images, fantasies and notions that we have about what love looks like, we see that we opt for the fantasy. But, when we do, then we are not coming from satisfaction and wholeness in our relationships of love. The difference is that a relationship that has gone beyond its own survival has the space to become what it has always been—an opportunity to experience and express the natural magnificence of the relationship. The value of such a relationship cannot be measured by everyday standards because this type of relationship is considered as miraculous. A relationship of this type is about creating the context for the conditions in your life that will manifest those miracles that result in love. It is only in this context that you will experience relationships that are alive with a brilliance as never experienced before and which are truly magical expressions of love.

Changes That Result

Once the problems that keep our relationships from working begin to clear up, then we have the space to create something anew. Then, one of two things can happen:

- We can create new problems that allow us to play "let's get our relationship to work" all over again, or
- We can step into a realm of consciousness that is beyond workability

The first possibility is the familiar one because that is the route that most relationships take. The second option is a realm in which we begin to express the potential for power, love and joy. This realm generates the experience of being in a state of communion with another person. It is the kind of experience that is beyond the sex, emotions or mental images, and that— for most of us—happens maybe only in our dreams.

Responsibility

"There are only two games in life. One is to expand—
to participate, and play wholeheartedly. The other is to
contract. There is no such thing as holding still."

On Being Accountable

Responsibility is the key precept in life. Whether or not you
assume the responsibility for whatever happens in your life,
you are still always subject to the consequences of your actions. You can't escape this fact—even if you give up the
responsibility for something. Thus, if you give up the responsibility for your financial situation in life, then when economic
adversity affects you it is hard to say that something else or
someone else is the cause in the matter. In a similar manner, if
you give up the responsibility for maintaining your health, then
later on—when certain conditions and afflictions begin to manifest themselves—you suffer the consequences of your past
behavior. Whether or not you accept the responsibility for everything in your life, the result is still the same: you are cause
in the matter—willing or not, aware or not.

The failure to accept responsibility in one's life doesn't have any
significance—other than shifting the "blame" to others and to
events. If you can't see that it is you who has ultimate cause in the
matter, then you will always be at the effect of everything that
happens. Events will happen to you "for no reason at all" in your
mind, but ultimately there is something somewhere that precipi-
tated every event in your life. This is not to say that you are causing
everything that happens to you because there are events which

occur that are way beyond the comprehension of all of us to perceive and fathom. But, your response—and all future responses—to events definitely have a profound shift in altering the effects of any circumstance in life.

What Is

"Obviously the truth is *what's so*. Not so obviously, it's also *so what*."

The Shift in Consciousness

The Discovery

The defining point of all reality is "what is." But, to have a game then "what isn't" is made more important than "what is." The rediscovery of this fact causes a shift in your consciousness because your mind then sees things at a very different level. For example, every business can be seen as a game of profit and loss although it doesn't lessen the blow of layoffs, mergers, bankruptcies and plant closings. Even war can be seen as a game—although it is one with very heavy consequences in terms of loss of life and the destruction of the environment.

The existence of all of these games is one of discovering your purpose in life. Since life is a game, then life is your partner and teacher rather than something that you are the victim of. Life then becomes a process of discovery, especially about what your purpose in life is. When you discover this purpose, then the action of the discovery creates a "space" that allows you to have an opportunity to make your life work. Creating this "space" begins a process in which things begin to happen in your life—magical things—such as having your relationships work, your finances be in order, and your work become meaningful. In the process a joy and satisfaction begins to happen, and you begin to experience an aliveness that is operating at a very different level.

The Transformation

But what does the discovery of "what is" do for you? There is a transformation of the self at a higher sense that establishes a willingness and ability to provide support for other human beings. It goes beyond the ordinary support level in the normal interaction between two human beings. Instead, it is a complete and total support for another that is always there—one hundred percent of the time. It is a support that has no strings attached to it, no conditions specified for it, no reservations held about it, and no sense of abandonment—no matter what happens. It is the type of support from which power manifests, energy is created, affinity is produced and from which love results. It is also a support in which the truth can be told in a way that is enlightening. Thus, it is opposed to the general situation in which each of us avoids telling the truth—the whole truth and nothing but the truth. This is because the truth may be uncomfortable, because it might hurt someone's feelings, because it may cause additional problems, because it might be confrontational or brutal, or even because it may be threatening to tell the truth. But, in telling the truth, the person gains the capacity of perceiving the way things really are. So in saying what's so about anything, you will discover the truth in a manner that is appropriate.

The Shift in Communication

The realization of "what is" alters your consciousness with regard to communication. The extent of this shift makes it possible to communicate in a way that even disagreements begin to be in alignment with each other—even though they may be diametrically opposed in position. This is because you will now communicate and come from who you are rather than from what you have done. This realization allows you to operate with viability in the world because it is now one that nurtures the people who are participating with you in life. Instead of operating from a basis of survival, you instead operate from total integrity. It is this context that creates the "space" for others around you to become "enlightened." But, this is something that cannot be figured out or analyzed by logic for it is something that you have to discover through the process itself.

The Discovery of Purpose

The discovery of your purpose in life will reveal the natural condition that already exists in the world—that people are already related—but which has been covered up by centuries of belief and inaccurate notions of who people really are. What people really want in their lives is to experience aliveness, to be nurturing in their relationship with others, and to make a contribution to other people's lives. This natural alignment is revealed through the process of participation, sharing, communicating, and by being who you are and letting other people know you. It is to allow yourself to experience life the way that it is, and not the way that you believe it to be—or think that it should be.

Changes both small and huge will take place in your life from the position of this new context of relationship. You will clear up misunderstandings, separate opinion from fact, resolve money situations, start your day with enthusiasm, and begin to communicate in a very different way with others. You will experience more of everything in doing whatever you do, have more love from others, more happiness, more intensity, and more exhaustion—but of the kind that benefits the spirit. The totality of all of your experience will be more aliveness.

The Ending of Effort and Struggle

Life does not care about your effort and struggle to make it work. No matter what you do, life only turns out the way that it turns out. If you look back at your life you will see that life has always turned out the way that it did and never in any other way—no matter what you have done. The truth is that there is nothing that you can do to force life to do otherwise because life is always the way that it is. Life does not work the way that you want it to—life works the way that it does and only in that way. Thus, what you need to do to get life to do what it is doing is simply nothing. To do nothing means to do exactly what you are doing. Hence, the first move—and the last move—in grasping the notion of nothing is to stop the effort and the struggle in your life.

Living

> "Your life has already turned out, and once you get that, life goes on from a position of it having turned out. That's called playing the game of life from a position of win."

The Confusion

Living

Living and life are two things that are often confused. Living is something that happens right now—not in the past or in the future. Living is not the story of your life because it is the process of experiencing in the here and now. Thinking, figuring, perceiving, arguing, reading and believing do not produce any certainty about living. The uncertainty about living goes away when you get beyond the symbols, beliefs, thoughts and feelings about the now. Beyond the effort and the struggle, there is observing, being and experiencing the now that makes the uncertainty about living disappear. This point is where you know the truth in the only manner in which it can be known— by direct experience. This experience creates the "space" that makes it possible to transcend everything and just be in the here and now.

The Experience of the Now

Anyone who experiences the here and the now can see the nature of reality because that is the way that it is. When you are being yourself—with nothing more added or nothing less taken away—when you are doing what you are doing and are allowing what is so around you to be exactly the way that it is, then you are in the here and now. Rather than going somewhere or being something or doing something, you are just observing it all exactly as it is without judgements, comparisons or evaluations. In the observation of what is, right now, you see things the way that they are. This does not mean that things will stay like this forever, but only that at this moment—in terms of experience—living is what is so right now. There is nothing startling about this realization—what is, is and what is not, is not—because it is nothing more than a so what! Nevertheless, that is precisely what you will find out, *except that it will be an enthusiastic so what*. This experience provides an enormous freedom because when you observe this fact, it will transform your entire ability to experience living.

Communication

"When one experiences love as one's own reality, then life is experienced as eternal."

True Conversation

Traditional Communication

Traditionally, society has not been structured to communicate. Throughout our history, society and its organizations have been structured to manufacture and deliver products, to accumulate commodities and wealth, and to represent positions—but never to communicate. True communication happens infrequently—and mostly accidentally rather than responsibly—since it is not a matter of simply exchanging symbols or words. Although we can say things, we generally don't notice the "space" in which we state them. The context for what is being said often determines the efficacy and potency of the message. So while people may be conscious of the facts or content of what is being said, they rarely have the intention for the context of their communication. Even if you change something in the communication and give it a new form, the situation will still persist.

Altering Your Communication

To alter your communication, you have to create the condition for transformation to take place. The "space" of true communication allows for something unsuspected in the ordinary course of events and it moves things without causing them to persist. With true communication you have the power of creation and disappearance—where the old disappears and the new becomes apparent. Real communication is thus an unusual phenomenon in life because it is done at a level that is beyond the conventions of our agreed upon reality. When you communicate at this level, there is a lot less struggle, sacrifice and effort involved. Things will also move faster and depending upon your intentions, this communication will reach deeper and will affect the more profound areas of your life. For when you are in true communication about what you are doing, a transformation will take place with your relationships, community, organizations and society.

Mastering Life

"Your total purpose in life is living. As you master life, what happens is there is more living in life, more aliveness, more experiencing right now."

The Context of Life

The Contents of Life

Life is different from living because living is what is happening right now whereas life is all of the content in it that defines it. In the realization of yourself—the process referred to as "enlightenment'—there is still life to handle. Since life is definitely an uncertainty machine, if you make the practice of life into a process of self-invalidation, then you will certainly not succeed in life. That is, when you do something and you don't succeed, then the next time that you perform this activity you will have lost some of the enthusiasm through the process of self-invalidation. This becomes a self-fulfilling prophecy in that if you do this activity repeatedly, and you are not successful, then the enthusiasm lessens again—until at some point, you literally give up.

If you are that way about life, then obviously you have definitely lost your enthusiasm about life. This makes your life a very mundane one because your life will now revolve around things like wars, political scandals, or performing a job that you may not like. Life becomes about the boring project that you are working on, your uneventful marriage, your humdrum family, trying to get along with people, and not really being able to communicate about any of it. Life is then a process of mere existence rather than one of living it at its fullest. The price is that the aliveness is lost, along with the happiness, love, health and full self-expression.

The Problem in Life

There is some certainty to life and in many ways it is very simple. The simplicity in life is that it comes in many different forms, these being clothes, food, shelter, transportation and all the other necessities that come with life. There are also rules concerning clothes, food, shelter, transportation and other necessities in life. You have to figure these things out, you may feel overwhelmed and you may not be able to handle these successfully. The feeling then becomes one of wishing that if the world would just leave you alone and let you do your own thing in your own little corner of the world, then everything would be great.

The basic problem in life is generated from the world by not obtaining any success—a state that becomes a self-fulfilling prophecy by giving you a false answer that the key is not to do anything. However, the nature of life and the rules that guide us in life—those about food, clothing, shelter, transportation and other necessities of life—are the fundamental ones for everything in life. They are the central rules in life, and they are *exactly* the same for everyone. Once you have discovered these rules for yourself, then life is no longer the great mystery.

The Fundamental Rule

The most fundamental rule is that *life is a game* in which *what is not* is more important or better than *what is*. Politics, economics, business, social concerns and just about everything else are games, and the truth is that all of life is a game. The importance of this rule is that when you lose the ability to play the game of life—and to master the game of life—then you forget that life is a game.

Understandably all games have various degrees of consequences. War, politics and economics are all games that have very serious and heavy consequences, especially when people wind up dead, vilified or broke as a result of having played those games. But, even the consequences of not playing can be heavy and serious also. To go through life, be at work and do your job when you don't really want to do it—or because you are not very interested in doing it—are all symptoms of this malady. The malaise then affects relationships, such as not wanting to be with the person that you are with. The relationship game then becomes one of the unfulfilled wish of not being free to decide who you want to be with, and the fantasy of being with another person whom you think that you really want to be with.

The Mastery of Life

To gain a mastery of life, you need to find out what the game of life is composed of. You don't have to figure out all of the rules for your marriage, job, relationships, finances and all of the other games that you may play in life. For if you understand the rules of life, then you will understand and gain the mastery of life. To accomplish this state you have to start from a position of a no-games condition—which is called living: where *what is, is* and *what is not, is not.*

First, there must be an agreement that a particular thing is more important than something else. The importance can also be created by disagreement as long as what is important is what is not. For example, money is important by agreement because it has no intrinsic value since it is merely a form of paper, metal or plastic. Second, *what is* to be important must be *what is not* because if *what is* becomes more important than *what is not,* then the game is over. Thus, life is a process in which wherever you are, that is not it because it has to be someplace else.

Since the real purpose of living is living, then life is a game about achieving a goal—and to always win. The goal that is set is what helps you know where it is, and becomes your destination—and defines the time for reaching it. The goal is merely a representation of anything that you have agreed to that allows you to play the game. So to master life you simply need to know what you want—whatever that may be—because it really doesn't make any difference what this goal is. If what the goal that you set does make a difference, then you are stuck with what you said that you wanted. However, at any point in time you can want something else. To master life, all you have to do is say what you want and know where it is that you want to go—to move from where you are to where you want to be.

The Flows in Life

In playing the game the only complications are the forces or flows that are either moving with you, opposing you or crossing you. You must include these flows in your life to be certain. In the past what has cost you your certainty has been when you have stopped to handle the cross flows and the counter flows—and sometimes even the helping flows. Including what assists, crosses or counters you is part of the mastery of life, and the only thing that keeps you from doing this is stopping to handle these flows. Do not stop to handle these flows because it will keep you from where you are going. Instead observe these flows, see what the situation requires, and include them in the game.

One of the primary flow problems concerns our parents. If your father and your mother told you to do things, and you didn't do them, then it was probably because you thought that your parents wanted to dominate you. What your parents really wanted to be were your parents—which included telling you what they thought was the right thing for you to do. If you opposed your parents all of your life, if you have stopped in your life to handle your parents (opposing, crossing and helping flows), then this has caused you to fail at your own purpose in life, and you have thereby lost at the game of life. This is the only way that you can ever possibly lose at life—by stopping to handle a threat, or a perceived threat.

Agreements are another problem in the flows and the game of life because they become solidified with time, and so the games that are associated with these agreements become solidified also. If you become "right" about these agreements, then that is not masterful because the mastery of life includes handling the agreements that you have already made. If you have made an agreement in which other people are involved, and you try to break that agreement, then in the process you become subject to the original agreement. Thus, you have to handle those agreements in a different manner—by getting the person that you made an agreement with to release you from that agreement. It may involve giving up something, or maybe acknowledging and communicating to that person that you made an agreement with them that you didn't keep.

If you have made agreements and you didn't keep them—even if these agreements were only made with yourself—then they are still important because it is your life that is bound by these agreements. The only solution is to make another agreement that it is all right to let go of those other agreements that you no longer want, for once you let the original agreements go, then they will cease to exist. You simply look at the things that you wanted to be, do or have and say that it is all right not to be, do or have those now—and then those agreements disappear. The reason for doing this is that the mastery of life includes integrity, and it includes the process of "cleaning up the mess" that you have made when you have not kept your agreements. Otherwise, these will become problems that are unsolved in your life and will be ones that keep coming up for you again and again.

Unresolved Problems

If you have left some problems unresolved in your life, then you can handle them by expanding your purpose to include solving these problems. Then, what was a problem before ceases to be a problem, and therefore becomes part of the solution. Essentially what you have to do is to expand your purpose of making your life work to include making the lives of others work also.

If you say that, "My goal is to make my life work and for your life to work too," then you have to "clean up the mess." This includes people that you have upsets with, people that you are out of sorts with, and people that you are not communicating with. That is the beginning of mastery—to "clean up the mess" that you have made, whatever that "mess" may be. To take the effort out of this process of "cleaning up the mess," you assume the point of view that your purpose in life now includes "cleaning up the mess." So if there are any problems in life, if there are things that you have done wrong, if there are bad things, horrors, secrets—if you have got any of that terrible stuff in your life—then it is not necessary to stop your life in order to handle it. All that you have to do is to expand your purpose so that in the process of getting from where you are to where you want to be your purpose includes "cleaning up all of the messes" that you have made. In this manner, the process takes all of the heaviness, horror, guilt, shame and everything else out of it.

It is always okay for you to get back into the game of life and to play it in its total extent. It is also all right to expand your purpose in life to get whatever you want out of life, including "cleaning up the messes" that you have made. The important thing is that you don't have to make up for all of the bad things that you have done in life in order to master life; all that you have to do is to be willing to "clean up the mess" along the way. If you can expand your purpose in life—to have aliveness, love, health, happiness and full self-expression—if you can allow that to be the purpose for which you play the game of life, then your life will transform in the process of living.

Failed Purposes

Another part of mastering life is to let go of all of your failed purposes in life. If you can acknowledge the things in life that you have let go of, and either rehabilitate your desire to achieve them or let go of the desire to achieve them, then they will cease to be "stops" for you. If you found something in life that you wanted to be, do, or have, then you can be, do or have that in your life. It doesn't matter that you think that you can't be, do or have that in your life because in actuality it is possible to be, do and have whatever it is that you want. All that you need to do is to expand your purpose in life to include whatever it is that is stopping you from being, doing or having what you want. All that is necessary is to see what it is that is keeping you from being, doing or having that.

The collection of reasons called your mind can complicate this situation to whatever degree that you like—but, life is still a game, with some of it having enormous consequences. However, if you get stuck in the importance of it, then you will no longer see that it is a game—even when the consequences are enormous. You need to realize that life is a game, and that everything in life is a game, except for living because that is simply what is.

Experiencing Life

Your life is composed of where you are and where you are going to be. All of the things that are problems for you—all of the stops—are part of your getting there. Thus, you cannot really fail, although you can make it take longer if you stop for barriers, because eventually you will get on with it. The only reason for mastering life is so that you can get beyond life to the thing called living, and once you are living, then you can do life itself. Ultimately, knowing what it means to live isn't the end of the game because you have got to get back to where you are. You cannot avoid the journey because it is a trip that has to be taken, but you do need to master life in order to bring more living, aliveness, and experiencing of the here and now into your being.

In experiencing out your resistance to confronting what is incomplete in your life, you will realize your true intentions. This includes experiencing yourself as the cause of your experience—and not as its effect. Also, in locating, experiencing and dissolving the areas of blocked consciousness in your body and mind, you will move in the direction of experiencing yourself as a buoyant, radiant and alive being. Finally, in locating, communicating and dissolving notions about whom you are afraid that you are, you will naturally open up the "space" for you to more fully express who you really are.

Experience

"Sometimes you will give up your possessions, your children, your husband or wife, you will give up everything, except for the one thing that you need to give up in order to experience something that you want. And what you need to give up in order to get that experience is the notion that you haven't got that experience."

The Substance of Experience

The Nebulous Thing Called Experience

Experience is something that comes out of nothing. Experience is not a form, is not understanding, and it doesn't come out of the world, your mind or your thoughts. True experience comes out of telling the truth—in a clear manner. Experience is when your mind empties out and you get to the thing about what it is that nobody can talk about. Experience is something that is outside the symbols that represent it.

You know something out of the experience that you have concerning what is going on around you and of what is out there in the world. This experience transcends the wishes of wanting to be saved, to become "enlightened," of being in a state of "nirvana," or of merely getting that flash of light called insight. Also, the experience is not what you think someone else has— and that you don't have—and more important, it is not one that you have to struggle for. What this experience involves is giving up the things that you are attached to—the things that you think that you need to survive in the world.

This experience is a process that never stops for at every moment in time you are subject to the forces of uncertainty in your life. However, there really isn't anything that is different about what is out there in reality—except for your point of view about it, and in terms of how much agreement that you get about this point of view. So experiencing is not about submitting to things or resisting them; it is simply a matter of "getting off of your position" about them. Having a position is okay, but being stuck in one is what robs you of your power.

Power in the world for an individual is represented by being able to operate in a condition of no agreement from a position in which you are not attached to—it is to be able to merely take a point of view about things. Thus, when that point of view is no longer appropriate or valid, it is easy to drop this point of view easily and instantly—as long as you are not attached to it or have deemed your survival upon it. This action represents true power: the ability that allows you to look at your own mind and to decide what is appropriate—or not. For experiencing the abstraction is what allows you to see the conditions in your life, especially the parts about where your resistance to things emanates from.

The Context of Experience

Experience is not a one-time event, but rather a process of "getting on" something and then "getting off" something—a process that is repeated over and over again. If you can be in a state where you can "get off of it" at any point in time, then you will experience that whatever comes up for you clears up in the process of life itself. Of course, this doesn't make it any easier once you are able to achieve this, but it does represent a certain level of ability in the mastery of your life. This ability represents a certain "space" that you command, a "space" where you experience being in control, and one in which you are able to be responsible for things. This experience gets you in touch with more of your resistance to things and events—but all that it means is that you get to handle more of it in your life. This is the way that life can start working for you, a process that makes it possible to share and to participate in your life to the fullest extent. Experience is really where to start the complete blossoming and flowering phases of your existence in life.

It may seem that by experiencing in this manner the only thing that will happen is that you will get massacred in the real world because life appears to be complicated, sometimes not very "clean," and oftentimes cruel. However, manifesting yourself through your participation in life provides an incredible constancy in your life. The world is organized on a "more is better" position, on scarcity rather than abundance, and on a similar set of other concepts and ideas. The only thing that is different is your way of handling this reality—and that is your constancy. For no matter how bad that you think things are—or how terrific that you think it is—it is all pretty much the same way all of the time. Coming up against that constancy is what enables you to keep growing, and what makes it possible for you to contribute to your own well being as well as to those around you.

Experience is something that is apart from the ordinary comparisons of education levels, of what school you attended, of how much money you have, of the things that you own, or the company that you work for, and so forth. Experience is also not about vacations, relationships, people, jobs, houses, environments or anything else. Experience is always there and it is something that you can't manipulate. Experience is something that comes up for you repeatedly and it is the one thing in life that makes it for you.

It takes great strength and impeccable integrity to maintain yourself against the odds in life. This is what separates the women from the girls and the men from the boys. Climbing mountains, jumping out of airplanes, river rafting and other life-defying events are not what kill people—*it is boredom that does it*. Even financial success has never made anybody anything. Instead it is the ability to keep coming back that has done it—and this is the one thing that has prevailed throughout the history of human beings. The tedium, the agony, the knowledge that people are going to die from strange—or well-known—diseases, and that everything in the world has been botched through blunders: all of this does not mean a thing in terms of your experience. For it is your ability to alter your experience of the world that will produce incredible results in your life. It is the communication of your experience that will produce more harmony, more enjoyment, more satisfaction and more interest in your relationships, work and everything else in your life.

Transformation

"Some people seem to think that getting off of it is like being a leaf in the wind. It takes strength to get off of it—power. It takes the same kind of power to get off of it that it takes to get on a position, and make it work."

Personality and Position

Who you Really Are

Your personality and position in life manifest themselves through anger, sadness, happiness, skepticism, indifference, belief and many other aspects. When life knocks you down, it sometimes takes great strength to be totally willing to let whatever it is happen. It is very hard to accept things as they are—especially when there is pain, confusion, resistance, upsets and unconsciousness. This is where transforming your life becomes extremely relevant and important.

Transforming your life requires participation since transformation is not an event nor is it content, but rather the context—or "space"—in which the event transformation occurs. Precisely, it is your experience that your ability to be transformed has been created. *Being transformed (i.e., "enlightened") is knowing that at any moment in your life, under any circumstances, you always possess the ability to transform the quality of your life—to "get off of it "(a position).* Transformation is being complete about things. It is the realization that creates the "space" for you to get off of it, and to hold it in the context of knowing that you are on it and are also able to get off of it (a position).

Those who experience transformation get in touch with their intention. The self's intention is to complete itself—to make a contribution to the self as other people's aliveness, to "clean up the mess" that you have made, and to make the world work. In all of this what allows transformation to be complete is your participation. If your participation stops, then your transformation never was for it becomes an event—an event called "enlightenment."

Transformation carries with it both the opportunity and the responsibility—but not the burden—for completion: the inclusion of all that is needed for the integrity or fulfillment of something for that transformation. The transformation keeps expanding into its own context and expresses itself as individuality on an initial level, and then in terms of relationship at the next level. What happens as you complete your enlightenment at one level is that you start to share yourself at higher dimensions of transformation. As you complete enlightenment at the level of individuality, and then share your self in relationship, you redefine your self at the level of relationship. When you complete enlightenment at the level of relationship, then the next step is to share your self in organization[1]. Thus, the quality of your life is a function of your enlightenment completing itself in a continuous fashion. Hence, your enlightenment of the self exists first within the context of individual. Then it manifests itself at higher levels such as those of relationship, organization and society.

Participation in Life

Participation is the crux of your enlightenment. Participation means simply that you can express your joy, anger, sadness, that you can complain, acknowledge or observe, that you can confront and handle an area of your life—and that you can "get off of it." Participation is the sharing of your experience with other human beings and to create the "space" for other people to share their experience with you. Participation comes from recognizing that there is very little difference between us and them. At some point, you will realize that you are responsible for your experience of all of it, and that you have the "space" to choose to be responsible—*or to not be responsible.* It all depends upon your willingness to participate and to share your self.

Participation creates an opportunity for you to experience the truth, transformation, enlightenment, satisfaction and well being in your life. It also creates an opportunity to participate in making the world work, and in contributing to the lives of others. What creates the "space" for you to participate is alignment with "source" (the self) rather than agreement with someone or something. For it is from source that you create all of the games in life. Of course, this does not mean that you have to be responsible for all of the evils and problems in the world. *You are only responsible for creating, causing, contributing and participating in your experience of it*—to get out of it as much as you give to it.

The one constant fact in life is that nothing is ever over, nothing is ever handled, and there are no ultimate solutions. As a consequence of this fact, participation is also never over, and allowing yourself to handle your "barriers" to participating is never over as well. When you are transformed, what you get to do for the rest of your life is to complete barriers to participation—just the same as when you were in a state called "not transformed." The only difference between these two states is your willingness to handle these barriers, and your capacity to be in the world—to take responsibility for your own well being and that of the world.

Of course you can also choose not to play for your individual survival is in no way dependent on your being. There is only your intention to communicate clearly. This clear communication affords you the opportunity to experience life totally in the present—in the here and now—with nothing added and without the constant "chatter" of your mind. True communication—as distinguished from the plethora of words and symbols, from the mass of explanation, argument and understanding—is the intentional and harmonious recreation of experience by one individual of another individual's experience. When one achieves the condition of true communication, the results are harmony, diminishing effort, expanding of understanding, increasing affinity in one's relationships, and the experience of love and satisfaction in one's life.

The Source of Strife

The source of the effort, misunderstandings, upsets and frustrations that often accompany the attempts to communicate stem from the barriers to communication. These barriers are the fundamental reasons that prevent you from experiencing and expressing your full potential for power, love and joy that is possible in relating to someone else. Thus, to make a relationship work, you have to experience and express the fact that you are related—no matter what the condition of your relationship may be. The essence of the situation is one of expanding the certainty and satisfaction that comes from experiencing and expressing your absolute relatedness to another.

To handle what may be blocking you from making a relationship whole and full, you must be clear about the purposes and goals of being in that relationship. You have to operate as *cause* in the matter of that relationship rather than being at the *effect* of that relationship. Eventually, you will work back to the completion of the fundamental relationship that is the archetype for all of your relationships in life—your relationship with your parents. For in working out your relationships in life, what you are actually doing is moving backward toward your relationship with your parents. *Until you complete your relationship with your parents, then you will have very little possibility of doing anything in any of your other relationships—except to dramatize your limitations about your relationship with your parents.* It is only when your relationship with your parents is complete that your life can be about having complete, nurturing and satisfying relationships with others.

Eventually you will realize that your parents always loved you and that all that they ever wanted for you (unless your parents were totally insane) was to experience satisfaction in your life. The total source of all the conflicts, upsets and communication failures with your parents is derived from the form that they put their love in for you. Almost everyone (unless they have been severely conditioned by their parents) organizes their life around an attempt to prove that they can "do it their own way." Since the purpose of a family is to provide an environment with some freedoms and some boundaries within which a child can recognize and discover who he or she is, then once this realization becomes evident you are no longer acting from your past. Then it is not a matter of trying to run away from your parents, it is no longer a situation of putting forth an effort to make it, and thus, you are no longer trying to be a "grownup." When you acknowledge that your parents completed their job in caring for you and nurturing you, it is then that your willingness to communicate will expand. Then you can let others know when things are working for you—and when they are not. You will also be able to state that there are things that others can do for you—even if it is simply a request for them to stay out of the way. You will know when you need support and when you just need the freedom to be where you are and who you are.

The Shift in One's Definition of Self

Transformation is a shift in the definition of the self from content to context. The shift is one of going from the identification of the self as a point of view, your life story, your personality and your body to one of recognizing the self as the context in which all of these things occur. Transformation is not an event, it is not a peak experience, and it is not about the conceptualization of your experience as a mental construct. Transformation transcends the law of things and events—and the limits of time and space—because it reaches back into the past and transforms it so that your experience of it is different. Experience comes from a set of abstractions while concepts only provide you with explanations of life. Abstractions have the power to create since they are generating principles.

Transformation is the "space" in which life occurs, and is the eternal change in relationship to the forces of life. Transformation is the recovery by the self of the generating principles in life with which the self creates itself. The shift is from identification of the self as a thing, position, event or process to just being who you are. The simple shift from trying to get satisfied to that of being satisfied makes any content in your life satisfying, nurturing and complete. It is not about getting better or about improving the content of your life, but about shifting the context in which all events occur. When this shift happens, the transformation enables you to create the real story of your life— rather than just be part of the narrative of the story or its events.

In transformation a self is complete and is represented by a self that manifests itself and expresses itself as being complete. It is not narcissism, it does not cut you off from other people, and it is not the result of confusion with the self as a position, body, ego or individual. The experience of the self is the full self-expression of the self in the world. If you are complete, then you are always beginning because it means being whole, being fulfilled and having entirety—that is, having all of the parts necessary to your integrity. Transformation exists on the level of *being*, manifests itself on the level of *doing*, and results in *having*. Transformation is given form by completing it continually—"be, do have" rather than the accepted belief of first having something, then doing it and finally achieving it. You simply start by expressing what you want to be, then you begin to do it, and finally you have it.

Endnotes

1   Organization refers to any institution. It could be government, the welfare system, church, medicine, the company that you work for, or the club that you belong to.

Functioning in the World

"An organization that works is one that is viable in the world, one that nurtures the people that participate in it, one which truly serves the people it intends to serve, and one which stays true to its original purpose. Such an organization operates with integrity and doesn't operate from survival."

The Context of Society

How the World Really Is

For transformation to be complete it has to be taken out into society at the level of self in the organization. This becomes the difficult task since there are no organizations in the world that work—those organizations being the ones that remain true to their purpose, that are viable in the world and that nurture the people who participate in them. Almost all organizations lose their purpose after they are organized and become instead mechanisms of persistence, survival and self-perpetuation. At worst, organizations sacrifice people and become evil—evil being the trading of aliveness for the purpose of survival.

Of course, only the self can be transformed because it represents the "ground of all being" from which everything arises—as wholes rather than parts. The transformed self works through the level of organization to alter society. Acting from "source" means that you are being responsible from choice to be "cause" in the matter. Through communication, you recreate someone else's experience, through relationship you create the "space" to doubt and question, and through integrity you reveal the truth. Without these elements being present, what happens is that evil crystallizes in the organization that you belong to. If the evil manifests itself, then you become a victim of it and then all that you can do is either hide it or resist it.

Dealing with Evil

To deal with evil—be it a violation of trust, disclosure of intimacy or misrepresentation of facts—you must confront it. Otherwise you will lose sight of the purpose of the organization, and you will then only serve for your personal ends rather than those of the organization. Eventually, if the evil is not responded to, it leads to a situation where the survival of the organization becomes more important than its original purpose. This then leads to lies, more lack of trust and a submerging of your true experience within that organization. You will then explain away and justify your participation in that organization by allowing the evil to further crystallize.

One of the biggest fears that anyone has is that of being conned—and worse, that someone else will think that you have been conned. If that is the case, then you will become defensive, you will negate your experience, and you will validate your fears. You may still be successful, but you will "hide" the evil and function from a pure survival game, defending your position through manipulation. This is precisely what happens to organizations that lose their purpose for being.

Moving Beyond Survival

Survival at the level of the self is expressed by self-righteousness, domination and invalidation of others, and self-justification. Instead of being concerned with your survival, you must realize that your being is already complete. Similarly, survival at the level of relationship manifests itself through entanglement and involvement. Again, the real context is that your relationship with others is also complete—even if it includes both love and hate, the latter being a barrier to that relationship. In the same manner, survival at the level of organization evidences itself as bureaucracy, effort, struggle and complexity—and produces work with no satisfaction for anyone. Rather than function in conditions of unreasonableness, it is best to function as "source"—the context in which everything occurs. Because this state extends to that of the organization, by your participation in it, you accept the responsibility for your experience of everything that happens.

Since agreements and disagreements are functions of the mind, then individuals, relationships and organizations will never work as a function of these conditions because the evil that resides in them will be buried. Rather than being merely successful, the point is to be in alignment—to function fully, freely and responsibly. *For agreement is merely a condition of content in which everyone is going to the same place. Alignment, on the other hand, is a context in which everyone is coming from the same place.*

The Past and the Present[1]

"If you look back over your life you will see life has always turned out the way that it did and never any other way—no matter what you did."

Then and Now

Completing the Past

It doesn't matter what you do in life as long as you participate in it—and acknowledge that you do so. Relationship is the most important part in the process of participation because in a relationship, the natural state is one of alignment—to live in the world the way that it really is. But, somehow as a child you knew that grownups were lying to you, and that things were not really the way that they said it was like. This created the dichotomy between the way that you wanted it to be and the way that it really was, and hence this created the inconsistency as you grew up.

So to complete your relationship, you have to let go of the past, including the resentments that you have stored in your mind. Besides, you can't go back since all that you have is the context of what happened from the basis of your experience now. While something may have worked for you in the past in some situation, more than likely it is now impossible to make it work in that manner in the present. Moreover, you probably don't even know what it was about it that worked in the past. So even though it is easy to evaluate the past—be it good, bad, fun or not—*the mere process of evaluation introduces a lie into the truth*—the truth being simply that it was the way that it was.

Endnotes

1 From an interview with the est staff as taken from the article "Then and Now at est" in the *Graduate Review*, January 1977.

On Sharing Yourself

"Since most people's lives don't function in our society, then you are on very dangerous ground if your life does function. Most people have a vested interest in not looking too good. And if your life functions, then that threatens those people."

The Process of Sharing

Sharing is Participation

Sharing is a big part of participation, especially if we have something valuable to offer. But, we never know how people are going to respond to what we say and so we start the process of making considerations. This is particularly true when these people are those to whom we are related and whose opinions we value. So the experience of sharing yourself is a process that you go through: an opportunity for you to look at yourself. Since you never know what people are going to say to you, and whether they will like it or not, the process can become uncomfortable and can reactivate moments from your past. This may even force you to go for agreement—especially if the reactions are hostile—instead of sharing yourself openly.

However, if someone else shares themselves with you, you may think of yourself as gullible if you accept what they have to say. In actuality, there are only two kinds of people: those who are gullible, and those who defend themselves against their own gullibility. In fact, a major part of your life is spent defending yourself against the fear of being conned. Thus, we won't tell someone that we love them because of the fear that this person won't respond—and in the process we will have been taken in. If we get beyond this stage, we won't make a commitment to that person because we are also afraid that this person will not keep their part of the bargain.

The Con in Life

We have an enormous set of laws and yet they can't prevent us from getting conned. But all of life is a con—a trap—and almost everyone avoids this fact because it is too much to confront. Marriage, education, love, money—we go into these knowing that we are conned. All that you can do is protect yourself so others won't find out that you have been conned. The fear and embarrassment of being gullible is what keeps you stuck in gullibility because you will not look at the person who you are afraid you really are.

It is possible, however, to go beyond the winning and losing—beyond all of the considerations in your mind of being conned. When you do, what you get is the experience of yourself and your own integrity. You can then share yourself with both enthusiasm and with compassion because all of the heaviness and significance disappears. For if you have something valuable to offer, sharing this with others is a natural thing to do. But, if you are unwilling to do so—perhaps because you may not get any agreement on it—then it results in a barrier in your life, especially if you have to handle rejection and loss of support. Nevertheless, communicating to others about who you are and what you do is the context that provides the satisfaction in your life and the joy in your relationships.

Getting Results in Life

To obtain results in life, you have to heighten the quality of your life. This means that you have to go beyond the barriers, doubts, embarrassments and all of your past conditioning—

119

beyond the so-called maturity which is merely a process of hiding the fact that you are not in touch with who you really are in life. Of particular interest is love because this is one thing that everyone wants to keep under tight control—rather than being spontaneous with it. A necessary part of love is that you must have the ability to experience yourself as being all right the way that you are, including all of the stuff that goes with it such as anger, rejection and loss of agreement. Another required part of love is that it is okay for you to expand and become more powerful and able than you presently are.

A prime requirement for getting results in life is to keep your agreements. The reason is not because your life won't work if you don't, but rather because you won't be able to see what is not working in your life. Continuously breaking your agreements confuses your field of vision and keeps you from confronting the things which may be very uncomfortable for you. But, you cannot correct things unless you are clear and are willing to be the cause of your experience—the opportunity "to be yourself." Otherwise, you will operate from effect, you will glorify effort, and you will stay rooted to the barriers and resistance in your life.

It is true that the world culture does not normally allow you to fully express yourself in it—to fully experience your well being. Most of the time you are invalidated for your experience, and you are countered with a lot of unfriendliness—especially if your life is working, you are enjoying meaningful relationships, and you are nurturing your aliveness. The world instead seems to support slick, clever and "successful" behaviors, and not necessarily "the decent life." Nevertheless, this doesn't mean that you have to alter the physical reality of life. All that you have to do is make it all right for you to express yourself and to be yourself in spite of all of the problems, barriers, lack of trust and openness, and difficulty of communication. Your experience will be different if you tell the truth about your experience for this very act will open other people's lives and enable them to experience what is so in the world around them.

Magnificence

"The only 'stuff' that is heavy is the 'stuff' that has mass and persistence—all the lies and barriers. Truth has no persistence to it. It's very light. Enlightenment is about lightening up."

Our Acts and Attitudes

The Spectrum

The spectrum of acts and attitudes that make up your life are completely controlled by whatever you are resisting. You are literally a "puppet on a string" because your resistance puts you at the mercy of the system. In this state you are not responsible for causing your own experience in the matter. Moreover, while some things may support you in life, the truth is that most things do not. This situation becomes associated with false cause, and it is what prevents you from ultimately being responsible for causing your experience.

When you support whatever supports you in your experience, what you end up with is more circumstances that verify, validate and provide more agreement in your life that you are cause in the matter. This realization expands your experience of life in an ever-increasing wave. The toughest part of this experience is in terms of relationships that always seem to start out very high when they are new and then deteriorate with time. Nevertheless, you are still responsible for making a relationship work.

The Discovery

When you take responsibility for a relationship, it is transformed into something that is greater than itself. It also opens up the "space" for the love in the relationship and manifests it on an expanding basis—as long as the two people in a relationship choose to create it that way. The primary problem that prevents this from happening is the root cause which is that of your experience as a child. For the most part, as a child you did not participate and communicate with others because of the conditioning to "hold back" with regard to life. The concept of scarcity became ingrained from the notion that if you gave everything away, then you would have nothing. This spilled over into relationships with the consequence being that you would always hold on to a little part of yourself so that you would never "run out." This is where the lies began to be told, and where we did the "bad" things, and where we learned to manipulate others—including that of being a "victim."

The real discovery in all of this is that if you put yourself out there completely, the truth is that you will keep having more of yourself—not less. Eventually you will find out that you have a reservoir that is literally limitless. This is not just a statement, or a crazy idea; rather, it is a matter of not resisting the way that things are in the world. The discovery of the "child within you," of what you have that is underneath it all, is what is necessary for you to experience yourself as totally responsible for your presentation in life. This includes everything in your personality such as your speech, gestures, body language, posture, outlook and disposition.

The discovery also brings with it a realization that the best way to function in life is to play it straight with others—and especially with yourself. If you break your agreements, then others will no longer count on you, and eventually the world will cease to count on you as well. The ultimate reality of seeing the reflection of the way things are in life will move you from being sad, protective and whatever else you use to cover it up, into a sphere where you can laugh at the whole thing. The process is one of recovering your ability to recognize that you are the cause of all of your considerations in life.

This is the state of being through which you will achieve mastery over all of the patterns in your life. By your word alone you will shift the guiding paradigms through which you live your life. Interacting with others will become a privilege when you are functioning at this level. The result will be a powerful and overwhelming sense of the magnificence of other people— and that of your own magnificence.

Being at Cause

*"People's actions are always perfectly correlated to the
way the world occurs for them."*

Our Common Culture

The Perpetual Struggle

Children and their grandparents usually have a wonderful relationship because they have a common enemy: the children's
parents (the grandparents' offspring). This cultural problem of
a family is the norm in this country, and creates much of the
strife between children and their parents. It culminates in its
greatest intensity when the children are in their teens, when the
negative-positive balance of energy creates a great deal of the
heaviness with which the kids have to deal with the rest of their
lives. All of the acquired and learned traits of behavior—including the extreme of a "screw you" look written all over the
face—is what makes everyone grow weary. Getting all of this
"heavy stuff" out of the way is what is required, and this is a
process that will take as long as is necessary until you get over
it.

All of the associated emotions with the heaviness in life only
makes these events more significant. Accepting the premise
that we are in a hopeless system where suffering is the way
only strengthens the notion of deficiency in one's life. It leaves
one with only the option of having mental "crutches" to make
the best out of the situation. Rather than being complete, you
instead come from lacking something—of having something

be wrong with you as being the cause of all your troubles. This is where the infamous trail starts of finding someone who can make you whole—someone who can fill the gap and help you—to find the person that is "the one." The flaw in the argument is that you know that no one is perfect, and thus that your search will be one that is impossible to fulfill. This is because "the one" is strictly in your head, and your picture of that person will never match anyone in reality. This unattainable position creates the bottom-up struggle in your life, with the hidden agenda emerging as one of knowing that you are ultimately "going to get better."

The truth is that it isn't about getting better, but rather about it being different. Only when you notice what is really happening in life will you be able to let go of it and experience instead what is really there for you. Thus, when you experience a relationship that works, it then creates the context for other people's relationships—and the possibility for them to work also. Confronting what comes up for you and being straight with others enables you to communicate the truth of what you see. It is the difference between fun and value. Value is satisfaction, acceptance, and allowing things to be. It is knowing that whatever happens is okay—even if there is no fun associated with it. Fun, on the other hand, is mostly a reactivation which is sometimes triggered by an upset. For most of us we only get value when we have fun, but the reality is to get value for its own sake since fun is a separate issue. The attempt to create value by having fun only causes confusion. In other words, you have to do something in order to have fun, but you only have to be to get value.

When the distinction between fun and value becomes clear, then you will no longer be at the effect of having fun. In this manner you will be free to create and in the process have even more fun than before. Within this context your relationships can sometimes be fun, but they will *always* be valuable. What you discover is that once you can experience the value in your life, then fun is an unnecessary—although enjoyable—luxury that is created on top of value. This transforms the quality of your fun.

Our Everyday Existence

Marriages are arrangements that are crafted from a carefully worded set of agreements, including procedures for divorce. What brings people together in marriage are their pictures and patterns—and what sets them apart are their pictures and patterns. Anything that reduces the aliveness of a relationship—including divorce—is a function of these mutual pictures and patterns. This is at the heart of all the unreasonableness, false cause and difficulties that people experience in relationships. This is what gets in the way and what diminishes all relationships.

The real strength of a relationship is for both parties to be willing to have it, or not to have it—or both. Thus, to have a workable marriage both members have to be willing not to have one. Until all possibilities are included (divorce and marriage) and made to be okay, no real commitment can be made—the agreement made out of choice. Only in this way can you share it all, not just the good and lovable things, but all the evil and hate as well. There is no pretense of "having it all together" because you simply use your own personal process and the things that you are moving through in your life to create the "space" for others to be.

This is literally the experience of the "magic wand." At any point it is possible to transform not only your life, but that of the world. You do this by considering it to be other than the way that you have considered it to be before—an event that causes the world to shift to validate your consideration. It includes recovering your original consideration—especially the notion of someone being "the one." Otherwise, the person that you are currently with may be the greatest and most wonderful human being, but that person will certainly not be your choice if you have the consideration that this person is not "the one." All that you have to do is consider it differently with this person, and by doing so you will shift the whole context of your relationship—by choice. For if you don't, then your whole life will be about not having found "the one" and you will be left alone and unhappy. You will invalidate yourself, you will go on searching, and you will be left at the effect of everything while you look for that mythical person.

The Essence of Being

Your true context is one of being cause and creator of your reality—including the creation of someone whom you can call "the one." The world will shift to validate that experience because it gets back to the transformation of yourself from position to context. The context is not about a destination but rather about how your life will naturally unfold from a place of satisfaction. It is not informational (what we know) but is instead epistemological (how we know what we know). It is the shifting of the story and content of your life to that of the experience of your life as an expression of satisfaction, wholeness and completion. It is also not a search for that expression because all of that will have persistence to it. It is about enlightenment—about "lightening up" from the heavy stuff of life. When you create this natural realization, you are then the context in which your life occurs, you generate all of the content within it, and you experience it as it unfolds in your life.

If you opt for attainment, you will just become attached to these things and then it will become a matter of survival for you. You will only see the content and not the context. You must look at yourself, tell the truth about yourself and then experience yourself. It is not a matter of following some discipline but one of discovering who you are—yourself as your own master. This doesn't mean that everything will be perfect for you afterwards, but you will be in a true relationship with yourself.

You may resist feeling bad, or sad, or mad or some other feeling, but you will find that this does not work. *All that you will discover is that when you resist something is that it will persist.* So the best action is not to resist something when you come up against a barrier—because otherwise it will be precisely what you get. The crux is responsibility—to experience yourself as being cause in the matter. Only then will things that have been persisting in your life begin to dissipate. You may not alter very much, you will still have the same energy and use the same communication—but you will be different in that you will not have the attachment to any of it. To emphasize, being cause at what you do means letting go of the notion of "making it" in life. You must realize that you are climbing a mountain that has no top, and that whatever value there is in doing it—it is all obtained from the process of climbing this mountain.

Truth

"The truth doesn't mean anything. It just is. If you experience it, it is the truth. The same thing believed is a lie."

The Basis of Truth

Obstacles to the Truth

Truth is like a flower because it doesn't mean anything—it just is. Meaning is something that is imposed by the mind while truth is not derived from the mind. When the mind "ceases to exist," then the truth becomes evident. Truth is thus an experience rather than a belief—which is always derived from knowledge. Anything said about the truth is a lie, and thus words can only get you close to the truth—but not to it. But getting nearer to the truth does not make any difference. Only when you make the jump from the lies of the mind will you arrive at the truth—the *"what is"* in life.

People are not really interested in being happy because they are always ready to sacrifice happiness for reasons of pettiness: anger, hate, jealousy, possessiveness and other nonsense. Of course, the opposite is true—that they will not sacrifice anger, hate, jealousy, possessiveness and other nonsense for happiness. The truth is that if you accept what is, then there is no possibility of being unhappy. Happiness is a simple phenomenon because there is nothing needed to have it. All that you have to do is be there and be happy. It is all up to you how you choose it to be.

Since happiness is a function of accepting what is, then it is also part of being healthy. Moreover, health is a function of participation, and the more participating that you do in your existence, the healthier that you will be. The converse is that being uncommitted and being merely a spectator in life will only lead you to a state of unhappiness—and unhealthiness. But happiness and healthfulness does not mean functioning out of ego-expression—which is irresponsible behavior that stems from one's "act" in life. Instead it is to operate out of a context of self-expression—which is a function of responsibility. In self-expression you are responsible for the whole and everything that you do affects that whole. It is to stand there without anything to hide behind. It goes beyond the expectations, entertainment and boredom to a point of excitement and relevance.

As long as you are an achiever, you will never be awakened to this experience. Experience is the only way in which you can truly function. It is only from that center that you can live up to your highest potential. You will tap that spirit within you to discover the power within yourself instead of looking to project it out to someone else. This is also not about adoration or magnification of yourself as an ego, but rather an introspection of all of your patterns, games and acts that prevent you from living in the fullness of life.

It is also not a matter of belief. Belief can be very powerful but it has failed for many people who have employed it. Originally, valid experiences are the ones that have given rise to belief. However, through time these beliefs are then passed on without the foundation of experience behind them. The trouble with this is that these beliefs then delineate what experiences are deemed as valid in the future. For if you have experienced a certain facet of truth, and have gotten locked into that particular facet as a belief, then you are not open to the newer possibilities of what you may experience next. Your survival

Truth is a
sphere — no one
fixed point.

becomes rooted in that element of truth—which is now a belief. The belief is a trap because now you are not willing to take responsibility for yourself. The responsibility is now projected to God, the "devil", the church, the government, your parents, the company that you work for, the organizations that you belong to, or to your mate—to everyone except yourself. Furthermore, operating from belief leads you into categorizing and judging everything and everybody into good and evil, and eventually you become bound by those judgements and categorizations.

The Awakening

It is much more fulfilling to opt for life, freedom and fullness by being responsible, by including other people's points of view and by giving them the freedom to be who they are. Instead of creating a climate of divisiveness, you will expand to be more active, alive and spirited. It will be a situation of presenting less to others and more a matter of what you are doing together. This doesn't mean that you have to be a fanatic or indifferent—although you may have to let some people go if they are not up to participating and your communication with them is not in a context of a return cycle.

There is no value in censuring your communication because if you tell your own truth you will experience clarity. This is your journey of growth in life: with your relationships, in completing your past, confronting barriers, shattering the illusions and taking responsibility for your life. It is the basis of reconciliation of yourself with your human heritage. It is about regaining your spontaneity instead of responding from the reactive mechanisms of the survival machinery of the mind.

Belief will not stand up to experience and the truth is what has real power in life. The belief systems that are attached to your human heritage are not what is real for you nor do they determine who you are in this world. Beliefs are merely concepts that are intended to share experiences, but at best they are symbolic abstractions that are used to convey ideas. The problem is that many of these beliefs no longer function and are no longer appropriate, with the result being an enormous amount of arguing and fighting in the human community. This only creates an environment that is totally off purpose and destructive. The real concepts are those that arise from your own experience of your human heritage. That is the real awakening of experience—and what constitutes the truth.

On Letting Life Work[1]

"Truth is guarded by confusion and paradox. One such paradox is that if someone says, 'I am telling a lie' and that person speaks truly, then that person is telling a lie and therefore speaks falsely. But, if that person speaks falsely, then that person is not telling a lie, and therefore that person speaks truly. At best, all that you can say is, 'Don't believe anything that person says.'"

The Suppositions in Life

Our Intellectual Functioning

Most of us have an intellectual apparatus through which we interpret the knowledge from social, political and economic systems and the events that are associated with them. Usually we are strongly attached to our ideas about the world and we use the language to express ourselves in the traditional way—of having answers for the positions that we take in life. We discuss things based on presuppositions that we then use to determine the truth or falseness of any given situation. The outcomes then become theories according to the statements of our original presuppositions. But we never seem to question the original suppositions that are all based on hypotheses and conjectures.

Creation is at the root of everything although the mind has difficulty in accepting this since its persistent search for answers threatens the beliefs of a lifetime. The reality is that in life everything is effect that is due to circumstances. Neverthe-

---

134

less, you still create your own experience at every moment in time, and if your experience is not a function of your circumstances, then you will be able to create your experience out of nothing. This goes against all tradition, conformity, family values and all other barriers that you use to protect yourself from whatever poses a threat to you.

Your experience of life is more fundamental than the personality, circumstances or culture that surround it. It comes from having the courage to tell the truth—even if it is only to yourself initially. This experience will support you in everything that you do, especially with regard to your relationships. Of course, this does not mean that you won't have problems, upsets or disagreements; however, these will all occur in the context of completeness rather than one of deficiency. Instead of struggling and getting caught up in needless introspection and self-questioning, you will be free to participate in the world and to sort out what is relevant for you.

Doing Nothing

Clearly, there is nothing you can do to force your life to turn out differently because the reality is that life is the way it is and it turns out the way that it does—and not the way that it should, or shouldn't. But, every human being operates out of a paradigm that colors all of the choices, decisions and actions in life. This paradigm states that when things are the way that they should be, then things are "right," and that when they aren't that way, then something is "wrong" with me, with others—or with the world. But if there is nothing that you can do to force your life to work, then the solution must be to do nothing—to be in a state of passive contemplation, defeatism, or even withdrawal from the world.

Doing nothing in order to "let life work" has associated with it some lies that become traps and prevent you from operating with an absolute and active type of integrity. One lie is the implication that life can work whereas the reality is that all life is suffering. You can attempt to transcend this fact by playing games of eternal salvation, "nirvana," heaven or other activities that promise a reward tomorrow for what you do today. But all of these games revolve about some other time, some other place and some other condition where ultimate value and fulfillment are supposed to reside. Thus, they constitute mere abstractions that hide the truth about the suffering in life. Another lie that is implicit in doing nothing is that most of us instead do something that we term as doing nothing such as surrendering to the inevitable or abdicating one's personal responsibility by becoming a "victim." Still another lie is that there exist alternative choices. Most religious thinking is centered around this concept with its attempts at explanations to promote ways out of this bind.

Content within Context

The indomitable fact remains that it is all content within context as regards life and its events. But, as long as you think that you are playing the game effectively, you won't question the need to play it according to the "right-wrong" paradigm. Again, the paradigm is that when things are the way that they should be, then things are right, and when they are not that way, then something is wrong with you, others or the world. To get beyond this "right-wrong" paradigm, you have to free yourself from the illusion that you can control life so that it turns out the way that it should. First, you reclaim for yourself the power to determine what is possible in the future instead of acting out of what you have granted to the past. Second, you create the possibility of a new way of being for yourself as a function of the commitment that you are willing to make. Third, you declare that there is no right or wrong way—and no fixed way that things should be or should not be.

The Realm of Possibility

The new realm of possibility that you declare is founded solely on your stand for that possibility. You bring it into existence as a possibility without any backing by precedent, argument, explanation, evidence, justification, prescription or proof. And, the only certainty in the matter is *your commitment* to take action, to be persistent and to have continued capability in the face of risks, quandaries and obstacles that will come your way. This is the "clearing" in which the future happens, and is what allows life to work.

Endnotes

1   From the article "Viewpoint: Letting Life Work" by Howard Sherman in the *Graduate Review*, August 1977.

On Education[1]

"Can we transform what appears to be the most impossible problems of humanity into the most useful and constructive tool for understanding the complex forces that limit our own lives? Moreover, can we, on the strength of that new insight, gain a sense of personal power over those forces—forces that increasingly diminish our own freedom of choice and our own well-being?"

Learning and Education

The Source of Learning

When people assume responsibility for their own reality, the results can be amazing—especially with regard to their education. Illiteracy, poverty and other thwarting environments are transformed so that learning takes place in ways that are useful. Some achieve mastery in their lives as they begin to see what it takes to make the world work for them. The ignorance and lethargy of their daily lives is removed by the realization that education is their primary tool for achieving practical action. This type of learning is done in a framework where the learner becomes aware of his or her capacity to make choices that then shape their specific environments.

This kind of knowledge is a process—rather than something static—and revolves around a consciousness of intention. It is a kind of problem-posing education that involves a constant unveiling of reality, and which sometimes entails critical intervention and a movement to action to create something that is of value to everyone. This situation is diametrically opposed to one that only has associated with it a brief emotional experience behind it—and one that only affects the particular individual.

An individual's personal experiences of life are given validity and acceptance by what is termed the "cultural circle[2]." This leads to an expanded understanding in a personal context and will include the experiences of other people in that circle. Eventually a wide enough circle is produced that encompasses the entire realm of a political, social and economic climate. But comprehension is only a small part of a wider pattern and the process involves a deeper investigation of the holistic aspects of the language that is being used to convey the experiences. The consequence is a reflection that enables one to be aware of the world, of your position in it, and of your power to transform it. In the process, it ceases to be external and becomes instead a creation from within—from source.

Real Education

This educational philosophy can be summarized by distinct and fundamental ideas:

- Everyone is an incomplete being whose task is to transform the world
- Transformation is used to change the social, economic and political arena
- The world is a problem to be worked on through freedom and observation
- Everyone is capable of looking critically at the world through dialogue with others
- Education either causes conformity or it leads to action
- Awareness grows as a result of meaningful dialogue
- People must gain their individual freedom from oppression

- Human beings and the world are in constant interaction
- Human beings are free and are not bound by a deterministic context
- Subjugation of human beings is accomplished through beliefs
- Human beings are capable of being agents of their own recuperation

Assistance that is directed to symptoms rather than to fundamental causes robs people of the necessity of being responsible for their lives and instead creates a chronic dependency in them. When people discover that they can deal with their problems through education—rather than through welfare—it makes them whole and they begin to function out of a set of ethical principles. They learn that if they apply the same world myths—those of inevitability, scarcity and lack of solutions—then they will suffer the same consequences in the areas of money, relationships and all other aspects of their lives. For the real education is in discovering the principles that are necessary to have the world work for them—instead of against them.

Endnotes

1   From the work of Paulo Friere as taken from the article "Education and the Return to Consciousness" in the *Graduate Review*, October 1977.

2   A culture circle is defined as a group of people who interact and learn together. The group uses key words through which they personally relate. Each member uses the key words to create, clarify and expand the meanings to other related ideas, concepts and experiences. The discussion leads back to the work that is to be done—and to the worker who will do the work.

Making It Better

"The purpose of life is to allow you to express and experience your alignment with the reality in the world so that you can find out that you are the source of it. You have to understand that wherever you are and whatever you do, everything that happens to you—you bring on yourself."

Our Relationships With Each Other

The Drama in Life

Whenever you find yourself in the middle of having a "pity party" or of developing a psychosomatic illness in response to some threat to your emotional survival, it more than likely emanates from your first experience of abandonment. The upset is produced by the subconscious recall of a pattern and is a way of "getting attention"—of eliciting the desired response for sympathy in others. However, if the response does not occur, then the "game" stops there because the emotional appeal does not work anymore. Only then will you be able to see the real problem and deal with it in a manner that is more truthful.

As long as others "plug in" to your drama, the "tape loop" will play again and again for as long as you want it to. The result will be that you will probe deeply to get to the real reasons for your behavior, and you also won't be able to treat the various "illnesses" that manifest themselves from the conditioned behavior. To achieve both physical and mental health, you must realize that there is a greater drama taking place in the world.

You must also learn and discover the rules as part of your quest for wisdom.

Reference Points

Everyone exists in reference to somebody else. When that reference point is lost by that someone not being in your life anymore, you lose the experience of identity through the presence of someone else. The result may even be an experience of being nowhere, especially in an emotional sense—and if severe enough may also constitute a threat to your physical survival. If so, then you will do anything to ensure that someone else is there for you as a reference point since no one really wants to feel like they are nowhere.

But, what will you do to keep this someone else there for you? Will the "payoff" be great enough for you to withstand any additional pain just to have that someone there? Will you do anything to keep that in place? It all depends upon the responses that you get from this someone else. It is especially so if they are ready to "care" by being concerned and worried over you, even to the point of perpetuating your "illnesses," depression, and everything else that is associated with this need to have that someone there for you.

The Cure

The antithesis of caring is loving someone, including that of providing the space for that someone to be sick, depressed or whatever. By simply letting that someone be, that person can recover from being "sick" depressed or from whatever else is bothering them. This leaves them with the "space" to be healthy, to become clearer—and to oftentimes undergo some dramatic changes in well being. The crux is that by allowing someone to see clearly where they stand in reference to others, you will also see how you stand in reference to yourself—and thus to your environment. To the extent that you are able to do this in your life, to that degree will your life be made more satisfying.

Making yourself better is something that is easily said—but very hard to do. For when you open up to someone else, and you reveal to them your inner nature, you have to deal with the exposure of yourself to that someone. You have to move past your fears, and to have the confidence to deal with any situation that may result as a consequence of the revelation. In fact, the more difficult that the communication becomes, the more satisfying it will be when you push through the barriers because it will force you into unfamiliar circumstances. All obstacles that present themselves to you will provide the necessary motivation for your true communication to occur.

Through this process you will see that the essence of communication is intention—and that communication is very different than just mere information exchanges. Making it better means having communication, cooperation, mutual acceptance and common purpose. The words that are used are merely devices of convenience; what has to be clear for true communication is your intention. Through this process you will experience love, health and happiness, and you will attain full self-expression.

The Result

The measurable result of this process depends upon the extent to which you can experience satisfaction in your communication with others. It is also dependent upon the extent that you commit yourself to that communication. You should be able to express the things in life that are really important to you. This applies to the job that you are involved with, and includes preparation, training and the ability to provide the service for whatever you do in your line of work. You also have to look at your shortcomings, break through any facade, and deal with these so that things become clear for you in the process. Otherwise, you will end up blaming others and making up reasons when something fails or goes wrong.

If you deal with others in a negative context, then the genuineness and openness will become lost. The security in a job lies in the comfortableness that you feel in dealing with others— without any apprehension or fear. You also will not use others because you will take responsibility for your actions instead of laying it on someone else. For if you come from choice, then you will do things well, and the stuff around you will work itself out in the process.

Creativity[1]

"Play is whatever you give yourself to completely."

The Magic of Creation

The Source of Creativity

There are moments in life when there is magic—when something happens that is quite unlike anything that has happened before. This constitutes creativity, a quality that almost everyone attributes as one of which only a few people are capable of doing. But real creativity has to do with being, with creating something out of nothing. The full expression of the self in the world—true creativity—is at a level of experience that is called "sourcing." "Sourcing" is the experience of creating your own experience as you are experiencing it. For if you are creating your experience moment by moment, it is always fresh and new for you—never old. This discovery allows you to take your manifestation into the world from where you can make a contribution.

Creativity is innate in all of us, and expressing it is a function of accepting it, of allowing it to be, and of letting it happen. You must let go of your beliefs and considerations to allow yourself to be a magician—to do things that are deemed to be beyond what our system says can be done. Creativity means that there is no separation between yourself and the thing that you are doing. It will all be a single flow in which you are creating each moment with wholeness and satisfaction. Creativity is the art of creating each moment as being perfect. It is the direct experience of being the one who creates satisfaction in your life. It is the context out of which your life is generated—which is what creativity is.

Endnotes

1   From the article "Viewpoint: Being Creative" by Hal Isen in the *Graduate Review*, November 1977.

Integrity

"In the interim, integrity is being true to one's principles. Ultimately, integrity is being true to one's self."

The Essence of Integrity

The Basis of Integrity

Integrity is a quality of profound humanness that is sometimes equated to moral uprightness and behavior steadfastness. However, integrity is more profound than this and involves a commitment and an ordering of every dimension of the self that is focused towards that commitment. Without that integrity, you are merely the effect of the various forces that impact you in our society. The true basis of integrity is a resolve that chooses your destiny through the decisions that you make—whether these are done consciously or unknowingly. To do so with awareness is to act responsibly and with freedom.

Integrity is the realization of being true to yourself and from that position looking at the values of your society. Integrity is thus beyond the opinions and codes of others. The person of integrity is engaged in reevaluating the values of society and reinterpreting them according to that person's life thrust. It is a fundamental obligation that transcends the conformity of living within the mores of society. Having profound integrity means acting in ways that are always appropriate—even when you are opposed and at odds with everyone. It is to be securely anchored—not with the currents and waves of present societal activity—but with the deep trends of human history itself.

147

Profound Integrity

Someone with profound integrity experiences an inexplicable rootedness in a long journey towards an object of resolve. It involves a wisdom that is centered around the adage: "Know yourself, and to your own self be true." Integrity also requires that your actions incorporate the following behaviors that form the base of it:

- keep your agreements
- do what you say you will do
- don't violate your ideals
- operate as a "tight ship"
- do complete work
- operate with compassion

The ultimate integrity is one of telling the truth about who you are. This means expressing yourself consistently and experiencing your life with the following qualities:

- sharing your integrity
- letting others experience your integrity
- letting others experience their own integrity
- experiencing the integrity of others

Profound integrity is about having "miracles" manifest in your life from your intentions. That is the purpose—to make *what is, is*—with aliveness being the underlying condition. Experiencing, manifesting and sharing your profound integrity in everything that you do is what will make "miracles" happen for you.

Making A Difference

"No principle exists in the abstract. Without its concrete application, it has no meaning."

What it Means

The Game

The game of "making a difference," which is what the lives of human beings are about, is to have "miracles" manifest themselves so that the world works and the planet is transformed in the process. In allowing others to experience that their lives make a difference in the world, you will establish the quality of "aliveness" as a natural state for human beings. What you will gain by making a difference in your particular role in the world is one of impact. The context is beyond pleasure, excitement or doing things that feel good; it is also not a process of getting credentials, accumulating knowledge or symbols, or one of achieving something—and certainly not one of manipulation.

To make a difference you have to take a position of leadership that is based on your own magnificence and then operate in a multi-directional and integrated manner in everything that you do. You also have to be clear about your purpose so that everything that you do works toward that purpose. In the realization that you are doing something that is incredibly valuable, the quality of your life will change through the experience of making a difference. Even if you don't succeed, it is important to do it so that others can also experience the same thing. Thus, you have to accept that what you are doing is worthwhile, you

149

must do it in an intelligent manner with intention, and you must display enthusiasm and excitement. You have to be committed one hundred percent and take the responsibility for the context that your life can make a difference.

The Options That Are Available

Your options in life range from making money to the possibility of creating real value. The realized self—who you and I and everyone else actually are—exists in an environment that is termed the "beingsphere." Making a difference is about transforming the "beingsphere" which at present is contrary to life. It is your natural birthright of joy, relationship and wholeness—that is, enlightenment. It is having aliveness be the natural condition that functions in your life. All other states of being that are concerned with events in the world are irrelevant to the outcomes. And, the opportunity to transform your "beingsphere" starts with making a difference in your own life.

Even if you are not "in the mainstream," you still have a vested interest in building a coherent life-support system. The dissociation with nature is at a point where we are polluting the environment—the air, land and water—to an incredible degree. By questioning the conventional wisdom that has been handed down to you, and by examining the unexamined in life, a positive turning point will occur in your life that gives you immense power. If nothing else, it will allow you to take control of your life. Ultimately, it will enable you to take responsibility for things in the world to the extent that you want. All that you have to do is acknowledge that this is what your life is about and then communicate it.

What is Relevant

You have to give up being liked and you may even have to give up the entertainment value during the process of making a difference. It is a way of changing that hasn't been worked out yet. Operating within this framework will also probably be incompatible with the belief systems that exist. You will have to grow, you will have to communicate to others about how you feel, and you will have to observe what is going on for you during the process of making a difference in other people's lives.

The process is most relevant with children because they are remarkably clearer and can work towards their goals much easier than adults can. Children understand the end and can keep it in sight as opposed to adults who must function with a lot of "clutter" around them. Furthering their independent lives is the most important thing in making a difference for children for eventually they will have to do it for themselves.

Transformation of the Body[1]

"We think we are our bodies. Consequently, our lives are determined by the consideration that we are finite, deficient, limited and damageable. Normally, what motivates us to involve ourselves in physical fitness is simply a struggle for survival that is born out of that consideration. When that is the starting point, what we get is effort and struggle—not aliveness."

The Temple Called Our Body

The Interest in Our Bodies

A great deal of interest exists in our culture with regard to the view of what our bodies are and for what purpose they should be used. Losing weight, looking and feeling better, improvement of health, reinvigorating sex lives, and staving off disease all constitute a means of camaraderie with others who are engaged in the same activities. Whether young or old, people are bound together on a common basis to attain the glow and feeling of well being.

There is a deeper and hidden dimension that is associated with these activities and which is derived directly from them. It is the adventure of body, mind and spirit that emerges when people stop fragmenting body, mind and spirit as separate entities—rather than viewing them as a connected whole. For when the body is separated as an object and mere content, then the context becomes buried in the desires of the body such as lust, food, drink, drugs, exercise and so on. Even some religious

152

traditions denigrate the body considering it as a necessary and temporary vehicle that will be gotten rid of in the future, at which time the spirit will transcend to a "higher dimension."

Looking at the body in this manner is viewing it as merely a machine that is being guided by the mind. But, vacating the body in this manner opens it up to harm and makes it vulnerable to pathology. The body must be incorporated with mind and spirit as an integrated whole, and as such it must be listened to from its many thousands of feedback circuits. Tuning in to the body makes you aware of your relationships to others and to your environment. Removing the restraints on our bodies that have been imposed upon us by culture starts the process of well being—and makes the "miracles" of healing occur.

The Relationship with the Body

The direct rapport with your body, with how the organs feel and how the cells function, makes you more attuned to the full range of your inner senses. The body has associated with it visceral feelings that provide a wealth of information—but only if one is conscious of these feelings. These feelings go beyond the visual and aural inputs and are expressed kinesthetically. In some sense the entire history of humanity is contained within your body—all the way to cell structures, DNA patterns and even to the atomic levels.

One can easily be convinced that something has happened to the body as a result of exercise, involvement in some discipline, drugs or other factor. What actually changes as a result is the structure of apprehension. With this change the feelings for life also change and are expressed through the look of the eyes, by body changes such as being flushed, or via voice inflections. Beyond these common changes, there are even more exotic alterations—changes in the cellular levels themselves. Sometimes all that it takes is a mere suggestion that is provided in the right context.

153

Healing Our Body

In our culture the healing process normally involves a consultation with a doctor, an outpouring of our symptoms, an examination and a consequent prescription for some type of medication to cure the "illness." This gives full authority to the medical practitioner instead of taking the authority for yourself for your body. This process traps you into beliefs and traditions, and it limits your experience of what is really possible with regards to the body. For without operating with deep insight you will not be able to discriminate and see the deepest truths that exist for humanity—and more important, you will not be able to utilize these experiences to transform your ability to heal yourself.

Looking at the whole metabolic system of muscles, organs, cells and so forth, we are able to see the endurance of the human body—and of the improvements that can be accomplished through sheer will by intention. The possibilities for well being are linked to self-mastery and to a re-inhabiting of the body as an unfolding experience of adventure. Otherwise, your ingrained attitudes toward life, your lifestyle and your state of mind can certainly create havoc for you in terms of illnesses such as ulcers, migraine headaches, heart ailments, cancer and so forth—all of these being forms of "slow suicide."

If you can produce damage to the body through your mind, then you should also be able to produce healing. If you can break down tissue and produce ailments, then you can also transform your body to heal itself. The majority of "disease" is psychosomatic *in origin*.

However, what is accepted is that we can make ourselves sick—but what is resisted is that we can make ourselves well, something that is relegated to mysticism and occultism. But, the process works both ways. The problem is that traditionally medical science has investigated pathology—rather than exceptional health.

That is why there is a negative stigma that is associated with the positive side of things, with the whole healing process.

In the natural process of aging, we have powers to make changes that will affect our longevity and well being. You can make life worth living beyond the culturally accepted points. You can experience feeling good and pass this heritage on to others who may then live a better life. Even the little things that you do such as good nutrition, having a positive mental outlook, and performing exercise, all acknowledge your body and add information about it. Your body is more than just a "tube" with input at one end and output at the other end. Your body is part of the "cosmic dance" that allows you to touch on those very deep levels of being where you can experience yourself in perfect rhythm with the Universe.

Endnotes

1   From the article "The Body as 'A Facility for Transformation'" by Michael Murphy and George Leonard in the *Graduate Review*, March 1978.

About Sex

"When you're hot, you're hot; when you're not, you're not."

The Activity Called Sex

The Experience of Sex

Experiencing yourself as the cause of your sexual experience and not as its effect transforms your awareness about sex. By dissolving your barriers to communicating about sex, you can then be at choice about it. Thus, communication is the key in the way that you discuss sex. When you communicate about sex, you create a safe "space" in which to discuss sex, watch sex (such as in the movies), share your sexual fantasies, and so forth—*openly*.

When you can communicate openly about sex, the honesty frees you from the significance and judgments that you may have "bundled up" with sex matters. The more that you communicate, the more that you will discover in terms of what to do to make it safe to talk about anything that concerns sex to another person. It will also provide the opportunity to locate and dissolve any barriers that may stand between you and the ability to communicate about sex. This ability—that you are willing to say what it is that you want—means that in regard to sex you will have a very good chance of getting it.

156

About Money[1]

"Money is the <u>symbol</u> of the experience of being whole ✓
and complete and is not needed to *be* whole and complete."

The Symbol Called Money

The Aspects of Money

The primary question about money is whether you have it—or
it has you. Someone who thinks that they are their money certainly is controlled by money—and they will trade off everything
for money, including love, health and happiness. <u>Money—like
love—has associated with it the idea that there is not enough of
it to go around.</u> But money is only a symbol, and its accumulation doesn't provide any more satisfaction in life.

If money controls you, then you will have to discover how to
handle it, especially if your ground of being views the nature
of money as being one of "scarcity." If so, then you will believe that it is inevitable that you will have money problems,
and worse, that there are no solutions to money problems. For
the majority of people, these assumptions underlie every aspect of their lives in their relationship to money. These
established beliefs about money are the source of distress in
most people's lives. In fact, it is easier for people to divulge
their sex lives than it is to disclose their personal financial situations.

Your ability and your competence are what allow you to do
whatever it is that you want to do. If you do what you want to

do without worrying about money, then you will put your energy and time into it—with the project being its own reward. However, once you start thinking about the money, your project will diminish—and maybe even cease to exist. This happens because you get bogged down in the money aspect of it rather than your goal. For the money cannot possibly accomplish your goal—only you can do it.

Money and Survival

You always have to deal with money in any regard as a personal issue. Thus, it is important to separate your project from anything that you are working on as a means of survival. If you predicate the survival of your project on your own need to be comfortable, then you will wind up failing in your project. Money is always secondary to what you are doing although you cannot ignore the power and subtlety of money. It is just that if you operate in the world and plan everything based on money, then you will not discover and pursue your project and instead you will do a lot of "running around."

This is the distinction between your project and your livelihood—that is what you do as a "living" as compared to what you do for pleasure, self-fulfillment and satisfaction. If you cannot make the separation and you cannot distinguish the priority of your project, then you will be stuck in a fundamental belief about the situation. This belief is one that states that what you are working on is the most important thing and that you have to survive at it. The coupling of these two ideas becomes a conviction which for most people leads them to believe that the world owes them a living.

Hence, it is important to consider whether you are capable of both providing for yourself and of doing your project also. Of course, if your livelihood and your project are integrated, then it is a simple matter since just by doing it the money will be there for you. This is where the concept of "right livelihood" enters the perspective. If such is the case, then all you have to ask is whether you can sustain your work for a very long time, and whether what you are doing is intrinsically good in terms of the greater community. If the alignment is there, then the pursuit of your right livelihood will perfect your skills and qualities—with a reward of deepening you as a person in the process. Still, there has to be enough passion and devotion to make a living at the things that you want to do. You cannot "drop out," "do your thing," and not worry about the money because that is an approach that has futility associated with it.

Almost everything that we do—and in every way that we interact—is related to money. All of the processes that are associated with money—interest, profit, capital, inflation, and so on—are visible everywhere in the economic world, and money is the symbol that is used to measure this success. We become absorbed in getting, having and exchanging money for things whose value is determined by their price. In almost all aspects, the world that we live in is one of money, and those who deny the role of money will find that the world becomes very unpleasant for them.

On the other hand, there are contexts in which no money is involved. Art, poetry, music, dance, sex and a multitude of other activities function without any dependence on money in the natural sphere of human action. The truly satisfying things in life—love, health, happiness and self-expression—are valuable beyond any price that we can assign to them. Nevertheless, the recognition of the role of money will come from the understanding of who you are in the world, and this recognition will greatly influence how you respond to the world around you.

Endnotes

1   From the article "In The Money" by Michael Phillips in the *Graduate Review*, April 1978.

Telling the Truth[1]

"Without integrity, things do not work. At best, things grind to a halt."

Truth and Transformation

The Expression of the Truth

Temporarily, some places are "safe" in which to tell the truth, and these allow mutations of consciousness to occur. In general, however, most of the institutions and relationships of society are involved with survival and hence do not foster honesty and frankness. They instead promote position, restrict the individuals within that environment, and are concerned only with content rather than context.

In an untransformed world, "evil" manifests itself through the selling of aliveness for survival. Governments, schools, companies and other organizations justify and perpetuate themselves by dominating the individuals within their sphere of influence. Very rarely do they generate a healthy community because "politics" becomes the end in everything that they do.

In such an environment, transformed individuals have very little room in which to express themselves. It is an unfriendly and non-nurturing place in which a transformed individual is invalidated and made to appear meaningless. Slick and clever behavior is rewarded as being "successful." Any attempt to express any type of transformation in such an environment only generates survival behavior from that environment. But, a transformed individual requires a transformed environment because

---

160

only in such a context can that individual express himself or herself in a natural manner.

In spite of the manifestation of hostility, a transformed individual cannot retreat from life—such as to some monastic endeavor or other activity that denies the world. The only way out of this predicament is to lay an effective siege on untransformed environments. You must combat the environments to create the conditions that allow a further expansion of transformation.

The Starting Point

Raising the pertinent questions about the social, economic and political environments is the beginning of creating the conditions which will foster and expand transformation. That is the means of identifying the mechanisms of survival and position, and it is the starting point in the search for the ecology of transformation. Some of the barriers in this journey of discovery are lack of communication, pretense, no acknowledgement and no correction. These ritual behaviors that only "go through the motions" create effort, struggle and complexity—but no satisfaction.

The key ingredient is intention for without intention, then everything that is done merely becomes a preoccupation about insignificant events that do not generate any interest. The pretense appears: that everything is okay, and all behavior is geared towards the prevention of attempts to tell the truth—to unmask and expose an environment for what it is—and to avoid fault. For in an environment in which one cannot express the truth, then one is not nurtured by it and the tendency will be to just "go through the motions." An institution that has such an environment will "stop working" and will no longer be "on purpose." The institution will survive—but its purpose for being will become secondary. Instead what will occur is the thwarting of communication that is intended to correct problems—and in turn, this will prevent the prospect of success-fully pursuing more ambitious aims. Thus, all that will happen is a dramatization of mistakes with no associated responsibility for them—only blame.

The Essence of Transformation

Transformation has to be mediated by transformed individuals through transformed relationships and transformed institutions in order for transformation to have a radical effect on society. Only then will our existing institutions begin to work to reground and transfigure the way that we relate to each other and to the world. Otherwise all that we will get is social re-form—which is not a very effective means of changing society. All that happens with social reform is a futile replacement of one group of leaders with another group of leaders, with none of them operating or functioning on purpose.

The essence is one of being revolutionary, not from ambition, but from wanting the world to work. The organizing principle is one of creating a context that nurtures, enables and empow-ers the institutions of humanity. Thus, it is not a revolution that is merely concerned with social change—which is only resis-tance, antagonism or revolt against something or someone—but rather a revolution that transcends this form of radicalism. While social values do change through resistance, it is only through social transformation that effective social change can take place.

Transformation goes beyond the political, social and economic ideologies and goals. It is about knowing where you are com-ing from—and not about survival and position. It is not about attachment to how things are going to turn out, or about narcis-sism—or about preoccupation with the self. All of these positions come about through escape from and at the expense of social, economic and political responsibility. True liberation is at the root of the necessary commitment in changing the social, economic and political aspects of our institutions. You have to give up the notion that you are already "enlightened" to go after a true transformation of the highest order. Through transformation you will produce results and become more powerful, especially as you "give away your power" to others. This genuine change starts with the transformation of the individual which then extends to his or her relationships, and that finally manifests itself in the institutions—from which it can then lead to a transformed world.

Endnotes

1   From the article "A Place to Tell the Truth" by W.W. Bartley III in the *Graduate Review*, May 1978.

Helping Others

"I don't know what your destiny will be, but one thing I know: the only ones among you who will really be happy are those who have sought and found how to help others."

Support and Assistance

The Natural Cynicism

Helping others may appear to be a waste of your time, especially if the tasks to be done are monumental and the reasons for doing them are "meaningless." It may even be held as so much brainwashing to attempt to help others at anything. At worst, the consideration is that helping others falls in the category of being dumb and of sacrificing yourself for nothing. In any regard it is an activity that has the implication of "entrapment" because it is looked at in a very cynical and sarcastic way. Thus, there is an inherent reluctance to help others—especially if past experience has resulted in frustration from the act of reaching out to someone.

What happens by not helping others is that you create a wall of separation between you and others so that their lives and emotions no longer are of interest to you. You then observe others at a distance so as to protect yourself from betrayal and possible harm. But as you conceal your emotions—by not feeling the extremes of pain and joy in helping others—you become a "cement block" and your mind will begin to consume you as a consequence of your many defenses.

Breaking through The Layers

If you act and speak with all of your feeling and express whatever arises, then your helping experience will transform itself into a moment-by-moment activity and the "heaviness" will begin to fall away. As you "peel the layers away" in the experience, you will reveal the untapped resources that exist within you. Your perception of time will also be altered in the process, and your communication will no longer be limited to words. The mystical will be altered to the ordinary, you will see no difference fundamentally between yourself and others, and you will naturally help others so that they can unfold and blossom like a flower. This is the realization that we are all responsible for each other's growth, that we all contribute to each other, and that we are all related to each other.

Of course in helping others you may sometimes be pressed beyond the limits that you may have established for yourself. When you do so, you will discover that these limits were placed there by you—just like everything else in your life. You can either choose to "burn out" or you can test your sense of trust in transcending these self-imposed limits. Helping others always represents an opportunity to turn your life around—even though you may hate it while you are doing it. Even if you think that something is beyond you, helping others is an opportunity to test your ability to get the job done by pushing all of your considerations aside.

The question still remains as to what do you get out of it by helping others? It is certainly not about getting better, but instead is a process of moving yourself from a position of being helped to that of helping others. You may experience fears, and you may even test your physical endurance to its limits by undergoing sheer exhaustion. If you experience it deeply enough by giving up your conveniences and pleasures, you may be altered more profoundly than you ever have in your life. This experience creates that exuberance that literally puts a "light that streams out of your face."

There are many people who jump out of airplanes or who climb mountains who in their everyday lives conduct themselves within a box called "be careful." This will literally cost you your life because playing at that level will prevent you from "going for it." Unless you are willing to take big strides you will never play at this level. In extremes, it may even involve risking your life—*or even losing it*. That is what it is all about in helping others. It is about participating at the level where you will have the necessary energy for a human contribution to occur. The outcome of all of this is that you will best help yourself when you are helping others.

Intention and the Body[1]

"Integrity is not simply another position from which to play the game—*it is the game.*"

The Process of Learning

Awareness

Although its application varies, wisdom is always the same and its use is invariable—to free the human spirit. Awareness depends upon discovering something fundamental about ourselves with respect to learning and change. Awareness is something that is sensed at an intuitive level and which has a very special meaning. It is a higher aspect of our consciousness—but it has to be cultivated.

Awareness is consciousness that is allied to knowledge and includes being attentive to both internal and external events. It is an intrinsic part of us but it cannot be taught in a verbal manner. Instead, it has to be experienced but in a way in which a particular learning situation is created in the process. This situation must stimulate awareness and pose problems for it—especially in a crisis—that only a heightened awareness can solve.

Learning

In creating this type of learning situation, what is also created is a new kind of learning—one that is non-cerebral and non-coercive. It goes beyond the "correctness," competitiveness and manner of doing things. The learning is as much play as it

---

167

is work, and it involves both mind and body in the process. The learning is self-directed without regard to an authoritarian framework, and it is free from anxiety and habit. Curiosity and pleasure are the two pillars of this type of learning and they replace the normal will power and compulsive effort that is normally associated with learning, especially one that is set in an authoritative rote learning environment.

Learning to learn produces visible and sometimes dramatic changes that affect the body and mind. It results in a heightened sense of self and replaces habitual and ineffective movements with those that require the least amount of energy. The inducement of flexibility allows a person to restore their dignity as a result of literally altering the patterns in the cortex of the brain. This movement—the embodiment of intention—is the essence of life and of the organism. Every thought and emotion finds its expression and outlet in the form of movement—be it rage, fear, sadness or happiness. If there is distortion in this expression, then it is incorporated in the message of the communication and the movement of this distortion creates a destructive repercussion in the body.

The Effect on the Body

The reversibility of these destructive movements creates a change in the very cortex of your brain that frees up the body from the old patterns. It is what makes re-learning possible, and what makes it possible to return to the native intelligence that you had when you were a baby. These alterations in movements are what produce a re-organization in the body that results in a new balance of intention and impulse. When you experience these movements, your eyes will be brighter, your body posture will be different and straighter, your muscles will be looser, and your self-expression will be altered. You may even walk differently and behave with feelings of exuberance and exhilaration. It is a discovery that when you "image the moment," you will automatically mobilize the body and its muscles for action.

Since the learning diffuses itself throughout the entire nervous system, the change will affect the whole self: mind, body and spirit. The difference in the outer manifestation will be a reflection of the inner change in attitude. The new learning is the crystallization of the experience of intention—whether it is verbalized or not. In ordinary learning, a confrontation with a new situation always produces a resistance to change. Learning with a new awareness modifies the ability such that new things are seen with a different perspective. To live every moment with comprehension is to mean exactly everything that you say. It is to have self-esteem, self-respect and strength—to supercede the inhibitions and ineffectual impulses of the old conditioned patterns.

If you become aware of your body and its movement and orientation in space, it will lead you to a new functional integration of your self. In some ways it is a return of the body to its childhood state. It acts to restore its physical function—and in the process treats a multitude of physical problems that have an emotional source. It is a realization that there is no limit to possible improvement in functioning, and as such, no limit to your human potential. Thus, the "damage" that you may have inflicted on yourself through bad emotions and faulty learning can be changed. A malfunctioning body that is caused by a distressed psyche can be freed from its forces of coercion and repression through new learning.

Recovering From Faulty Education

Once you realize that you are functioning under faulty education, you will not regard yourself in the same manner and you will "cure your sickness." It is the difference between feeling dull, awkward and shameful to that of feeling free and uninhibited. You will behave spontaneously and in the process you will correct the distortions that exist in the brain by breaking the old patterns of response. Once you have managed to achieve this, your behavior will begin to change—sometimes dramatically through which previous conditions of deformities, injuries, congenital illnesses and feelings of impotence clear up miraculously.

Our civilization demands increasingly finer adjustments to continue to function in a human way. Yet this same civilization represses us from the time that we are born. To develop the qualities that we need, each of us must undo the emotional and physical havoc that is caused by the suppression of our most vital impulses. You can better the functioning of your nervous system if you hold it in the context that the possibilities are immense. Since all life is a process, if you improve the quality of that process through your intention, then the manifestation of this intention through your body will be taken care of as a function of this process.

Endnotes

1   From the article "The Teaching of Moshe Feldenkrais" by Layna Verin in the *Graduate Review*, June 1978.

Beyond Medicine

"When you allow something to be, it will allow you to be."

The Doctor-Patient Relationship

What Doctors Do

The field of medicine requires involvement with organic, bio-chemical and complex factors of a human organism rather than with its existence within a social context. All doctors are taught to dissect, to treat symptoms, and to focus on the microcosm rather than on the patient's existence in the macrocosm. Rather than caring for the psyche of the patient, the emphasis is less on candor—because it is inappropriate to admit not knowing—and more on enhancing a physician's reputation. It is a practice of evasion through technical jargon that constitutes the professional life of a doctor.

If doctors become responsible for both what they know and—more importantly—for what they don't know, then the field of medicine becomes more rewarding for everyone who is in-volved. The patient then becomes part of the medical decision process, the physical well being becomes a responsibility of the patient, and the health provider now has the responsibility of guiding the healing process. The health profession practice then becomes a partnership between doctor and patient—a context in which "miracles" occur. This process makes medi-cal institutions have real power as a consequence of the communication, participation and intention that is displayed by the patient.

Our Medical Reality

But, the reality of medical institutions are that they are largely impersonal, and that doctors are not that interested in having relationships with the patients that they treat. Sometimes there is a lack of trust that occurs through incomplete communications and this produces barriers in the actual delivery of health services to patients. The medical concern is more about staying within the role of a medical practitioner—of being "cold" and not showing any feelings. The end result is that very little difference is made in the life of the patient—something that becomes a source of frustration for doctors.

As far as the quality of a patient's life is concerned, an illness can be cured—but not without the wholeness, completeness and sufficiency that is required from that patient. Even miraculous technological innovations can be futile if the quality of a patient's being is not considered. What has to be countered is the notion that illness is inevitable and that nothing that anyone does really makes any difference. Otherwise, health becomes the avoidance of illness. To make a difference in the quality of life, it is necessary to hold health as a context that allows for all positions—rather than just *being ill* or *not being ill*.

If you hold illness as a content in the context of health, then the very illness becomes a contribution to your experience of health. Rather than having an illness be an *invalidation* and a statement of *inadequacy*, it is instead regarded as a condition that exists in our total sense of being whole and complete. As such, everything contributes to the manifestation of well being—with the result that nothing is held as a devastating or invalidating illness. One then has the opportunity to experience wellness and wholeness—and with it, the elimination of an illness.

Health in a New Context

But what is necessary to transform the context of health so that the experience of health becomes a natural manifestation of the individual? What has to happen in the environment (relationships, institutions and society) in order to express that well being? What is the real alternative to avoiding illness and getting health from doctors, hospitals, drugs, therapy, exercise programs, nutritional practices and other established means? What is necessary to create a context in which actions are no longer the tactics of avoidance, but are instead contributions to the realization of one's essential health and well being?

What is necessary is for one to take individual responsibility for the persistence of the condition called ill health, and to make a commitment to the creation of a context of well being. It is to illuminate our human predicament, to see the conditions in which we live our lives, and to allow ourselves to see what works—and what doesn't work. It is to make a significant contribution to the institutions of health through our individual transformation so that health professionals have a new platform upon which to stand—one that allows them to experience satisfaction, completion and wholeness. The process is one of alignment that results as a commitment to the creation of a context of well being. It is to make real a context of health in which well being is the natural manifestation of existence—rather than the exception—and as a natural expression of who each of us is in this world.

The transformation into this context will create shifts in your awareness that may include a new intimacy, warmth, closeness and pleasure—pleasure not as a way of avoiding something but as a way of recovering. It will be something that is true and spontaneous and which is available at any time for it is a pleasure of the joy of being alive. You will be able to look at your life and see what causes "miracles" to occur. For if you notice them when they appear, and you know where they come from, then you will know the truth about miracles: that what causes your life to be miraculous *is you.* Of course, there are no models that exist for this transformation. However, the biggest shift of awareness in you, and in your relationships, is the recognition *that there is nothing bigger that produces more miracles than the words "I love you."*

Acknowledgement

"Too often, we either put off telling the people in our lives what they mean to us, or we tell them in a way that is incomplete."

Aspects of Acknowledgement

The Failure to Acknowledge Others

Acknowledgement for someone occurs whenever we speak about that person's magnificence—without any reservations. It is an expression of their true value that says to that person that he or she is appreciated for all of the magnificent things that that person has done and for that person's way of being in the world. Sometimes we do see someone being presented as a marvelous and wonderful person—*but only after that person has died.* For almost no one creates a wholly supportive piece about anyone else while that person is still alive.

This state of mind reflects our inability to appreciate, nurture, love and support each other. It is a case of not being entirely supportive and appreciative of another human being without some "but" being interjected in the statement of acknowledgement. Thus, what has to happen is that acknowledgement must be done so absolutely, so totally and so completely that the person who is being acknowledged lives out the rest of his or her life knowing that they are truly magnificent. It is this experience that breaks up the reality that keeps us from being able to acknowledge each other totally and without reservation. This also has the effect of breaking up the "survival structure[1]" so that instead a context is created in which there is absolute love and support for one another.

Expressing Acknowledgement

Because acknowledgement is a statement of what's so, it can sometimes be negative—such as by stating that something worked and produced results even if it was not in alignment with some purpose. However, this is totally different in just being "positive" about someone—such as merely telling a person that they are wonderful. Such a statement is in fact an evaluation rather than an acknowledgement. For when you acknowledge someone, you have to tell the truth about your experience of that person, and you have to do it in a way that the person gets it. This is very different from just trying to make another person feel good—which comes off as being condescending and manipulative. Instead, it is simply telling that person that they did something for which they are appreciated.

When people try to express true acknowledgement for some person, they often wind up suppressing it or rationalizing it away. Even if someone does something that contributes greatly to your life, it becomes very difficult to acknowledge that person under these conditions, with the result being that the acknowledgement never gets expressed. There is a prevailing feeling that it is threatening to acknowledge others for supporting you. Of course, there is also the concern that others will get acknowledged instead of you.

In all of this, you will find that you either care about people, or that you care about what others will think about you. True acknowledgement comes from the self and it disappears once it is expressed. Thus, it is not about owing something to someone for what they did to contribute to your life; it is simply the full expression of recognition for someone in a way that honors that person.

Fostering Acknowledgement

The environment in which we live does not allow the expression of another's true worth and value. There is always a resistance that has to be penetrated in letting others know. It may even require the accumulation and presentation of a massive amount of agreement just to have someone be recognized in a way that you and others know about that person. Acknowledgement is to be recognized in the fullest extent possible, such as for the difference that some teacher or mentor made in one's life. It can take the form of an expression of loyalty and commitment—of a special bonding of faithful adherence. In any case, the act of acknowledgement transcends factors such as appearances and circumstances.

Acknowledgement is the creation of a context in which to recognize each other's magnificence. It is something that is done in the spirit of absolute love, trust and openness. It is about the expression of beauty, of being together and saying it to one another with no holds barred. Acknowledgement is about the discovery of the magnificence of people—as something that can be part of your life always—and about the realization that all other things are irrelevant.

Endnotes

1   Since the purpose of the mind is to survive, it will make itself right and others wrong. The mind will thus add to its survival by making the contributions of others less.

Enlightenment

"Live your life as if your life depends on it."

Why You Cannot Apply It

The Experience of Enlightenment

The attempt to apply "enlightenment" directly to the world doesn't really work—no matter how hard you try. All that you can really do is communicate naturally and be aligned with whatever your purpose is in life. The ground rules are very simple: keeping agreements, participating in life and being responsible. It is about communicating and about doing whatever seems appropriate—even if you never get acknowledged for it.

The experience of enlightenment is not about things, but about the context and the experience of the self. It is about transforming you to do whatever seems natural and appropriate for you. However, if you convert your experience of enlightenment into things such as beliefs, ideas or philosophies, then you will only wind up in a process of refining your views and imposing these on the world and to those around you in your life.

Of course, the responses that you get from your experience of enlightenment can range from love to hate. But, you have to remember that enlightenment is simply a context for holding things, and that the context is nothing itself—and thus cannot be applied. Any attempt to convert that context into something that you can apply will only turn it into content—and this clearly will not work. Above all, it is wise not to make a rule about this also because *life doesn't have any rules—it just is.*

Ecstasy

"A miracle is something that validates who you are—instead of reducing who you are. It expands your awareness of who you are."

What Ecstasy Is

The Transformation of Relationships

Ecstasy in relationships means creating a transformed context in which they become brilliant, alive and magical. It is to express your magnificence in a way that mutual acknowledgement of each other occurs. It manifests itself through gentleness, inclusion, lightness of being, and passion. It is the basis of the "ground of being:" the place where you can celebrate the miraculous and the magical. It is about being—not about doing. It is about creation rather than explanation. It is about context from which your experience emanates. It is about being the light and the fire—and not about being illuminated or warmed by them.

Ecstasy is beyond being male or female for it is more fundamental than just being lovers. It is about letting go of all the ideas about relationships and opening yourself to the unknown. It is to surrender into the experience—to fall out of the reality and fall into the mysterious. As you let go, you will always land in the same place as before, but you will arrive in a new, sparkling and brilliant place of your creation. This realization of ecstasy is beyond that of joy and pleasure for it is not a measure of gratification but an expression of love. Ecstasy is the loss of personality and of something more profound: the emergence of one's true self. That ecstatic experience is brought about by the loss of one's self as a position in life.

Rather than ecstasy being something to achieve, a way to look at something, or a component to add to ourselves, it is instead a "space" to come from—the context in which things occur. At this level it is possible to experience the magnificence of others and to celebrate that magnificence in a profound relationship. All problems simply disappear in this "space" of unconditional love. It goes beyond the feeling of being compelled to work hard on any difficulties in a relationship because it transcends the doubts, misunderstandings, perpetrations, pettiness and upsets that are normally associated with a relationship. Ecstasy includes these but in a light that is so brilliant that these issues pale in comparison. Ecstasy moves us from a position of "hanging on" to that of a "space beyond words."

In a state of mind such as ecstasy, one may be inclined to think that such things happen only by chance. But it is a state that is beyond mere chance because it constitutes the very essence of the power to create the "space" in which the mastery of relationships occurs. The context is not about being in ecstasy—or of working towards it—but about willing to come from that "space". It is a "space" that is created by simply considering it as being created in your life. Ecstasy is definitely not something that is created in opposition to a condition, such as that of misery, but is a creation at the level of dichotomy and balance where every "yes" and "no" co-exist with one another.

Ecstasy as Context

At the level of context, one creates by consideration alone— by waving the "magic wand." With this wand you consider ecstasy to be the "space" in which everything occurs, including all of the circumstances and conditions of your relationships. Then you see everything as evidence of that—or you don't—

181

depending upon your consideration of it for that is the only thing that makes a difference in how you hold it. What allows for ecstasy is the creation of a context for the context, a commitment of your relationship to something larger than itself. This commitment is to the quality of relationship in the world where you devote your life to a purpose that is larger than everything else.

Ultimately, this is what makes life work because a relationship that is truly whole and complete makes a contribution to the world that is far beyond its existence. Rather than hiding in it or keeping some of it in reserve, the context of ecstasy demands that you hold nothing back. But, you have to be willing to do it—without any sense of protection or place of refuge in case "something goes wrong." When the "space" is that of ecstasy, you have everything that you need to be satisfied. All circumstances in life are contained within it, and everything is released into it.

Manifesting and sharing your expression of love for others is not one of sympathy. It is not about being afraid that others will take advantage of you or that you will lose everything that you have. It is not about being cautious or about being afraid to make mistakes. If you have doubts, then it is impossible to function at this level. It still may be true that you will experience fear and losing when others do take advantage of you, but these events will happen no matter what you do anyway.

In the context of ecstasy everything is possible and you will realize that love is not bounded by time or space. It embodies magnificence, brilliance, aliveness and truth. This is not to say that people have no flaws or that everything is perfect in the world. It is to admit that there are people in the world who make a difference in the world because of the greatness of their hearts. Ecstasy is about taking responsibility for your own worth, and it is about admitting that you are both magnificent and noble. For when you can communicate from that "space," then you will be communicating to others to their magnificence—rather than to where they have positioned themselves in life.

So what is it that you have to give up in order to get the context of ecstasy? It is certainly not your job, money, family or health—or anything else that you can think of. What you have to give up is your recognition of the self as not being body, mind or emotion, but as the "space" for everything. Ecstasy is the supreme context in which you can exercise your selfhood with total responsibility and freedom for it is your acknowledgement of yourself as an individual manifestation of an infinite majesty with total power of intention.

Identity

"To make sure a person doesn't find out who he is, convince him that he can't really make anything disappear. All that's left then is to resist, solve, fix, help or change things. That's trying to make something out of something."

True Identity

The Search for Identity

In the universal story of the search for true identity, what is at issue is your personality, life and education. Identity is a description of your life for which you must take full responsibility—especially for completing your past. It goes beyond the exploration of your childhood memories, your archetype, and your symbol of existence. It is also beyond the simple quests of working on yourself to promote a better self-image of yourself to others (improving appearance, losing weight, etc.). In its essence, it is the expansion and the transformation of consciousness.

But, it doesn't stop at the level of individual transformation because its root is that of an ecology of consciousness that permeates throughout the environment and manifests itself in relationships, institutions and society. Thus, individual transformation cannot be seen when people are hungry, when massive layoffs are occurring, when wars are being fought or when disease is widespread. It is a matter of getting to the truth rather than one of proving the correctness of a position. If not, then your life and the events in them do not contribute to the quality of other people's lives.

But what does the individual human spirit have to do with the general human condition—with inspiring, transfiguring or explaining human behavior? Certainly, the mistakes of the past do not negate that at any moment you have the power to transform the quality of your life. No matter what has happened you always have the opportunity to make your life work by choosing to transform, enhance and nurture your life. In doing so you reveal your identity and you discover your ability to make a contribution to the world. Whatever happens in this context provides the insight that offers you real transforming power.

The search for true identity involves finding out about the "impostor" part of yourself—the "acts" through which we identify ourselves in our stressful or worst moments via the repertoire of emotions, arguments and responses to events. To go beyond these limitations involves an inherent power and innate sensitivity to everyone around you, and the ability to deal with everyone as they present themselves to you. It is not about engaging in a routine, pattern, technique or argument—especially to protect your feelings. Nor is it about betraying logic and reason, about pleasing or impressing someone, or about capturing their attention—or about "trapping" them. Instead, it is to emerge from the self-deception in your life—from imitation—to become compassionate and caring with a sense of spontaneity.

What Must Happen

To get to this identity involves the puncturing of illusions, the unmasking of motives, a probing of rationalizations, and a humorous view of hypocrisy. While this may evoke pain, shock or even surprise—depending upon the "buttons" that get pushed—the "payoffs" are discovered through the process of these reactions. By staying focused and not losing the attention, this "truth process" can be used to dig deeper into the associated body sensations, emotions, attitudes, states of mind and memories of your life. As the truth is told, the problems vanish, and a new context is created in which it is possible to deal with one's own ills.

The obstacles to understanding our own identity stem from the lack of spirit that views aggressiveness and intrusion as mysteries, fantasies, beliefs and other unknown factors. This can also become a battle between will and intellect. This then becomes the reason for the lack of vigor and imagination which in turn robs us of our vitality and enlivenment. To break free of these obstacles requires "working close to the material" to promote the release of anxiety by "coming close to the bone" in all matters. This represents "final cause" in which worlds are created and governed by intention, goals and purposes. It is a context in which an idea is the most powerful thing in the world.

Identity thus begins with "taking care of yourself"—not in a selfish manner—but as a healthy and openly expressed self-interest that prevents you from being dependent or from assuming the role of a "victim." It is very important to realize that *what we intend happens, and what happens is what we intend*. There are no chance events since each of us is the architect of creation, and because all things are connected through each of us. In true identity, the ego is transcended as each of us moves in the playground of reality where through direct experience each of us is creating all of existence in an effortless manner.

Beyond Personality

"Being cannot be explained in terms of doing and having—it has to be explained in its own terms. A rule about being is that you need to be willing to allow yourself to be, without having to do something to deserve it. If you are yourself, you will naturally be useful in the world. And, incredible things happen at the level of being—'miracles' occur."

Who We Really Are

Patterns and Behaviors

Personality is a set of patterned behaviors through which each of us acts with other personalities. It represents the habitual way in which each of us represents themselves and it can manifest itself in many varieties of behaviors. These behaviors can range from being funny to avoid an issue, being outgoing to avoid intimacy, always having a comment as a compulsion to fill up all quietness with incessant talk, of "going through the motions" just to have a social interaction, or even "being stupid" so as to not get the point. To become aware of these behaviors what must be revealed are the mechanisms that keep these in place. When you touch upon your natural integrity, the effect is a breaking up of these patterns. Going deeper into one's personal integrity breaks up more of these patterns in a spiral that uncovers the pretense in life.

The circumstances under which one's pretenses are in operation are there because we are pretending to succeed—even

---

187

though in fact we are only "getting by." Rather than having mastery over the situation by creating according to our potential, we instead rely on our good ideas and plans. Thus, instead of telling the truth absolutely so that things will happen like you say they will, we resort to words that never fit the situation—and which therefore are lies.

The Peak Experience

The truth telling is an important preparation for an immense and mystical "peak experience" that sometimes occurs. This peak experience is a self-actualizing realization—a profound, concentrated, intense, accepting and comprehensive feeling of unity and wonder. It is an experience which is beyond language and which therefore cannot be described. It is, in effect, an *experienced experience*: one that is beyond the everyday experience in our lives. It is something that breaks through the "wall" of theories and concepts—one in which everything drops away and is no longer mediated by your position. You find out who you really are because the peak experience penetrates through the screen of concepts and your hierarchy of values into a more detached, objective and intense context.

A "peak experience" is related to others, to your work, to nature and to art—as well as to anyone or anything else. A peak experience profoundly affects your life and is one in which you are able to perceive in a larger context. But, a peak experience of the self is *not* related to anything for it is a profound sense of self. This peak experience becomes the context for all states—*the context for all contexts*. As such it goes beyond all of the conceptual and intellectual framework for it is the "high noon" of the spirit in which all "shadows" disappear.

Telling the truth then is what wears out your concepts and allows you to go beyond into a peak experience. This blaze of clarity puts you in a new state of being and makes your life "magical" as it totally alters you and reorganizes your values—

especially the ones that you have functioned with from the time that you were growing up. You transcend the ideas of success, of security, of "making it" because you see the folly, stupidity and hypocrisy of conventional values. A healthy skepticism is infused as you shift the focus of your values from that of success to that of growth. You realize that life is not about success—but rather about fulfillment and satisfaction. And, the concern is no longer with reputation because you are only interested in the truth.

The Conversion Experience

This "conversion experience"—the shift from one's old values and a rebirth into new ones—happens because what was previously considered to be important no longer is so. The conversion kindles the interest in the search for enlightenment— to live in a perpetual state of potential— where you are ever changing, ever growing and ever becoming more conscious. You live in a state of constant alteration until you finally have that extraordinary experience in which there is no form, but only timeless eternity and unbounded space. *It is a realization that you know nothing and that you know everything.*

The realization that everything that you know is skewed toward some end is the awareness of the fundamental skew that exists to all knowledge—the skew of the "unenlightened" mind towards survival of itself. Thus, the skew is towards success, towards all goals from the material to the mystical—and even to that of self-realization. Of course material things can still be enjoyed, but they no longer have the meaning that they had before—a false meaning that exists only for its own sake. What you see is that there are no hidden meanings and no secrets for everything is just the way that it is. All knowledge that is amassed merely acts to obfuscate the simplicity of the truth.

All of the identifications with personality cut one off from the experience of living. Surely you are not your thoughts, emotions, ideas, intellect, perception or beliefs. You are also not your accomplishments or your achievements—or what you have done, whether it be right or wrong. Most of all, you are not what you have been labeled, either by others or by yourself. You are simply the "space," the creator, and the source of it all as you experience the self in a direct and unmediated way. In this state you hold all of the information and content of your life in a new way, mode and context—from direct experience and not from having learned it.

Experience is simply evidence that you are here, but it does not define who you are. It is your self as the "projector" and everything else as the "movie." You recognize yourself not by seeing the "movie" but by seeing yourself prior to it—not as the person who has done something or as one who has an identity[1]. You are also not your mind or your set of patterns as unconsciously established by your parents. You are whole and complete as you are, you can accept the truth about yourself, and you are "at source" because enlightenment means that you have found truth and your true self all at once.

Endnotes

1   All identities are false since they merely tell lies about others from your wanting them to be different or yourself wanting to be other than who you really are. In the same way all attachments come from lying about who you really are. When you don't have any real identity of your own, then you will fault the identity of others. In short, you won't grant "beingness" to others as they are.

The Ultimate Liberation

"The quality of life does not depend upon the circumstances. And, you possess within yourself, at every moment of your life, under all circumstances, the power to transform the quality of your life."

Beyond Freedom

The Necessary Transition

The emergence from any struggle into an expression of humanity happens in situations in which resistance is waiting to be transformed into responsibility. When we have an opportunity to play a role in which we have to give up our security, we recognize that our positions entail comfort and fear. If we acknowledge our sense of choice and personal power, and we examine our positions, we can then sacrifice the expected for the attainment of experience that is untried in our relationships with one another. As we experience limits and constraints, each of us turns towards positions which advocate full social, economic and political equality for everyone. This, in turn, has the effect of releasing a tremendous amount of energy that allows each of us to expand to a fuller and less constrained expression of our common humanness.

In this transition, there is always the danger that we will exchange one position for another, sometimes with a resulting disinterest or apathy. In other cases it may even result in a more limited and confining position that is rooted in resistance. Only by examining a position and by moving the resistance does

---

191

one take responsibility for one's own liberation. By doing so one creates a new purpose, commitment and joy by virtue of the animation process that occurs via the transition.

Resistance always constrains the transition because it leads to the persistence of that which is wished to be overcome. The experience of taking responsibility for something is what ultimately makes the action more effective. On an interim basis, a stance can involve a resistance to some perceived negativity that consequently leads to a readiness to treat that part of humanity as the "other." This distancing acts to guarantee our survival, with the end effect being that we function largely out of what we reject. This confines the clarity to that of knowing who you are not like, and thus anchors each of us in the very stance that we are rejecting.

The Real Struggle

The real struggle in life is not to seize power, but to transform it. We must be clear about who we are not so that we can begin to create who we are—oftentimes with a new reality and even language to describe it. It is not a matter of measuring the seriousness of our commitment by how much energy we spend in resisting something because then we inherently avoid the responsibility for the issue. In such cases, all that happens is that we become a "victim" of the circumstances.

The reaction can be troubling because in reality people in power have much to gain by telling others to assume full responsibility for their situation. The advice of "blaming the victim" serves to direct attention away from the oppression—a very dangerous path since if no resistance is offered the oppressors will continue in their position. And, if we don't make them see their position, then how can they possibly change what they are doing? And yet, to continue to resist only makes them wrong and colors our position and perception with sarcasm.

The profound insight is that we cannot make people change or make them take responsibility for their own lives, much less for the world. What we can do is to communicate our experience, accept the experience of others, and create the changes that we argue for. The worst position is to resist another's resistance for this will just prolong the situation. Instead, it is a matter of re-creating another's position and of fully understanding and accepting the world as they see it. Otherwise, our positions will anchor us until some new wave washes away the old "certainties" and lands us in a space where we may no longer know what it is to be a "true human being." Clinging to our anchors has a cost that is no greater than the risk of letting them go—the only advantage being that anchors offer us safety. However, the big difference is that clinging to our anchors has the effect of "weighing us down."

The Decision in Life

The decision in life is whether we spend our energy on making people wrong, or whether we spend it on making things right. In moving from resistance to responsibility, we transform a position into context. Thus, when you make a commitment to something as a context for your life, even the resistance that takes place is within that context so that opposition becomes part of the process rather than an obstruction. The willingness to be cause in the matter is one of taking responsibility for our liberation and to create it as a context instead of a position of resisting oppression.

You don't need to sacrifice the clarity of your vision nor the intensity of your commitment. You also don't need to deny the existence of what seems "wrong" to us in the recognition that those who wield power on this planet have come to endanger our survival. Acknowledging the facts without blaming others or forgiving them enlarges our experience to include these facts of a world in which oppression occurs. Neither is it to hold back from the suffering of the world for perhaps it is the one suffering that you have avoided—possibly because it would incite you to outrage, remorse and indignation, or worse, to become rooted in a context of hopelessness. But, it is still the responsibility that is the underlying seriousness: to dare and achieve greatly. It is the dedication to the "impossible dream"— whatever it may be.

The "enlightened self-interest" and the frank concern with problems is what makes one trustworthy. It involves a rejection of everything that serves to disguise the opposition. It is the very process of the form of change itself that is the means and the goal of justification. It is the experience of polarities in a cooperative manner. We no longer identify ourselves as the past and this choice is one of the most freeing experiences that the transition provides. While resistance protects us from the challenge of creating something that is not simply an opposition, and thereby guarantees our survival, it is responsibility that guarantees our growth. The transition is one that involves going beyond the limitations to create opportunities for transformation—rather than as sources of resistance. Once we have experienced this transition, the struggle ends—and the movement begins.

Thinking for Yourself

"There is a particular state of being in which one achieves mastery over the patterns or models of one's life. In such a state, it is possible, by consideration alone, to shift the context within which you live your life."

The Real Power

The Truth of Matters

Suppose that you had the power to heal all of the ills of the earth and to turn it into a garden for all humanity. If you had such an opportunity to make a difference in the world and to shape the future of humanity, it would be a clear message that not only would your life work—but that everything else would work. But, since we don't experience it as working, then obviously we are not seeing the truth of matters. All that happens is that we try to match the truth against pictures, opinions and expectations that we have been given about the way that it is supposed to be like. What is worse is that if we assume that this view is correct, then the truth—especially when it fails to match these pictures, opinions and expectations—is then held as wrong and thus becomes junior to these ideas.

If the idea that you can't make a difference and that you are not that important are your reality, then you will not be able to contribute to the quality of human life. Moreover, if you are not even handling your own life, making the world work is in a realm that is out of your possibilities. All that happens is that

---

195

a self-fulfilling prophecy is created in which the evidence states that you don't make a difference, and therefore, that it is useless to attempt to make a difference. This paradigm becomes a structure that fosters the conditions in which we live, including all of the associated limitations that shape our behavior and thinking. For if you never examine the paradigm, then you think *from* that paradigm—but never *about* the paradigm itself. And, if you come into life through that paradigm—the one that states that *we are all born into in a life which is inherently incomplete and that we don't make a difference*—then that paradigm influences your life and it gets more solidified every time that you say that you don't make a difference.

The truth is that some people do make a difference. Every time that a particular person has the courage to express that view, that person is hailed as a genius because of the unattainable position that surrounds such a view. It is a position that hardly anyone else ever hopes to achieve. Probably as a child you might have experienced that what you said and did made a difference. But, in the process of growing up, you were subjected to and eventually grasped the "horrible truth" of the world. The effect is that you no longer regarded yourself or the world very highly, and you thus began to accept the notion that you didn't have a chance of ever making a difference in the world. This is what creates part of the pain of adolescence— the struggle to reconcile the deeply felt experience that what you do does matter against the overwhelming agreement of the world that you don't matter. And, if you succumb to this paradigm that you don't make a difference, then the result is that you become attached to making money—to becoming what is referred to as being an "adult."

Regaining The Lost Power

But what happened to the big "YES" that you possessed when you were a child—when you thought that you mattered? Rather than being something that is lost forever in adulthood, it is instead well hidden by your genius that does not admit to the possibility of making a difference in the world. The only way to retrieve that former ability is to not allow anyone else to tell you what to think. But this is not as easy as it sounds since the culture that established the paradigm that you don't make a difference shapes your attitudes and opinions. It takes courage and hard work to think for yourself—even if you make mistakes along the way. It definitely will not make life easier for you, nor will it gain you any popularity.

However, if you want monuments built in your memory, then don't dare to go outside the cultural set that has given you the paradigm of not making a difference. It is easier to go for agreement since you probably won't get any statues built in your name if what you want to do is to make a difference in the world. What you do get for making a difference is workability—the monument to yourself that states that *you will not accept anything less than a world that works for everybody with no one left out.*

If you want to make an impact in life, then you must get the truth for yourself by being willing to do your own thinking. This entails the examination of your beliefs, going beyond your opinions, acting beyond the functions of agreement and disagreement, and not defending your position against other positions. You may still arrive at a conclusion that is consistent with your old conclusions, but the difference will be that you will have arrived there out of your own experience—rather than from your opinions. You won't have to prove it for it to be so, for you will be at choice about it, not as a position to be held but as a context in which all positions are included.

197

Ultimately, the context is beyond leaders and followers because the only thing that is needed is to follow your own experience. This will lead you into an alignment with others who are also following their own experiences. In turn, this will lead you into a natural discovery of the purpose that we all share together: *the experience that we all stand for a world that works for all of us.* If you dare to think the unthinkable, if you dare to see that you matter, and you dare to act consistently with that thought in mind, you will create a new paradigm that says that you are essential. It does require faith in your own process, a trust in your own integrity, and a reliance on your native intelligence. Above all, you must have the courage to give up the endless attempt to find certainty by looking outside yourself for answers that only you can provide from within yourself.

Extending Your Limits

"When you go beyond your limits, you get in touch with the incredible magnificence that you have as a human being."

Your True Capability

The Context of Our World

When you experience an increased ability to determine the quality of your life, your sense of purpose also expands with it. However, there is still a tendency to feel inadequate whenever we are confronted with a new, exciting and profound opportunity. Some of this feeling of inadequacy comes from having been committed to notions, patterns and behaviors that are contained in a "you *or* me" world. Another part of this inadequacy is the ignorance that prevents us from functioning intelligently and effectively in which the possibility of a "you *and* me" world exists. Finally, at the deepest level, the phenomenon of critical mass has to be attained—one in which enough things happen to make the process a self-generating one.

In freeing yourself from the patterns of survival that are expressed in a "you *or* me" world, the opportunity is opened up in a broader sense for you. There is also a contribution when you apply this same freedom to your relationships. However, a threshold—a critical mass—is not reached at the level of institution because that functions out of an untransformed environment. The main result is that at this level the tendency is to make you revert back into your old patterns and

away from your transformation. A much stronger communication process is needed to allow people to realize within themselves the qualities that they need to fulfill the opportunity to make the world work for everyone. Four qualities that are especially useful in this endeavor are as follows:
- a partnership to make a difference
- mastering the circumstances in life
- an awareness that there are opposing forces
- responsibility for all of it

Making A Difference

People who have made a difference in the world have discovered a way of transcending circumstances while those who have not made a difference offer the circumstances as an explanation why they are not effective. Also, they don't go into it knowing the answers—for if they already knew the answers, then they would definitely be applying them. Instead they discover within themselves the qualities that are necessary to make a difference in the world. To emphasize, if someone else determines these qualities for you, then it won't make a bit of difference in your life—much less that of the world. The world is full of people who know the answers, but around whom no able and capable people can be found whose lives work.

The search is thus not about finding the answers, but about empowering people with the answers that they find for themselves. Also, if all that you have is an individual sense of responsibility, then you are probably not going to make a difference in the world. While you may be admired and respected, you will probably tend to stay out of situations in which your reputation may be called into question. The process goes far beyond the acts of success, survival, getting along, earning a living, or constructing a reputation. It also isn't about meditating, contemplating, working with scholars, or using the mastery of a particular discipline. Instead it is to clarify that your contribution to life, your nurturing of life and the appropriateness to it are in tune with life itself. In this process the ultimate enlightenment is knowing that life is just as it was in the beginning—*except that there is now a different quality to it that was not present in the beginning.*

The Ultimate Pursuit in Life

Of course this does not mean that you have "made it" or have "arrived" once you have made a contribution for there is always a continuing growth and expansion as a fundamental part of being human. The *struggle* to achieve peace and tranquility—"nirvana," "enlightenment," etc.—is still just an interesting game. But, it is senior to just pursuing the game of making money which is mostly an arrogant endeavor. Accumulating money just for its own sake is pure nonsense; the real pursuit is one of being engaged in a game in which you have the power of choice.

Ultimately, the pursuit of making a difference is like climbing a mountain with no top. On this mountain all that exists is the act of climbing, and the value that exists is in the climbing itself. In choosing the commitment to climb this particular mountain, you demonstrate the most profound of human qualities—where you press yourself beyond the ordinary limits. By doing this you discover and realize more of your natural abilities. More importantly, in testing yourself on this mountain, you make yourself more available to support others in their quest of climbing the same mountain.

About Support

"Life is not a problem to be solved, but is instead a reality that is to be experienced."

The Greater Possibility

The Unworkability That Exists

For the most part, who each of us is and the fundamental choices that we make in life seem to matter very little in the world. Significant acts of great courage and intelligence seem to exist in the apparent unworkability of the world. Even the greatest technical achievements do not seem to fundamentally alter our experience that we don't make a difference in the world. No matter how admirable or inspiring an action may be—even if it galvanizes the world for a few moments—it seems to disappear from our consciousness.

It is apparent that the rules for living successfully have shifted and a new opportunity, or context, has begun to reveal itself. In this context, the possibility for a person's life to truly make a difference in the world begins with the question: "What is my life going to be about?" The way in which this question is answered by each of us has the possibility to alter the course of humanity. This possibility—the creation of a context in which people's lives really matter—is undoubtedly the most profound opportunity that is available to anyone at any time.

This context involves one of support, but it is not about agreement or opinions. It is also not a matter of trust, faith or belief in someone or something. Instead it is about the experience of support and of a process in which the truth will set you free. Everyone is up to the task of making the world work, but there will always be obstacles that will give rise to judgements or to reservations about breaking through these obstacles.

The Universal Desire

Deep down inside, everyone has an intention to make a contribution to others. Each of us possesses a desire to be happy, to be satisfied and to have all of their relationships turn out okay. But, the inadequacies and the struggle to deal with them inhibit the making of these contributions to others. Taking the effort out of this struggle involves looking at the inadequacies to see what is really appropriate in this effort. For the matter is one of telling the truth about your experience, and to keep on expanding that experience so that you keep alive the knowledge that you are making a difference. It is definitely not about following someone or something, but a commitment in your life to make a difference in the world. Sometimes it may not even be about being in agreement with anyone, and it may involve being confrontational. It is only in this manner that all objections, interests, questions and other responses can be included—by being able to talk to everyone and by being willing to say anything.

If you are willing to interact in this fashion, it will be because of your responsibility to communicate—and because you will be willing to have that be generated in whatever form that it takes. Out of that context, a common experience will occur in which anything can resolve itself. The actual communication will be the means through which the problems are resolved, and that is where the support will come from.

So the question that you have to answer is this: "What is your life *really* about?" If opportunities never conceived possible before suddenly became available to you, then what would you do? Moreover, suppose that these opportunities for new experiences were so empowering that the quality of life would naturally expand, not only for you, but for everyone else; then how would you react? Of course, if these opportunities are not available for you, it may be because of the fact that you have placed limits on the definition of what life is about.

For each of us there may be a moment of truth when the choice about how you live your life becomes very clear—and irrevocable. For there is a context, a way of being, in which you are completely adequate to these opportunities in life. It is a context in which what you do matters, and in which you will do what matters—a context which will enable you to fulfill the possibilities that are available to you in the world. If you are ready for the rest of your life, if you can clearly see the unprecedented opportunities that there are for you, then you will naturally assume the responsibility for your experience of your commitment. It will be a state that is far beyond your position, personality and economic situation, a state where you will recognize your own magnificence and the possibilities for real meaning of your life in the world. Once you do this, you will only be able to say, "How could I possibly live my life in any other manner?"

Expressing Yourself

"There are no problems to which communication is not the resolution."

The Power of Words

Communicating with Intention

The fundamental question to ask of yourself is, "How does who I am affect my environment?" This is part of the process of discovery about self-expression, the real communication that lies beyond the verbalizing and sharing of feelings, desires and emotions. It is far more profound than just talking because self-expression does not involve *doing* but instead is about *being*.

The greatest form of self-expression is that of love, but the difficulty lies in being yourself, in telling the truth and in trusting what is true. There are always fears that erect barriers—the fear of being rejected, the fear of being wrong, the fear of hurting someone, the fear of being foolish, and so on. If you acknowledge the fear and accept *what is* about any situation, then you will act differently than if you were to resign yourself to a fear and the associated act of self-invalidation.

Responsibility for Self Expression

The responsibility for self-expression begins with the willingness to experience yourself as cause in the matter. If you see that you create your own reality, then *being responsible is an acknowledgement that at some level you wanted it that way.* Accepting this does not mean that you have to like it that way;

it is only a realization that this responsibility includes the ability to transform your environment by simply expressing yourself. You can even include your emotions for they are the source of energy that will power your intention to create a new reality through self-expression. For it is the desires that you feel strongly about, and about which you communicate with intensity, that will manifest the things that you want to happen in your life.

Self-expression then is a function of responsibility and involves creating your reality through freely expressing yourself into it. Rather than your environment being something that is "out there," it is instead the way that you set it up to play your particular game in life. Less fear exists because you are expressing into an environment of your own creation, and the less fear that there is, the more that you will create out of that context. Everything that you are, do and have is an expression of the self. The degree to which you are responsible for having created it measures the extent of your power and your ability to express it. And, expressing yourself freely is the most important thing that there is in making yourself—and others—happy.

Doing What Matters

"Paradise is not a place to go to; it is a place to come from."

Changing the World

Power and Evil

In examining the possibilities and in reaching for the future, one has to first face the present—which offers as much darkness as it does light. This is not to say that the world will end, but it is to keep in mind that unless some of the basic values that we hold are turned around, each of us—and humanity as a whole—may have gone too far to correct the evils that exist. Trying to deal with these evils a little bit at a time only results in goals that are aimless.

It is easy to identify the ills of the world: war, famine, pestilence, overpopulation, degradation of the environment, racism, and so forth. As humans we control everything that we touch, and for national honor—or some other reason—we are capable of blowing up others. Even simple protests can turn ugly as heads can be whacked by military clubs. In the name of progress we pass a death sentence to wildlife, and we destroy the environment by polluting the air, water and land around us. Under the guise of power we begin to affect our own evolution in a way that we may wind up by destroying each other. In any case, for the first time the choice is up to each of us—to humanity at large.

Being the Author of Your Life

But does this mean that nothing in the world has changed? In the world of agreement we count votes, weigh opinions, compete against one another, and deal with each other over the circumstances of life. It is all about food, shelter, clothes, money, affection and of getting a place in the whole scheme of things. But while the circumstances may not have changed much over time, there is a difference in how it is all perceived. To move away from the trap of the world of agreement, you have to possess an inspired sense of life.

Instead of reacting to life, you will instead take actions based on motives that are effective—and which will stem from something that you bring to life. That something will be the ability to determine the quality of your life—to be the author of your own experience—regardless of what is going on around you.

The world of agreement in which circumstances don't appear to change is distinct from the world of experience. This is not to say that you never fall into the realm of agreement where you let circumstances run your behavior. It is also not a realm of pure experience where you can lose touch with the world around you. It does involve the ability to discern between the two worlds, and to create a third world for your life—that of context. In this manner you can include any circumstances in your life's purpose—no matter what is happening—and then use them to keep yourself moving forward in life.

Nevertheless, after all is said and done, will we still be dealing with an experience that is essentially an individual one, and therefore, one that is limited? The personal success of each of us as individuals appears to leave us without any fundamental shift in the experience to have our lives mean something in the world. For all intent and purposes, the world just appears to be a place in which human beings are incapable of being nurtured. Even if we deal with each other one at a time, it seems that only a few of us know the meaning of context, and that even fewer of us have the desire to empower others on the planet.

Only you can choose to make the business of others—that of humanity—as your personal business. Only you can be audacious enough to take responsibility for the human family. Only you can choose your love for the world to be what your life is about. Only you can choose the opportunity, have the privilege and make the difference in creating a world that works for everyone. Only you can begin a transformation in the quality of life on our planet. It does require courage and an unbounded heart—and it is much more radical than revolution or reform. You literally have the power to fire the proverbial "shot heard around the world." For if it is not you, then who? And if it is not here, then where? Finally, if it is not now, then when?

Being Ready for the Future

"Argue for your limitations, and sure enough they are yours. Also, whatever you resist, persists."

The Rest of Your Life

A New Context

Whatever negates what is constructive or promising is mostly the excessive interest in one's own appearance, comfort, importance and abilities. This is a cultural projection of traits that involve wealth, image, health, status and so on. If all that we do is "look out for number one," then we look at other human beings as mere obstacles whom we need to get past. If we are leery of everyone else, it is because we have fragmented ourselves into an "inside" and an "outside," letting only certain people into that "inside" and shutting off everyone else. Who you are—as determined by you—defines the narrowness or the breadth of your world.

The real self is the awareness that we are all responsible for one another. As an individual you have the unique opportunity to make a difference in creating a world that works for everyone. This may seem to be naïve and idealistic—particularly when viewed against the inhumanity that exists in the world. In spite of this, a vision of what is possible for humanity can still be viewed as practical, even if the way to achieve it is by being tough-minded. This is a world in which the rules for living successfully are based on a principle of a you *and* me context rather than on a you *or* me position—a world in which no one and nothing is left out. This is a world in which individuals can experience their power, have their purpose, and make a difference, not merely as an idea, but as a way of life.

You are always at the beginning of something—and it is at that point that you are in the process of recovering your power to determine what your life will be about. Instead of simply reacting and responding to the circumstances in life, the challenge is to break out of the old and limiting paradigm, and to deal with these forces from an entirely new structure of our own creation. In this way you will discover the truth for yourself as you encompass a radical new way of thinking. You may still be struck by doubts, presented with arguments, and even challenged by questions—with the prominent one being, "What am I to do?" But, instead of being told what to do, *it is about being empowered to do your own thinking, and thus to determine your own answers.* Therefore, instead of an agenda of things to do being presented to you, the context becomes an experience of a way of being in which the appropriate action to pursue will be revealed in the process.

The World as It Really Is

Before you can consider a world as it could be, you first need to view it as it is. For the most part, our lives do not give an indication that we make a difference—or that anything really counts in life. In the big picture no one and nothing seem to matter because it is a world that only works for a very few of us. Most of the people on the planet are poor and miserable while the rest have so much that they can appear to be joyful, but, in fact, most of these are also miserable in their lives. It is in such a world that each of us attempts to live a meaningful and purposeful life, and yet, the truth is that we mostly fail at this task because we do so in a condition that states that none of us makes any difference.

Is there any indication that any of us has a real impact on the quality of life in the world? Even after all of our social and technological progress, is there any proof that a fundamental shift in the world has taken place? Is anything really different as a result of all of the events that have altered our experience? We do make some progress and some things do improve, but these occur in a space that is left over to us after we have totally given up on the idea of ever making a difference.

If you could go back to your childhood—when you had dreams and visions—you would also discover the time when you gave up, when you learned not to care so much. This time was when you began to learn that you didn't count, a time when you bought in to the agreement of values—and most probably, it was the time when you began on the journey of accumulating power, money and status. Thus, rather than your life mattering, it instead became about making yourself comfortable and successful. At that point you organized your life to hide the aspects in which you didn't have any impact, and at the same time you probably began to prove that you did have some impact. Still, by participating in the conspiracy, and by involving yourself in inconsequential pursuits, you began to lead your life in a manner that stated that nothing that you did really made a difference in life. On this path all that you can do is move day by day towards an apocalypse, the abrupt and final destruction of everything—or *doomsday*. However, the real danger is even greater than doomsday, an outcome that will probably be much worse than the "end of the world." This scenario is that *it is more likely that we will continue on the way that we have been doing, creeping along at a petty pace—forever.*

The Root of the Problem

To create a new beginning for the rest of your life, you must determine for yourself, with all of your true intention, what your life is going to be about. But, before you start, it is necessary to examine the "unconscious" premises upon which you have based your life. Within each of us is a fundamental principle that shapes one's life and which determines the scope and boundaries of one's life. The principle is how each of us looks at every aspect of life—the "box" that each of us lives in—and is what sets the limits of thinking and feeling, what shapes the personality, induces the reactions, and determines the extent of expression.

The basic decision—the fundamental principle—is usually formed in childhood and is related to some incident that thereafter shaped the outlook for the future. It may be that you must have the approval of others—at all costs—or that you always have to "win," or that you have to be right—no matter what—or that you must always "play it safe." Whatever it is, until you become aware of this fundamental principle in your life, you will forever be at its effect. Until you transcend it and take responsibility for it, you will not be able to determine for yourself a new direction and purpose for your life. For if you continue to deal from the past, you will only experience more of the same in your future. All that will happen is that you will experience futility in trying to manipulate the circumstances in your life in an environment in which you are at the effect of forces that are outside of yourself—as well as by the unexamined assumptions that lie within yourself.

The Needed Transformation

For a transformation to occur in your life, it is necessary to break out of your old paradigm in life and to create an entirely new one by using the "highest function of your intellect"—the ability to create a *context*. Then, rather than being controlled by *content*, you instead generate a process via the creation of a context through which the content—all of the forces and circumstances in your life—reorder and realign themselves within that context. And, while the circumstances may not change, they will take on an entirely new meaning. In time, these circumstances will change and the situations in your life will begin to reflect that new context that you have created for yourself.

If you *"consciously"* create a new context in your life, it will allow you to determine, with total intention, the new fundamental principle that will now operate in your life. Instead of the previously adopted fundamental principle that was based on predetermined patterns of behavior (reactive, defensive, immature, etc.), you will function in a self-created context through which you will experience a new freedom and true power. Since the source of this context is you, then it comes into being when you create it for yourself—when you say, *"So be it."* You merely have to take the responsibility for creating this context, without any attendant reason or evidence of proof, with only the power of your word behind it. For when you say, *"This shall be,"* in the process *you will give meaning to your life.* Thus, *the meaning never comes from the outside; it always comes from within.*

The context does not evolve from the process which preceded it. It is not one of having more, acting different or being better in comparison to what went on before—a mere rearranging of the circumstances. The new context is outside the scope and the limits of the previous condition in which each of us has lived their life. The transformation has everything to do with daring to think the *unthinkable—to be the creator of your own world.* But, can your life truly be transformed, especially in a world that does not seem to support or nurture people? Such a notion seems almost idealistic, naïve and delusional.

To create a new context, one must be radical enough to think for yourself and be willing to stand on your own. While there is no proof of this stance, there are results that can be pointed to. It takes great courage to be committed in this way, especially if no credit ever comes your way. Creating a context is more radical than a revolution—a phenomena that has mostly been associated with destruction in the dismantling of the old structures. A creation of a context does not attempt to replace the old, or negate what has gone on before, but rather is meant to act as a fulfillment of all that has transpired so that things make sense when viewed against this new perspective. Then, rather than having senselessness and cacophony be the result of all of our activities, the context instead provides meaning and dignity that serve to guide us into the future. And, in this new context it is possible to replace the ways of competition, manipulation, hostility and struggle with the values of compassion, harmony and love.

This context does not constitute a position of altruism—nor is it a selfishness of desire for things to be other than what they are. Experiencing yourself as the "space" in which all things occur is to live beyond the world of altruistic "gestures of good will"—actions that only serve to strengthen the status quo. Rather than just sharing our surplus, it is a process of maintaining our world *by sharing the ability to produce a surplus.* True generosity means empowering people to produce for themselves rather than perpetuating a world of "haves" and "have-nots."

We need an entirely new way of thinking, and a very different set of rules for living. We need to get back in touch with the qualities that really matter—nobility, humility, courage and compassion. Although these qualities may seem archaic to us, and which we have mostly relegated to the dustbin of legends and fairy tales, they are what are missing in our daily lives. Possessing a *noble purpose* is not the exclusive domain of only a few extraordinary individuals; it is a *choice* that is available to everyone.

Living in Nobility and Humility

To live in a noble fashion, to determine for ourselves that our lives have purpose and meaning, can only be accomplished by

being *humble*. The quality of *humility* does not mean one associated with religion, or one of being shy and retiring, but instead
is a recognition of being bold—without being arrogant. It may
entail intruding into something, especially when it may be
embarrassing, in order to reconstruct a situation into a win-win
scenario. Even if a person attacks you, it is imperative to give
up figuring out what is possible and to stretch the mind to see
what is really possible—and what can be done. For if you play
it safe, then you merely stay within the bounds of what you
can succeed at. Only by being humble and willing to risk failure by thinking the unthinkable, is it possible to do the
impossible.

Humility is derived from the recognition of the value of each
one of us, and from *compassion*—the deep sensitivity to the
plight of all people. Rather than being sympathetic, compassion is to know that no one is insignificant. It is being willing to
ask others to stretch even more, even if you know what it takes
for them to do so. Heart, commitment and self-discipline are
the qualities that are needed to be compassionate to those who
are poor and in desperate conditions. It is also to know of the
emptiness that sometimes lies behind the comfortable circumstances of those who are "successful" in life.

It takes courage to approach living from this context because
you have to open up to your own magnanimity, and to subdue
your pettiness whenever it manifests itself. You also need to
accept yourself as an "evolving master"—even in the face of
failures, doubts, fears and uncertainties. You must consider
every obstacle to be an opportunity for a breakthrough in which
failure is transformed to enliven you into making a contribution.

The New Rules for Living Successfully

Since we have been raised in a you *or* me world, we are not
aware of the rules for living in a you *and* me world. Some of

216

the perceptions for these new rules—or operating principles—are as follows:

- respect the other person's point of view
- consider all of life as a privilege
- give up mediocrity pettiness
- take a risk and put your reputation on the line
- work for satisfaction instead of for credit
- keep your word and commitment

To utilize these rules requires the ability to use skillful means and to apply the effort needed to achieve results—results that are far greater than what would be expected from such an effort. This is done by using the principle of leverage—to enhance individual effectiveness in applying one's energy to produce the greatest results. It requires that your life be oriented beyond your personal desires and to shift your sense of self from personality to that of "space." It is in this manner that you will discover what is wanted and needed in a you *and* me world.

Finding out what actions are appropriate is difficult since there are no answers, actions, plans or list of things to be done that are available for this context. The solutions must be arrived at by thinking for yourself, and must be gathered by a special kind of observation so as to provide what is missing. This action applies to your life, your relationships, your organizations, and your community. In doing this the biggest difference that you can make is to empower others—to enable them to discover that they make a difference, and to master life for themselves. It is not just about sharing your success, but about sharing your ability to succeed. Contributing to the quality of another human being provides them with the ability to contribute to the quality of other people's lives—a self-generating process that becomes a chain reaction.

The Resistance to the Process

Operating from this context generates a lot of resistance and confrontations. Doubts, fears, arguments, questions and reactions will ensue, along with statements that say that something cannot be done. Even the dedication of thousands or millions to a task may not make any apparent difference in the world if a job is considered as too big. Also, if the task to be done is considered to be an abstraction or ideal, then it may be relegated to something that is inherently unworkable. Worse yet, the situation may be considered to be just too corrupt, people too greedy, and the task not worthy of the sacrifice that is needed to live in this manner.

But the context is not contained in a neat package because that is not the adventure in life. For it is the adventure in life that keeps you uncomfortable and off-balance. If your life is one of thinking for yourself—instead of from the view of the "thought police"—and if it is one of generating your own answers, and of trusting who you are, then you will enjoy a deep certainty in life. This will be true even if you may not know what you want to do in the future. In any case, you will recognize that whatever you decide to do will come out of your intention of providing what is wanted and needed.

The Ultimate Realization

What is involved in this process is taking a risk, of allowing yourself to make mistakes in the attempt to undertake the impossible. Rather then it being a struggle to "get it right," it is about something that is born out of the mistakes and the errors. Creating the foundation comes from seeing every failure as an opportunity for a real breakthrough instead of just another event. In all of this you have to choose to make your concern for others and for the world be what your life is really about. The creation of this context is a solitary and personal act, but it has the power to resound throughout the world. As your life shifts, a whole new array of options, opportunities and outcomes are revealed to you from this context.

When you make this choice, you will experience a deep and

profound connection to everyone and everything else—in a you *and* me world. Each of us has the opportunity to make a choice about whether life is about "making it," or about making it work. If you continue to keep your visions to yourself, then you will not bring these dreams to life and they will be buried with your potential still intact. If life seems like "only a brief candle" to you, then you probably hold it as not worth living. Only those who are bold, venturesome, and who have the humility to deal with what is possible will enjoy an exciting and challenging adventure in life. Rather than living in a "predictable" environment, you will have a life that is not defined as a "brief candle," but which is instead one of living in a world that can work for everyone, and one in which you can make a difference. If this is the case, then you will truly have a life that is worth living—and *that is what being alive is all about.*

Life and Organizations

"Organizations and people are basically incompatible. Have you ever seen an organization that nurtured people—that didn't make people smaller? Did you ever see an organization that worked and could tell you why it worked in a way that would allow you to duplicate its success?"

The Common Denominator in Our Lives

The Characteristics of Organizations

Organizations are a common denominator in our lives because almost everyone belongs to one, whether it be a company, a professional society, a social system, a political party, a community association or an ethnic group. Also, almost everyone deals with one or more organizations that are to be found in the arenas of government, business, military or social institutions. Organizations have been studied, much research has been conducted about them, a lot of theories have been put forth about their functioning, and much conjecture has been said and written concerning them. Some organizations—such as corporations—have amassed great wealth, power and influence in the world.

Fundamentally, organizations are social systems because they combine people and structures. The addition of technology to organizations complicates things even further because the result is often an immensely complex social system that almost defies understanding. But, it is important to understand organi-

220

zations, and to use them well to achieve the benefits that such understanding makes possible. Without this knowledge it becomes impossible to achieve world peace, have successful school systems, create beneficial economic structures, and pursue other desirable goals that individuals seek for the betterment of the world.

To make a difference in the world, it is almost guaranteed that you have to do it through organizations because they are the bridge between individuals and society. In this endeavor, any attempt to transform an organization involves the attempt to empower all of the individuals who belong to this organization. This involves making whatever you and others learn available to others in order to achieve a significant difference. Otherwise, an organization can be very effective, and yet not act in a transformed manner. Context, creation and generation are the important entities—and not the reactions to forces and circumstances that an organization faces in its existence. It is to function in a natural manner out of what is wanted and needed, even if it involves risk or puts you at odds with the organization.

Functioning in Organizations

An organization has a life of its own that makes it an entity that goes far beyond the collection of individuals within it. Individual changes in its management and operation manifest themselves in different ways depending upon the context in which these changes occur. The fundamental question that has to be asked is, "What does the transformation of an organization have to do with its general business nature?" Identifying yourself at the level of organization requires a high degree of commitment because it is senior to that of identifying yourself as the context for your life or as the context for your relationships. To identify yourself at the level of organization requires that you be responsible for the whole organization, for everything that happens—an awesome task indeed.

Thus, it is important not to invalidate the structure of the organization that got you to where you are. It also goes beyond discovering what is wrong and replacing it with something that is either different or better—an improvement, but not a transformation. You even have to get beyond the efficiency of the organization and realize that if it stays that way, then it merely becomes a well-oiled machine for doing repetitive jobs. Hence, while it may be very efficient, it will cease to produce real value for the individuals who belong to the organization and for the recipients of the services or goods that the organization provides.

What Works

An organization that works remains true to its purpose, is able to support itself, creates the effects that it intends, and nurtures the individuals who come in contact with it. It also allows individuals to make the contributions, to be fully responsible for their actions, and to function in an environment where they can fully express themselves. But, the force that makes an organization work is the people that are in it for it is their qualities which define an organization. These type of individuals have "awakened" to provide an opportunity for others to move from being at the effect of things to a much bigger and more complex context in which they are at cause.

People who want to be empowered and nurtured within their organization need to discover and express their full responsibility for their organization to make it work. If you are just a "victim," you will not take the necessary action to collude with others within the organization to maintain the nurturing state. This is not to engage in anarchy or revolution, but simply to assume the responsibility for creating the opportunity for a transformation of the organization through the means of fully expressing yourself. Otherwise, you are helping to keep an unwholesome condition in place by colluding with the status quo instead of being responsible for it.

Constraining yourself and setting self-imposed limits on yourself only serve to keep things in place as they are. To envision what is really possible in life, to know what you really want, you have to make your knowledge available to the organization, especially to its leaders. Some of the fundamental principles that allow an organization to work are as follows:

- not be attached to the past
- be free of its structure
- eliminate all suppression of intention
- provide for everyone making a difference
- allow full and responsible expression

Organizations are systems of relationships for processing information that are based on communication. In any organization, information is power, and the amount of information that any individual has within it is directly related to that individual's power to affect that organization. Thus, the manner in which information is handled in an organization is crucial to the understanding of that organization, especially as it relates to its effectiveness. Power—and not force which is simply making others do something against their will—is the quality of reaching out by using energy, intelligence and creativity so that other persons gain in strength and ability.

But a process that intends for an organization to work by empowering the people within it may be uncomfortable, have a sense of discontinuity, envelop ambiguity, and even contain some contradictions. Other feelings that may stem from this process may include the shock of being challenged, inertia over having to expand, and the awesome accountability in having to be responsible for the whole organization. Other effects that may be experienced might be those that are associated with traversing new areas that are unfamiliar and unexplored. How-ever, the process opens the way for the involvement of everyone who is concerned such that instead of organizations "using up" people they instead allow them to make a contribution. In this manner, an individual can make a difference by expand-ing to do that through the organization—by being responsible for the whole thing. But, unless you get it to work, whatever you do as part of an organization is not going to make any difference.

The Examined Life

"There are only two emotions: love and fear. Love is being our true essence and natural inheritance. Fear is being something that our mind makes up and hence is illusory."

Self Introspection

The Story of Your Life

In examining your life, you have to ask yourself the question: "Who is writing the story of your life?" Further, you must also pose the question: "Who has the ability to distinguish yourself from your circumstances?" You either see your past for what it is, or you are a prisoner of your past, trapped in a mental concentration camp. If you put undue pressures on your life as to who you want to be—or worse, as to how you want others to be—according to how it is "supposed to be like," then you will wind up blaming others for what has happened in your life. You may even wind up blaming yourself for having been born to "bad parents."

Living life with a "false identity," and then becoming aware of it leads to your liking yourself for who you are. To simply realize that what has happened is what has happened is the beginning of a totally new awareness. It is no longer a matter of having to prove to anyone else who you are because your past is your past, and that is it. If you are willing to be one hundred percent of who you are, then you don't have to run "acts" in which you try to be like someone else. In this process

225

you will experience being more open and direct, you will not be separated from the people that you have chosen to be with, and you will find the results to be quite remarkable. Your communication will be less isolated as you share with others what you are about—*and in doing so you will discover that your vitality will increase as a direct result of this sharing.*

The Key to Life

Much of the sadness in life comes from not knowing what you want to live for. As always, you have a choice to make: are you content with just existing, or do you want to give your all to a purpose of your choice? The purposeful choice that you make is what literally turns your life around, and it is what makes your life flourish—rather than burn out—*because it is the creation of a passion for living your life.* Above all, *you can choose to have good mental and physical health.* You can choose to trust people and ask them for their support rather than using them to bolster your ego. You can also have relationships that are built upon a foundation of love, respect and self-expression. The key lies in telling others what you know, and in letting them tell you what they know. From this you will see the true roles of men and women in our society, and most of all you will learn about yourself and who you really are.

Real Success

"Work is play for mortal stakes."

Altering your Being

Shifting from Content to Context

A transformed person is not necessarily a changed person although that person is certainly more intense in what he or she is at the level of heart, mind, spirit and body. The shift in the way that one defines oneself from *content* to *context*, alters one from a personality with a point of view in an accumulation of events to that of an encompassing "space" in which events in life occur.

Once you have experienced that shift, you will see events—all of them—as contributing in various ways to the completion of your life. You will be nurtured, have enjoyment, be enlivened and derive satisfaction in everything that you do. You definitely will not see yourself as a victim of events, but rather as their observer—and perhaps as their author. The feelings of apathy and hopelessness will come under scrutiny, and will shrink in importance, and possibly even disappear. The notion of separateness and no responsibility for others will cease to exist by recognizing in others what you see in yourself.

If you break up boundaries and open up opportunities for others who may want to participate, you will do this without forcing anyone to join a group, take sides or agree to a position. If you translate what you learn into your own area of interest, then you will become endlessly creative in generating expressions of yourself from this context. Moreover, if you engage in dispersing and vitalizing human effectiveness, then you will experience nobility in the way in which you live. In the scheme of things, it is your attitude that has the interesting effect to refresh your sense of doing what you want to do.

If you pay attention to the evidence of your own experience, then you will appreciate equally both acclaim and attacks. While an inaccurate description by someone else of what you are doing can be an obstacle, it will not prevent you from continuing to contribute. Transformation, rather than leading to narcissism—or identifying yourself with a position or ego— takes you into a world of self-expression. The end result of doing this is in the quality of the many opportunities that open up for you—just from being able to stand on your own.

The Nature of Reality

"A culture that recognizes and appreciates each contribution to the quality of life is one that ignores no one's needs, pains or discomforts. It is a culture in which it is all right to dedicate your life to greatness, to excellence and to humanity. And, it is a culture in which the dreams of our innocence are occasions for action rather than causes for embarrassment."

From Structure to Potential

The Fundamental Reality

We used to believe that a solid structure was a fundamental reality and that its abstraction—the word for it—was but a secondary reality. Through the years, it has gotten down to smaller pieces of matter, down to the atom and even inside of the atom to the level of quarks. Beyond this it seems as if there is nothing except energy with a potential to transform itself. Hence, this is a very different world of structure than the one that we started out with centuries ago. This world is defined as a dynamic network of events and emphasizes change rather than fundamental structures. It is a world in which interrelationships with a potential to act with each other transform entities into energy that can be experienced in a concrete manner.

On a Personal Level

If we take this physical context and apply it to our personal world, we can see that it is a matter of asking yourself what you really want without any restriction—not what you think is possible under the circumstances. The answer that you get will tell you who you are and where you are at in terms of full self-expression. For if you could have the world be what you wanted—in every detail—then how would you create it if you were to have a completely fresh start? If it were possible to clear away all of the boundaries, the rivalries and everything else, then what would you want life to be like?

But you can't answer a question that you can't even hear, so the task is to get the question heard. Although language is part of this communication, it is not sufficient by itself. In addition, there has to be a *demonstration* behind the words—not as a collection of good works—but in terms of what we must do to enable our good works. Otherwise, the difficulty in hearing the question will remain. It is a matter of letting your "light" shine in the darkness so that the perplexity of the current situation does not lead you into despair. The perplexity does have a way of humbling your pride, but in that you will see more clearly what you have to do. It is to move from being determined by the circumstances in your life to that of using those circumstances to express your vision of life.

Participation

"The real opportunity is to participate in the transformation of your life and of life itself. The context of transformation is a context of freedom and opportunity, of empowerment and human joy, of contribution, and of participation. Participation in this transformation is the highest and fullest expression of being."

Making Your Life Count

The Predicament of our Lives

When others tell you to take part, to pitch in, to make your vote count, and to have a voice in what happens—to participate—there is a tendency to consider this against what is going on in the world. What usually happens is that you arrive at a conclusion that there doesn't seem to be much of a point to it. And, when you look at the predicament that we live in, it is very hard to see how your participation in it will make any real difference. Thus, each of us just keeps doing the same things—the ones that don't work.

This wonderful planet is capable of supporting a world of wealth, ingenuity and promise for everyone on it. Yet, the world that we have made seems to be ready to close in on us due to the incredible acceleration and complexity that has occurred in the past few decades. The new technologies tempt us with visions of new ways of organizing, working and relating—and even to imagine great leaps in human abilities. But, as individuals, communities, nations and as a planet we tend to concentrate mostly on "getting by," on just settling to avoid destruction. While a few of us do take on the problems of hunger, war, economic peril, and human dislocation, most individuals only wonder what real influence that they might really have on events. Even if you want your life to count for something, it is very easy to succumb to the feelings of hopelessness and of uselessness.

Most people see the world as one of "participating in an accident"—that it is going to happen no matter what you do. This justifies the notion of just "getting by," of getting what you want and then sheltering yourself into a world of solitary retreat. It seems to make perfect sense in that if the whole world seems to be going out of control, why endanger and expose yourself by jumping into the melee? But, the world is not "out of control," and *we are the world*. Fundamentally, most of us want life to have value and to matter. And, while none of us can ignore the evidence of our predicament, the opportunity for each of us extends beyond the predicament. The opportunity lies not in manipulating conflicting ingredients into new combinations, but rather to see beyond the obstacles to create a new realm of possibilities. If not, then all that you will wind up with from the predicament is a justification for not participating fully in life.

But what does it take to have promises, problems and breakdowns operate in symphony as a whole and coherent opportunity? It takes an ability to see the whole—to have vision. It also takes an inexhaustible resource of the ability to create—at every moment—the value that we bring to the circumstances that life presents to us. It is interesting to note that whenever something of significance is announced to the world, we tend to focus on the accomplishment that was produced—not on the person who did it. We imagine what use the achievement could be to us rather than partake in the acknowledgement of the one who created it.

But, it must be remembered that great advances in the quality of life are created by the partaking of our fellow human beings in the substance and nature of our reality—in participation. Rather than it being an isolated activity, those who create the achievements in life are precisely those individuals who have listened to the collective voice of humanity. Their contributions are part of their greatness, their knowing that they could do the job even if it was thought not possible of being accomplished, and their refusal to not waver—even in the face of stiff opposition.

All of the evidence points to a deep connection: that we are the world and that the world is us. This is our natural condition in which participation can appear in different forms. It is not problems, circumstances and the processes in people's lives that are important; the crux of the issue is what you bring to what you do. The framework—the context in which things occur—is what should be operating at every moment in our lives, under all circumstances. You are the person who determines the context—but not the circumstances. The circumstances are contained within the context in which you respond to them in a *responsible* fashion.

This context is senior to experience because it is a fulfillment of experience, of going beyond the experience to enable and to realize your ability to observe, listen, think and live. It is you who brings forth the ability and the effectiveness to support your most profound purposes and those of others as well. You are the one who creates value for yourself and for others, and it is you who possesses the power to bring things into being—and who passes this power along to others.

There are certain principles that contain the essential power of participation. These principles are fundamental to any activity that people share in, and they are what nurture and enable the people who participate. These principles can be applied by anyone at anytime and anywhere, and are as follows:

- recognize your deepest commitment
- make it safe to take risks
- take a stand that you make a difference
- know that you are distinct from your circumstances
- focus on what people value
- provide the freedom to create

The first principle is about finding out what statement does your being alive make to others. The second principle is knowing that life is risky, and that the environment is one of support, and not that of comfort. The third principle is about knowing that you *are* the difference as a genuine, humble and responsible person. The fourth principle is that circumstances exist independently of you, and that they are only useful in pointing to the opportunities that exist in life which can be produced from ourselves. The fifth principle clarifies the issue between value and want—that what is important is what produces value for others. The sixth principle opens the door to possibilities by the nurturing of an environment where others can experiment and practice.

The way in which these principles interact serve to close the gap between the way that you observe things to be from the manner in which you envision how they could be. When you bring forth all that you are, what you do functioning within that gap is up to you. If you make it an opportunity—whatever you choose it to be—then you act as a spark across that gap to make something happen that makes sense in the world.

Taking a Stand

"What is at stake here, in the present moment, is not the future. What is at stake now is the stand that you take now for the future. By taking a stand, each of us can make a difference in the quality of life for all of us."

The Domain of Distinctions

Thinking for Yourself

Taking a stand is different from choosing sides, forming resolutions or collecting evidence for a position. What it entails is working in the domain of distinctions. A crucial distinction is that between the power of answers to that of the power of "living inside of a question"—where you are committed to the question instead of to the answer.

But just what is a question within which you can live a worthwhile life? You find this out by *thinking for yourself*, as a matter of creation by *bringing forth* the issues that make a difference, and not by merely taking sides on the same old issues. The question is not, "Will I survive?" but rather, "Does my life matter?" The latter question leads to an opportunity to take a stand, leads to knowing when to act, and results in seeing the decisive time in which to make things happen. Taking a stand is to demonstrate a domain of possibility in which an individual life can make a difference in the world.

235

The Reality of Things

Of course, the reality is that not much makes a difference. Monetary systems, military weaponry, advanced technology, space exploration, advances in medicine, and so forth are all great—but do they really make you have a deeper appreciation of your life? Living in the world today is much like being on a train where the people inside are having a terrific time. But, the train is heading on tracks that lead to disaster down the line. When the people on the train become aware of the impending calamity that awaits them, they start to get organized. However, nothing that they do makes a difference because the train is still on the same tracks and they are still on board. Thus, what must happen is an opportunity to get out in front of the train and lay down some new tracks.

It seems impractical to keep trying the same old worn-out ways for generation after generation, each time just exchanging one economic system for another, or replacing one political system with another. The realistic and practical thing to do is to think for yourself. Rather than taking sides on issues, it is instead to bring forth new issues. That is what is important. Posing new questions is also important because they are more empowering for others than the provision of answers. For when you are committed to a question—when you live your life out of that— then you get lots of answers. Nevertheless, you are never stuck with any particular answer that you may have at the moment because your commitment is not to find "the answer," but rather to live your life out of that question.

Questions to Ask

But just what are the questions in which you could lead your life—the ones that your life could be a reflection of? Are there really any questions that could make a difference, and if so, is there a way of posing them so as to make a difference? In any case, it is up to you to create these questions for yourself, for your relationships, for your community, for organizations, for society and for the world. Of course, the one question that is on everybody's mind now is this: "Will we survive?" This question is especially relevant with the threat of global wars and the proliferation of nuclear weapons. The power definitely exists with human beings for the capability to annihilate the world. At this time you are unlike any other human being who has ever inhabited the planet before. The reason is because you are living in a period when there is a real threat of ending the experiment called "the human being" with an all-out nuclear exchange among the various nations of the world.

Of course, the answer to the question, "Will we survive?" can be answered other than through nuclear weapons if the response is in the negative. We can also do this through economic means, by environmental damage, or biologically as a consequence of introducing deadly and incurable diseases. Electing "good" people to work on this question might not do any good if they don't realize that it is an important question. Hence, a more *useful* question may be this: "What if we do survive? Then what happens?" This type of question may prompt you to experiment instead of just looking for answers. You may even find yourself excited and inspired by it—enough to start living your life in the presence of making a difference.

Concept versus Presence

Inevitably, what you do becomes a memory and a *concept* called "making a difference." It all turns into feelings, attitudes, behaviors, movements and actions that are altered but which now are contained inside of a concept. Once you are no longer in the presence of making a difference, you are relegated into filtering the moments of your life through this concept—and your life becomes one of living it through the concept. This applies poignantly to love for it is the difference between loving as a concept as compared to loving as a presence. This is the real distinction, for the person who loves in the presence of something is totally different from the person who loves out of the concept of things.

If the answer to the question: "Does my life matter?" is "I doubt it." then you will become trapped in a vicious circle. Since you can never get the unequivocal proof that your life really matters—the resounding "yes"—your life then merely reflects the following answer: "I doubt that I make a difference." In the vicious circle, the presence of making a difference always turns into a concept. The distinction in all of this lies in the assertion that in being transformed, you make a difference *in the presence of it*. This state of being is outside the vicious circle which is the concept called "I make a difference."

The Realm of Meaninglessness

Living your life out of the concept—instead of its presence—leaves you with a fact that your life is essentially empty and meaningless: that nothing that you do really matters. However, the assertion that everything is empty and meaningless can be viewed as one of stating that it is also empty and meaningless to say that it is empty and meaningless. What takes the "heaviness" away from all of this is your contribution—because that is all that can be, and that is all that can show up. If you stay with it long enough to observe it, what you are left with is that instead of looking *at it*—the emptiness and meaninglessness—you will begin to look *from it*. From this you will see a new domain that you could not observe before as a consequence of avoiding the presence of your own emptiness and meaninglessness. Something opens up when you are left with just "naked being." This is the opportunity, the possibility, and the domain beyond those which everybody knows. It is the breakthrough that allows you to see the whole—the "clearing" in which things show up. When you take a stand in that clearing, your stand becomes the place for whatever it is that you are standing for to show up. It is not that you become it, or a matter of accomplishment. Instead, it is a window that enables you to build not only an alternative dimension, but to build a dimension that can be referred to as "dimension building."

The Domain of Possibility

This domain in which a difference can be made comes into existence by its own act—by bringing it forth. This domain of taking a stand is not one of taking a position—it is the opening up of a possibility. There is no evidence behind it, it is not based on any feeling or revelation, it has no legitimacy, cannot be justified or explained, and cannot even be considered as "right." It is simply the place where that on which you have taken a stand can appear—the "space" for its presence. In this domain—the possibility for possibilities—who you are is the stand that you take. The domain exists only by virtue of itself, and that existential act is the act of taking a stand.

Now the future will look like the past, but it will be different. Of course, a future that is brought out of the vicious circle will also be different—but the difference is that it will be the product of that vicious circle. Even if we "don't blow ourselves up," it is important to be empowered by the question: "Do I make a difference?" If you live your life out of that open question—not as a demand for an answer—but as a stand with no evidence or proof, then what will show up is the difference. Since there is no path, you need to be willing to take a stand with courage alone. The path that you embark on will be made by your walk because you will literally "be out in front of life." *Life will happen in your wake.*

It is not about taking all of this as an answer nor is it about inspiration. Even though you may feel good for a while, you will inevitably revert back into the vicious circle—and you will begin to doubt. You have to trust yourself, be open, think for yourself, master it, create and bring forth by taking a stand to create the issues that make a difference. It is about the possibility of something, the domain of distinction. For this is the domain of possibility—the domain of context.

Your Contribution in Life

"It's a matter of cognition, of understanding, and of experience. It's up to you, and you have to find the resources to do this. You have the one essential faculty that nothing else has that we know about—the ability to reflect on, and to transform the world around you."

The Difference That You Make

Your Place in the World

The Universe is made up of matter, energy, spirit—or whatever else you may want to call it. On this planet, nature has produced human beings—not as something separate and distinct but as part of itself. In this creation each of us possesses one essential faculty: the ability to reflect on the world around us. In this endeavor we gather evidence, pass judgements and change things—all of these being qualities that distinguish us from the animal, plant and mineral kingdoms. Although similar in some traits, we are still very different from other species such as chimpanzees, dolphins and elephants—even though these are supposedly "intelligent."

This being your essential characteristic, the greater extent to which you can develop your ability to transform the world around you, the more fully you will enjoy your human essence—and the more fully it will make a mark. *Quantitatively*, the size of your contribution may be irrelevant—especially if it is never recorded or remembered—although some people's contributions are regarded as those of rare greatness. But, *quali-*

tatively your contribution belongs in a class that defines a difference.

The world is different for your having lived, and that difference is the mark that you leave—something called "immortality." That is what endures, and the bigger the mark, the more people that you can make happier and freer because of your contribution. If this is really your conscious purpose while you are alive, then it doesn't matter to what degree you are able to achieve it. The fact is that you will live in the achievement of this purpose through other people after you are no longer here. Thus, the fact that someday you will no longer be here does not cancel out the contribution that you have made through your life.

That is what defines "immortality," the matter of leaving something (the "soul") which doesn't turn to dust. It is something that is permanent that has to do with goodness, purity, beauty and the eternal. All of these subjective feelings are the real sense of exaltation, and it is where you see the widest range of truth—as well as all of its little details. Rather than being in a state of mindlessness, you are on a level of human understanding that relieves all of the unease in the world—and in you. And when you feel this release, you will get what is sometimes referred to as the "mystical experience."

On Having Parents

"Your well being depends on how all right your parents are. And, if you want to make your life work, then you have to make your parents all right."

The Fundamental Relationship

The Source of Conflict

As life progresses there is a need to be without any conflicts, but it doesn't always turn out that way. Usually, you can let go of old difficulties with parents, but invariably some old upset occurs again. Whenever that happens there is a tendency that probably makes you even more determined to have the circumstances be different—to have them be "flawless."

This is because there is something in parental relationships that expresses the doubts, the resentments, and all of the upsets that happened in the past. If you become more determined to prove the point, you may become impatient, and even unforgiving of these past occurrences. The more that you resist, the more angry and upset that you become. In the process you become the very thing that you so wanted to avoid from happening again.

Instead of feeling despair, the thing to do is to "wake up." You must realize that you are in a process of working through those issues in your life. Your parents are who they are, and you are who you are—but, it doesn't change the facts of what you have to learn from these upsets. The parental relationship provides the opportunity of the learning process in which the awareness of it changes the entire context of the parental relationship.

243

You no longer have to feel guilty or inadequate in seeing that you are the way that you are. It is to feel grateful by dissolving the old "screen" of failure and guilt and replacing it with an expanding awareness of love and friendship between you and your parents. It is then no longer necessary to have the circumstances and the interactions be different from what they are. In this sense you will view your parents as *teachers* whose purpose is to keep revealing your childish patterns of behavior until you finally let them go. This has a power of its own because the truth reveals the relationship that your parents and you have had all of your life—for that is precisely what it has always been for you.

There may still be conflicts in your interactions, but you will observe them instead of doing something with them. If you commit yourself to being the best student that you can be, and you use the opportunity that the relationship with your parents has provided, then you can let go of the lifelong resentments and reactive patterns. In their place you will gain a deep sense of appreciation for your parents, plus the real meaning of loyalty and support that is part of a relationship.

Parents are the fundamental—*and perhaps the most important*—relationship in our lives for most of us since life begins with our parents. Thus, until you complete your relationship *with* your parents, your life is very much *about* your parents, for only then can you stop resisting being like them. Only then can you finally be yourself—rather than someone who is avoiding being their parents.

Language in Action

"The most potent domain available for the transference of transformation is the architecture of being able to cause change without persistence. Only communication can do that—which means the architecture of being able to translate intention into reality and be responsible for it. This really means the architecture of yourself making a difference in the world which means opening up the domain of the technology of yourself. This is what is called a 'breakthrough.'"

The Meaning of Responsibility

Bringing Forth

One way to know that you are excluding people is by using terms that don't create anything for anybody. These terms act as a battering ram, such as using the word "*responsibility*" as so much jargon. Just saying that "you are responsible" for the things that happen in your life is a lie if it is expressed in a context in which you are at the *effect* of things. True responsibility only happens when you are at cause in the matter; otherwise, it becomes a context in which you are either right or wrong about something. The only place that responsibility acts is in the domain of declaration—that of bringing forth, not as a prior fact, but as a creation.

One brings forth responsibility as a statement of empowerment. It is not making a statement of blame, burden, guilt, liability or manipulation. It is also not a statement about feeling bad for something that you did. This is pure jargon and does not work because instead of serving to communicate, it only belittles you. Using the word "responsibility" in this manner also belittles the use of the language. When you use words to create new possibilities for others, then you are bringing forth new distinctions for them. Thus, there is nothing "to get" in the use of language, for the experience of "getting" only lives in the moment that you bring it forth.

Knowing and Enlightenment

"You don't alter what you know; you alter the way in which you know it."

The Experience of Enlightenment

The Indescribable Phenomenon

The experience of enlightenment can be considered to be a quasi-religious phenomenon. Although it is something that seems to help people, there is an aspect of it that makes it suspect—something that has a certain kind of fervor or revivalist nature about it. In that sense, enlightenment becomes everything, and in that light it becomes a substitute for spirituality. Enlightenment is not the end of something nor is it a substitute for a particular path. At most enlightenment is a process to *examine* whatever path that you happen to be on—and it is definitely not about telling you *what the path is* or *what the path should be* for you. It is also not something through which you get an answer. Rather, it is an ongoing process, and the only things that are necessary to keep it going are the normal everyday circumstances and events in your life.

The most difficult part of the enlightenment process occurs when a certain state of mind or experience is reached. It is possible for you to have other experiences like that again, and then behave in the same manner again by relating to a kind of enthusiasm for these experiences that you have had. As you integrate these experiences over time, you then only bring them up when it is appropriate—instead of all of the time. But, en-

247

lightenment is not associated with being religious, or with being involved in religious exercises, or with any other spiritual practice. For the experience of enlightenment is not about worship, a code of beliefs, a theological body of knowledge, or any particular dogma.

The practices, truths and nature of religion are fundamentally different from the experience of enlightenment. Enlightenment provides a very different opportunity to both discover and recover the natural ability to discriminate between the different ways that you can know and be. Through the process of enlightenment you deal with your expressions in a way that you get a different hold on them. You are not obliged to respond to something in some manner—whether that something is recent or a distant memory. You can behave appropriately to that something by "completing the experience" of it. This experience constitutes a shift in the domain from no discrimination about something to discrimination about that something. In this shift, what is known is not altered; rather, it is the *way* in which it is known that is altered.

The Enlightenment Domain

There is a natural enthusiasm in enlightenment because of the excitement that happens within the experience. But, the fervor can be pernicious sometimes although it is a phase that passes quickly. The experience takes on a high profile initially, and then subsides into a quiet process. Neither the experience nor the process is enlightenment because one does not become enlightened through a long practice or great struggle. At some level *you are already enlightened*; all that you have to do is realize it in an instant that is outside of time and space. *People will give up everything and anything to "get enlightened." What they usually won't give up is the idea that they are already enlightened.*

Nevertheless, thinking that you are enlightened can be a danger in itself. Discussing enlightenment is not enlightenment, for those who know don't tell, and conversely, those who tell don't know. There are also no degrees of enlightenment, it is not something sacred, and the mental structure of questions and answers cannot hold it. Moreover, it is futile to sit, meditate or practice some discipline to become enlightened for there is no exclusivity, idea or path to it. There is no place to get to with it, for when you are enlightened, then you simply do what enlightens people. It is about *being* enlightened—not *believing* that you are enlightened—so that each step in your life is an expression of that enlightenment. Enlightenment only exists in the domain of context.

Another facet of this domain is that if you comment about someone else's state of enlightenment from the context of your being enlightened, then that statement *enlightens* that person. However, if you make the same comment to that person to get him to be enlightened, then that statement *darkens* the "space" for that person.

The Power of This Context

The power of context is not one that can be understood. There is a distinction between the belief and its actuality. As a *belief*, it ceases to be a context and instead becomes a barrier to enlightenment. To be the truth—to be so—it has to be *experienced*. Believing that you are enlightened is a totally different phenomenon. If you are enlightened, everything within that process is an expression of your enlightenment—even if there is a lot of inaccuracy in your life. The awareness that you touch on in the state of enlightenment enables you to *know* what is true—instead of just *believing* something to be true. You will also discover the distinction between *concepts* about living and the *experience* of living. The primary discovery is that the experience of something has a very different outcome than the idea of something. And, once you discover that you have not been experiencing life, then you will definitely know that you have been conceptualizing life.

Another part of the process of enlightenment involves doing nothing. In this state you can observe all of your thoughts, fears, concerns, pretenses and other things that you carry in your mind. To the extent that they operate in your life, to that degree they will impair your ability to be with other people. What will become clear to you is your act—your individual collection of patterned behaviors, actions, feelings and thoughts about whom you *surmise* you are. By being clear about whom you *actually* are, a whole new set of possibilities will open up for you in your way of being. The crux of the matter is that the process will reveal a fundamental inauthentic mode of living, and thus it will allow for the possibility of authentic living.

At some point within this process of enlightenment, a "breakthrough" experience will occur that will make your life profoundly different. It will affect your life with a deep sense of compassion, commitment and respect for others. It will enhance your life because you will have a real sense of the dignity of human beings—a deep kind of respect that lets you know that you would be willing to be "in the trenches" with the person alongside of you. The most empowering thing will be to discover where you have been relating to people that you love out of the *concept* of love, and to instead begin to love them out of the *experience* of love.

The Problem of Authority

The most powerful part in the process of enlightenment is when you break away from the authoritarian environment. This process involves letting it go, seeing that it is counter-productive, and observing that it isn't useful to others. When you have authority over people, they usually can't hear what you are saying—much less whether it is useful. The communication has to come from a place that is open, honest and complete.

You may still need a support structure, but it has to be one of strict confidence so that you are not "damaged" by your expressions. For if your structure can't "protect" you, then you will not feel inclined to tell the truth—and you will no longer say what is on your mind. That, in essence, is the basic problem with authority in the position of leadership, especially if the source for the authority lies outside of those with whom the authority is exercised.

To emphasize, a leader that has been given authority over a group by designation creates the potential problem because the authority is based on something that is inaccessible to the group. In contrast, if the authority of a leader is based with the people over whom the authority is being exercised, then it is clear to everyone within that group that this is the case. Since *they* are the source of the authority, the situation avoids the evils of authoritarianism because the group understands that there is really no natural leader. In other words, there is no outside authority that determines that particular leader, and hence the group is always empowering the people who are being empowered. What is recognized and respected is what allows the truth to prevail. This empowerment goes beyond the ideas, slogans and beliefs that are used to manipulate people in an authoritarian environment—one in which untruths arise because of faulty concepts.

Although attitudes still exist within this framework, they are allowed as part of the domain called the *context* of attitudes. This serves to reduce the deference, attention and adulation that is normally attached to a leader in the position of authority. Otherwise, authority only serves to make people right instead of nurturing them. Thus, within the context the point is to have a healthy, expressive, able and capable environment so that the evil of authority does not prevail. This is the only way in which empowerment can exist in a structure that contains a central place from which decisions are made and passed on to the group.

But, as long as your intentions—no matter what they may be—are expressed in a structure of authority, then you will probably not achieve your ends. A more useful structure operates as a network in which the center can be anywhere. In such an arrangement what gets decided and how the information flows is out of the whole network in an environment of partnership. It is only in this manner that ambitions, forces and energies can all come together to produce both individual and group efforts that work. Still, to achieve something important requires that a plausibility structure such as this not break down. A group gets into trouble when the perception appears that nothing is going to change. Inquiry has to persist throughout the endeavor in order to bring about power, value and the work itself.

About Promises

"Instead of looking for ways to dodge the risks of living, could you instead empower yourself in the face of those risks, and take on the opportunities that come with them?"

Living as Your Word

Making and Keeping Promises

Living as your word has to do with making—or not making—promises. Most of us do not consider making promises as a crucial issue in our lives. However, when you make a promise, the underlying premise is that you will be held accountable for that promise. The context of accountability may induce feelings such as fear or anxiety if the pressure is strong enough for you to keep that promise. And, if you can't keep that promise, then what shows up is that you can't be trusted.

If you live as your word—by giving promises, and by making requests, declarations and commitments—what comes up is the question of being trustworthy. But the question of being trustworthy is the wrong one to ask; rather, it is one of whether you are committed. The matter of trust is resolved by your integrity. The validity of a declaration of being trusted depends on its being said and on its being listened to. Your subsequent behavior—whatever it may be—will show up in that "space" of being trusted.

Commitment

The question of commitment is directly related to how you make yourself accountable whenever you make a promise. *Accountability is a matter of commitment.* In other words, when you are called to account for something that you have promised, what is at stake is your *accountability.* To emphasize, not keeping a promise is not a sign of your trustworthiness—it is one of your commitment. Are you really committed—are you accountable—to the promises that you make?

As a matter of fact, you won't keep all of your promises because if you are, then you aren't really making what are called promises. A promise involves a risk, something that is less than a one hundred percent certainty. If something is a surety, there is no risk; it is just a situation of "playing it safe." These types of "promises" that you do make become smaller because you reduce yourself to less commitment.

Being Accountable

The real accountability is that if you make a promise, and you find that you are not able to keep it, then *you* make the declaration that you didn't meet the condition of satisfaction for that promise. You don't wait for someone else to tell you that you did not live up to your word. Thus, if you cannot possibly keep a promise, your accountability means that you must *revoke* that promise. This doesn't justify your not keeping your promise; it is just a matter of speaking the truth instead of associating it with hope or justifying it around some excuse.

When you become powerful at promising something, the issue does not show up until the moment of either satisfaction (you kept the promise) or dissatisfaction (you revoked the promise). The concerns, worries or other considerations that may be associated with the fulfillment—or non-fulfillment—of the conditions of a promise disappear. This gives you absolute freedom in dealing with promises—even if not keeping them results in a situation that may not be favorable to you. The final word on things is that either you make a promise or you don't; either you are committed and accountable or you are not; and either you keep your promise or you don't.

Talking Straight[1]

"Things happen when people talk straight. Something
gets done."

The Vital Act

How We Really Are

If every person told the truth in a manner in which he or she
was not trying to prove something, then that person would acknowledge that something major happens –a possibility that
he or she had never seen before. Yet each of us is filled with
preconceived notions, assumptions and decisions such that the
truth of one's life is not objective. Although it is not separate
from whom you take yourself to be, the truth shows up only in
absolutely straight talk. This is what produces action and what
moves a commitment forward.

But, instead of living as our word, we analyze people's motives, we judge and we evaluate—all the while looking at life
through a particular filter of our own creation. It is "how we
see things," and it is based upon the evidence that we have
accumulated over the years. The problem with living this way
is that life becomes essentially a foregone conclusion in which
you can predict how you will respond to any given circumstance. This is not really living because there is no risk—and
no creation.

256

The Alternative

When we deal with life by pigeonholing and characterizing things, we don't allow a purer perception to operate so that we can see how things really are. If we agree to talk straight, and more important, *to listen straight*, then we will be willing to challenge our own version of reality—including all of the assumptions, motivations and notions of cause and effect. In this realm we have to be willing to create a condition of trust—a hard commodity to come by these days. Otherwise, you will be stuck in trying to figure people out, to find out what causes them to act in certain ways, and to investigate their backgrounds in terms of "what makes them tick."

The process of talking straight doesn't necessarily turn you into an extrovert, but it does allow people access to your being. As an individual phenomenon, it has the power to impact your health by increasing your well being. *You can uncover the awesome and very powerful recognition that you always have a choice to live life truthfully—and creatively.* At the deepest level it is about you—about a breakthrough in the possibility of being human.

This doesn't mean that you should have all of the attention on yourself because this only leads to personality changes, personal acquisitions and movements that affect your status in life. It is also not attention that is focused on your feelings or wants. Instead, it is attention that is centered on authentic expressions of your self as a function of creating the truth—not simply talking about it or searching for it. To do that you have to say it the way that it is—and be responsible for it, including the way that you are. That is authentic speaking at its core.

There are choices that you have made in life that reduce your vulnerability but which also diminish your power. Every time that you withhold your real expression by not standing up and being counted in what you are committed to, then you confine and limit the possibility of who you are. All that happens then is that you hide in self-doubt, you become "reasonable," and you tarnish your integrity. Your life is now reduced to coping with it, and you only strive to "get ahead" by attempting to reduce the risk in life. This state is one of being bound by the decisions that you have made, and by your psychological responses to life. It is to be relegated to opinions, likes and dislikes, wants, and what you think is right. It all becomes explanation, eventually you are molded into this psychology of motivational analysis and assessment, and for all essential purposes you are imprisoned in your own mind.

To discover another response to life—one that is created by an authentic expression of the self—is to bring forth life as a possibility and as a creative act. This shift operates every day, being created in full by expressing yourself truthfully. Your work is not about "knowing about," nor is it about "knowing," but rather about "knowing knowing." This is a fundamentally different way of being which reorganizes the way that everything shows up in your life. The way that this state of being is created is by speaking it. This state of being only lives because you say that it does.

Fundamentally your being knows that this is true because it is then that you are fully alive, free and turned on to life as you are literally *living on the edge*. It isn't a matter of sacrificing or of being charitable, but one of *living your vision*. Your life can be a great adventure—and that is when you feel complete and fulfilled.

Our Human Culture

We have suppressed most of our authentic expression in life—to the extent that we are no longer aware of it. We get used to the way that it is, we bow to the gods of appearance and image, we bargain our souls to careers, we compromise our integrity to get ahead, and we yield to popularity to gain social acceptance. Pretense becomes the way of life, and we resign ourselves cynically to our fates as the prevalent mode of being. We mask our enthusiasm, we submerge our caring, and we "sell out" for approval and agreement. The effect of this is to denigrate our spirit, and worse, to kill our self-respect. All that happens in this environment is alienation from one another.

This "inward turning" becomes brittle and rigid. You turn a "blind eye" towards the problems of hunger, war, disease, poverty, crime and ignorance. In an elite sense of things you hide in the worlds of wealth, knowledge, personal opportunity and self-satisfaction and you totally ignore those who are living with a much lesser standard of living than yourself. You look at those who are living in total deprivation as "the great unwashed." Even the news only leaves you with explanations about what is going on, but it doesn't generally move you to action. Even if you take a direction right now that may show up as a reversal in the future, for all intents and purposes you just don't know if any of it will really make any difference in things. So you continue to live your life in an inauthentic and non-committed way, and in the process of doing so you contribute to the predicament in which we all find ourselves.

Living in Authenticity

The shift that we need to make may require one thousand, one million or even one billion people in order to turn things around. It will take courage to be authentic—and most people are not willing to choose it because they would rather live in the pretense. Living in authenticity is an act of volition, of choosing to talk straight, and of telling the truth. You can't get stuck in the notion that there are only certain ways in which you can relate to others because then you will have no real relationship with people.

Authentic speaking—or straight talk—is talk without any concern for your survival. Your survival exists in an entirely different and separate domain, and who you are is separate from that domain. When you speak to others in that way there is value, you put forth a commitment, and things get done. But, living in this manner goes against your conditioning—of your consideration as to how others will interpret and assess what you are saying. However, if you are being true to your self, and you express yourself with integrity, then you will stand up for what matters as a way of *being*—and not as a way of *doing*. Otherwise, you will undermine the validity of your own experience.

Sharing your experience is a matter of your own authenticity. It is a matter of your honor, your integrity, and it is always a choice that you have to make. For if you don't, the one who pays the price is you—not the other person. Thus, you can either play for aliveness or you can play for survival and position, for "looking good." Standing for authenticity may make you uncomfortable, for *whenever you opt for authenticity you stand alone in an existential "space."* You can only create it moment by moment with nothing to prop you up—and this is what you are most afraid of doing.

What being fearless is like is something that probably nobody has any idea about. However, it is only in such a state that real satisfaction, self-expression and love can show up. Otherwise, your life is about being born, existing for a while, and then dying. In the short time that you are around, you can choose to be authentic. And, you may not know what it would be like if people lived their lives authentically, but you certainly know what it's like when people live their lives in an inauthentic manner—it is all around you. Nevertheless, it always comes back to a choice.

Endnotes

1   From "Telling the Truth: The Vital Act," an interview with Arnold Siegel in *The Network Review*, May 1984.

Out of the Sea of Humanity

"There are rare moments in life when you stand before a window of opportunity, when what you can see and experience alters your being in making rigorous distinctions, in inquiry about the nature and possibility of being human, and a fundamental shift in your way of being becomes available."

The Domain of Creation

The Culture That We Live In

The questions that you ask, and the perspectives from which you deal with the issues in your life depend upon how serious you are about living. If you can support, enable and empower yourself, and you can commit yourself to recreate anew, then a new possibility and a grander way of seeing will allow you to recognize what is available to you in life. The impact that true and rigorous thinking can have on your life comes from creativity—from the ability to abstract.

As human beings we live in a sea of myths, superstitions and beliefs about what a human being is. These myths, superstitions and beliefs hamper our effectiveness, keep us imbedded in them, and solidify the structure to keep us convinced of the way things are. As we motivate, analyze and describe ourselves, and as we keep on telling our stories, we become even more rooted in the incomplete grasp of what it means to be human.

261

Coming from Creation

To bring forth a creation that is inclusive and participatory implies that it must also be effective and ethical. Some sources of suffering are not in the circumstances, but rather are in the interpretations that people bring to these events. Realizing that these are interpretations produces transformation—and a more authentic expression of the self. Being authentic means more according to the nature that we really are. It is not to have "the answer" to everything, but to have it *all* be in the questions.

We are the kind of beings that we are because of linguistic phenomena. We commit to certain possibilities in such a way that we bring forth a relationship between language and being. This represents our freedom—to commit to possibilities. In the act of creating, we cannot distinguish between building our selves and building the society. The language that we use to create with is not fundamentally representational, but is instead a bringing forth of something.

The domain of creation is called existential participation. It is the domain where we create meaning for ourselves—with intention. It involves living, working and coming to grips with life amid the prevailing conceptual reality. Existential participation is the ability to come back into life in a generating mode. It is to realize the relationships that exist among language, commitment and the possibilities for being.

Where Does a Human Being Live?

Ultimately, a human being lives in language, and in the questions that are generated by using the language. As you become aware of your assumptions and unexamined commitments regarding living, the participation allows you to discover your ability to make a difference. This is in contrast to living your life as if it were a collection of choiceless and random moments. But to discover who we really are, we have to be willing to risk ourselves to obtain the clarity about the limitations of the prevailing conceptual reality.

As human beings we are language creatures, but not just in terms of words. Our self takes place in language—in the fact that we are committed to something whether we are aware of it or not. The extent to which we are "thrown" into our lives depends upon the time and place that we are born, the circumstances that we are raised in, and the established traditions, cultural heritages and beliefs of the society of our particular environment. We have nothing to do with any of these notions in terms of having created them. Thus, we grow up in this framework in which we don't create our lives, and as a result life has us—and not the other way around.

We show up in the thoughts that we have, through the language that was handed to us in infancy. This language set includes all of the assumptions about the nature of reality, and the very construct of the means of communication itself. In some languages, processes are more important while in other languages, it is things that prevail. The language makes a big difference in how each of us sees the world, how we perceive it, how we listen to it, and most important—as to what is possible for each of us.

Getting beyond the constraints of the language gives one an enormous possibility of power and freedom in one's life. The primary commitment is that truth is what makes a difference. The central distinction is that instead of using language as a representation, it is instead used as a declaration—words as actions to bring forth something. Instead of using the language in piecemeal fashion in a limited domain, we can use the language to expedite the affairs of our individual lives—and thus, to effect change for all of humanity through the network by which we are all connected.

Functioning in the Network of Humanity

The human network is centered in the power of language—but not in that which emanates from the past. Rather, it is a commitment that is dedicated to the uncovering of our mutual myths, superstitions and beliefs that serve to debilitate us. It is also about demonstrating the most fundamental faculty that human beings possess—of opening up the possibility for being.

The starting place for these activities is in the making of distinctions—those that are involved in the process of telling the truth about matters. This is where the distinction is made between the language of experience—of presence—and that of the language of justification, conceptualization and narrative. The possibility begins with a fresh and powerful approach to language—one where you can risk your assumptions and beliefs. One of these risks is making a promise, and then being afraid that you will fail. Another type of risk is existential in nature—that of being willing to stand and be in life without any props to hold you up.

It comes back to taking a stand that one is the stand that one takes. It is to never abdicate the responsibility for that stand—and to never use it to avoid the essential nothingness of being. A stand is only true because one says it is so since in the saying of it, it is coming from the being of language. What you say to yourself about yourself—over and over—shapes your possibilities for being. Say that you are a machine, and speak consistently about this, and that is what you will become. State that you are your thoughts, emotions and feelings, and that is the being that you will relegate yourself to in the world. Take the stand that you are the stand that you take—that you are your word—and that is who you are because you say so—and for no other reason than this.

In participating in this manner, you will observe yourself clearly, including the fear that emerges with making promises, and the patterns of avoiding risk that reduce your aliveness. Once you take one risk, then another, and still another, what you will discover in that action—in the moment—is who you are. Of course, this notion of possibility is difficult to relate to because it involves achieving what wasn't there before. The possibility is wide open—including the possibility that your life can work in a natural way—with intention. For what is unthinkable can still be true—and it includes the possibility that one person can make a difference in things.

The Responsibility of Every Person

The responsibility of every individual is to empower herself or himself. Forwarding thought is the concern of every person— not just those pundits who reside in the "ivory towers" or the political experts who dwell in the bureaus of governments. This kind of responsibility extends beyond the immediate network to society at large. You can't wait until you are smarter or more influential to make a possibility actual and real in the world. It is your job, it is hard work, and you are obligated to do it if you are truly responsible. Otherwise, the lack of action will extract a heavy toll in terms of cynicism and suspicion, especially if it is heaped on anyone who dares to challenge the prevailing conceptual reality.

The thrust is to challenge the faith that human beings have in their own "common sense"—in being able to count on their senses and reasoning powers to arrive at "the truth." The reactions of humanity to every new idea that comes along, especially those which are confrontational, produce great skepticism and resistance. Just as evolution took us from sea creatures to land animals, the possibility exists to evolve from the "sea of humanity" into the "land of humanity"—to create possibilities for being that were never there before. It is not a matter of when or what, but rather one of the evolution of the meaning of being human.

Since none of us knows what this will look like, we are literally on the edge in the sense that we don't have an answer. All that we have is a stand, along with all of the considerations and positions that you will have to deal with in the commitment to do the impossible. But, the basic commitment remains—that it is possible for human beings to create new possibilities by stepping out of "the sea of humanity" with no blueprints or rules for doing it. You will be doing it solely out of your intention to do so.

The work that you do lives in the commitment to bring forth new possibilities for being human. This is done by creating new possibilities in language—*by bringing forth life*. This is also not about a special possibility—it is about a possibility for humankind as a whole. To benefit from the language that defines who we are is to locate the source of value that is within you. The fundamental qualities in the network of humanity are those of participation and intention. To provide opportunities and possibilities that were not available before, requires participation by taking a stand for the reality and the power that is inherent in taking that stand. In that stand, not only does one benefit oneself, but one also brings forth a new possibility for others. And what could be more human than that?

On Possibility[1]

"There's a sense in all of us of the possibility of living—that life could be a great adventure, something created, like a work of art."

A New Adventure

Choices in Life

What is a possibility, how does it show up in your life, and how can you bring it forth? An impact in one's life is not created by change or alteration—it is brought about by facing the choices in one's life, and then replacing the current set of circumstances with a new possibility for living. Even though you may carry the same personality, history and mind, a choice of a new and limitless possibility will transform your life tremendously. It will allow you to creatively respond to each moment as it comes into being—authentically—instead of being stuck in the same structure. It is as a result of this new opportunity that you can respond in different ways to the circumstances that surround your life.

If you face your own responsibility, and your own choice in the matter, you can never ignore or use a disclaimer to the possibility of a new vision. The possibility affirms the challenge to transform your relationships, your organizations, your society and yourself—especially with regard to your spirituality. Your involvement in your community, the manifestation of your cultural expressions, and the resolution of global issues will all become part of what concerns you.

267

How We Structure Our Lives

We structure our lives to win and to succeed because that is how the game of life is played according to the rules that govern it. This prevailing view of reality provides coherence and an ability to function in the world so as to appear successful to others. The concepts and ideas that exist serve to form the set of cultural agreements that we abide by. Together they comprise to form the reality that "everyone knows" to be true. The particulars of the reality may vary according to place, family, culture and country, but what does not vary is that it is human to have such a reality. And certain aspects of this humanity are universally shared such as the concepts of death, time, the future, the use of tools, and the beliefs about beauty, truth, justice and love.

While it is very human to construct such a reality, we tend to "forget" that we constructed the reality as a function of the structures through which we organized it. We constantly interpret and filter what is real to us, and as a consequence it contributes to our inability to see our own role in constructing that reality. As a result, we are at the effect of this reality, a perspective that serves to burden us with restrictions and limits—especially with respect to our thoughts and judgments about ourselves and others.

This is particularly germane if we consider ourselves to be unworthy or afraid. Because of the limited range that these interpretations allow, we end up with decisions that seemingly make our lives safer and more predictable. However, living "out of this box" robs us of our freedom and of our ability to create. We can't move forward in our lives if we don't learn, notice, or ascribe new meanings to situations that arise in the course of our lives. Despite some moments of clarity, our common opinions will continue to prevail—even if they are unreasonable.

Speaking a New Possibility

A possibility is made real by our speaking it. One way that it is brought forth is by creating an environment that argues for commitment. Another way that a possibility can be created is by thinking for yourself—no matter what the environment around you is like. You can't look to the world to validate a possibility that has never been because all that is contained within the existing environment is a current system of beliefs. Also, possibilities are not a matter of evidence or assertion. A possibility is a function of a declaration that reorganizes that possibility. The truth about that possibility is brought forth in the speaking of it alone. From this initial declaration, further possibilities are brought into existence by more declarations.

The possibility of transformation is brought forth when the distinction between being and mind is made as a shift in our consciousness. Our thoughts and beliefs are something that we *have*—rather than something that we *are*. With this shift comes an enormous power in how we hold and nurture our "knowing." You can still reclaim old values and participate in established traditions. The difference is that instead of being mechanical or habitual in nature, they are now expressions and celebrations of being itself—with authenticity and passion.

The Origins of Mind

Our identification of being with mind began with primitive beliefs, when human beings considered themselves to be part of nature. Their strength and power arose from this link, and their arts, work and religions became appropriately structured to nurture and enhance that power. Whenever human beings observed an internal process parallel the external events of the world, especially one that could be used to predict future events, a context of self-consciousness of being was born: thinking.

The flowering of thought that followed became the foundation of civilization. The invention of the distinction of the intellect—the rational mind—became the power in promoting the mastery of the world. Humans began to identify themselves as "beings who *think*." The ensuing philosophies, religious doctrines, works of art and influential literature proceeded from this distinction as an interpretation of ourselves—the identification of human being as mind. This identification of being with mind seems to have reached a static conceptual state rather than evolving to a dynamic and experiential context. This identification has led to a life of survival rather than that of creation, a state of being where explanations are more important than aliveness, satisfaction or accomplishment.

To illuminate a possibility is to have an awakening rather than to search for an answer. It is to welcome inquiry and risk in order to bring forth the myriad possibilities through the creative power acting from the commitment to questions. Empowerment is attained in the power of questioning, in giving up the assumption that we have it figured out, and in remaining open to renewed possibilities. These act to reorient and reorganize the problems of our lives. The questions about what could be possible for the future are handled more seriously—without hiding in the intellectualism of the context. It means quite literally to live in the set of open questions: "What do I believe is true? What do I stand for? For what am I willing to be responsible?

Being a "Master"

Being a "master" means living face-to-face with the possibility of being—without ascribing meaning where none exists. It also means living with total responsibility, of taking actions that are grounded on the strength of your word. Such a way takes courage—of standing facing the question, "Who am I?" and drawing an answer solely from the stand. This is the essence of being a "master."

Being a "master" means that there are no rules, elements or explanations to guide you in your actions. It is something that can't be talked about; it can only be demonstrated in its existence as a possibility for others through their observation. A "master" can only make available through dialogue an awareness to others of their own innate ability to create being—rather than to impart "knowing about" being. From this sharing, others are then open to the possibility of bringing forth being in their environments.

But, the challenge is still one of being in the world as it is. Thus, it means exposing the structures—the assumptions and presuppositions—that mold us as to how we see each other and that determine the range of current possibilities. To live an authentic and committed life is very difficult in the present-day situation of things in the world. It is certainly easier, more comfortable and less embarrassing not to commit yourself in a world that seems largely indifferent to everything and everyone.

However, the current world environment—one that can be described as "the house that is on fire"—undeniably argues for an urgent need of possibilities and creative thinking to address today's massive problems. It is not a panacea, nor is it about reason, choice or ethics. The primary question that has to be raised is, "What will you create?" This means creating for yourself from within—regardless of the environment around you. It is a matter of thinking for yourself whereby you choose the limits, definition and direction of your life. The commitment is to live consistently with the responsibility of choice—a new kind of *binding* ethic that reveals itself in action.

The Necessary Commitment

The possibility does not appear as a prescription or as a formula, but as a commitment—to commit. Given the responsibility in the matter of your life, what will show up as a result of your having lived? Instead of trying to prove something or to fulfill some desire, what risk are you willing to take and what is the value of it that will guide your action? It is up to you to bring the possibility to the world rather than demanding it from outside of yourself. Both the freedom and the responsibility in doing so will spring forth from your determined goal to achieve something.

When one makes a choice between two options, as soon as one course of action is taken, the other is no longer available. However, other possibilities come into existence as a result of having made a choice. Making a commitment is an acknowledgement of choosing from a set of possibilities—rather than as a situation of fate or circumstance making these choices. Where we have chosen to bind ourselves in life—in our commitments—lies the freedom that we have. The inauthentic quality in our lives comes from pretending that this binding is imposed on us. The authenticity manifests itself when we chose it as the manner in which to live our lives.

This is the ultimate choice and responsibility. This goes beyond doing something from compassion, service or duty. It is a commitment that is done for its own sake and as a resolution of fulfillment. The reluctance to speak of our commitments signals a lack of harmony within ourselves. It is, in fact, a lack of integrity. The truth is that there is a commitment that is involved in living authentically and responsibly because it is to continue the engagement in the question of your own being. You don't necessarily avoid life because of it since you still have your family, work, society and your personal dreams. However, the actions that you take are not those that are designed to diminish risk, but rather they are a matter of actions that are taken in the face of these risks.

Endnotes

1 From "A New Possibility and a Choice to be Made," an interview with Arnold Siegel in *The Network Review*, September 1984.

About Service

"Who we are as human beings is manifested in the practices in which we work."

Communication

The Use of Language

The work that we do has a lot to do with communication—which is commitment by language. Language is not just a collection of symbols but is the product of interpretations of who we are in action. With the use of language we love, hate, think, admire, acknowledge and respect each other. Without the use of language, we simply do not happen.

The practices in which we work are the manifestations of our distinct expressions of who we are as human beings. Our service work is produced by the meaningful conversations that we employ. The language that we use expresses directly what we do, whether it be in oral or written communication, either formally or informally, and either face-to-face or via impersonal means such as through the media. For the most part we work with obsolete practices instead of inventing ourselves for the future and creating new opportunities through our own intelligence.

These opportunities deepen and strengthen our abilities to be of service in a way that will empower us. The heart of the matter still lies in the communication that we use—of the ability to make something vivid and alive. This is authentic self-expression, the ability to communicate about who you are, especially with regard to your intentions so that someone else can recreate these in a powerful manner out of their experience of you.

The Basics of Communication

Communication is not just an exchange of symbols or information, nor is it a collection of skillful techniques, or a force of persuasion. There is a way of speaking with commitment that makes for effective communication—the kind that empowers people and alters the course of history. This type of communication brings forth what has never existed before, and actualizes it as a real experience for others when the intention of the communication becomes translated into action.

Committed speaking—as well as committed listening—are very powerful forces that produce results in the world. Through communication—and the associated participation—the intention and the commitment show up to cause an impact. Communicating effectively and masterfully in your life and work *is* the service that you provide to others.

The Deeper Self

"The world that we have made as a result of the level of thinking that we have done thus far creates problems that we cannot solve at the same level of thinking in which we created them."

Your Place in Life

A Personal Choice

Nothing is ever what you expect it to be, especially in a situation where you commit yourself to a possibility of a vision that is much larger than that of your own private concerns. In this endeavor, without making that personal choice and without shattering the deep disbelief, cynicism and the "baggage of past failures," you cannot proceed towards making a commitment to the possibility that things can be different from what you have known them to be all of your life. In this endeavor, you will also make mistakes, wane in enthusiasm for the possibility, and diminish the commitment through a lack of expression, especially at those times when powerful communication is needed.

You must risk what you know in order to find out what your life—and world—might become. No matter what your beliefs, expectations or fears are, you have to make a profound commitment to discover for yourself what it means for you to be alive. Rather than just focusing on your life, you have to see what contributions you can make for others by sharing yourself. Your active participation and your creative actions will determine what all of our lives together can be like—a possibility that is brought about by one person at a time. In its largest scope it is to entrust your life—to put yourself out on a limb for humanity with all of your magnificence—to find new solutions for harsh realities. For even though there is plenty of evidence for discord, violence and war, you must persevere without the loss of vision, courage or heart.

The Connection to Others

There is a deep awareness that what is available to each of us as possibilities is intimately connected to the possibilities of every other human being on earth. Our actions and choices in life may appear to be "altruistic" or as being conducted for our own "self-interest"—or even just for the sake of "doing good." However, there is an underlying clarity and maturity that are born from the authentic compassion for the circumstances in which all of us find ourselves in our human predicament.

Every interaction that we have with every person touches their lives and ours. Each of us can be an example of looking out into the future to create something new. The fundamental issues that lie at the heart of living are deep-seated and are intrinsic to our lives. We are profoundly moved when a momentary glimpse of them touches us because there is something deep within our humanity that is awakened during these moments. These moments contain the seeds of true vision—the ones that can alter the course of our lives, and maybe even that of the world.

The studies of theology, philosophy, science and psychology have all examined and have directed their different approaches and perspectives to this same inquiry: to uncovering the nature of humanity. Unfortunately, the power of the inquiry has not been able to penetrate or to integrate the core of our innermost concerns. The pathways that have been made available have not allowed us to move forward and to contribute to the inquiry itself. Although you can study long and hard in your own way about this inquiry, the inquiry becomes viable only when it becomes a clearing in which insights—and their full expression—can occur that profoundly affect your being.

This is not an event that happens, nor is it a state to be attained, but it is one of living in the "space" of possibility for life. It is a stand of what is possible for each of us. No matter what the circumstances of our lives are like, engaging in this inquiry will give new meaning to our lives. The action to actualize a new possibility becomes part of the fabric of the culture. The manifestation first becomes evident in each of us, and then the manifestation becomes part of the culture itself.

Actualizing Into Being

To take part in creation—into an expanded and deepened inquiry—is to look outward into a realm of an infinite number of possibilities. It is born as an expression of a deeper self—that profound relatedness of being human. The impact is experienced on both the individual and society through the communication that alters our institutions. By the generation of an active relationship with the issue of being, it is feasible to create a possibility as an opening in which to live. Then, instead of it being a process of selecting options and then forming strategies about these options, it becomes a possibility of creating a possibility, an experience that has power and efficacy accompanying it. It is an approach to being that promises—not a future free from risk—but rather a future of empowerment in the face of risk. It is a place to stand from which to see clearly for ourselves what can be possible.

The Network of Humanity

"The benefits of profound inquiry into everyday living are that they produce a result of real mastery in living and in life. In the network of humanity, the breakthroughs are allowed for through vitality, or being alive; creation, or living at risk; commitment, or being the power of your word; and accomplishment, or getting from vision into action."

The Definition of a Network

Characteristics of a Network

What is a network, how is it organized, what are its operating principles, and just what is meant by a "network"? In one sense a network exists as a structure of empowerment that allows people to contribute to it in the form of themselves. A network is different than a hierarchy in that it only depends upon the common participation of those who comprise the network. A network, as such, is built around no one. Thus, the center of the network is everywhere—and it has no boundaries since it is open to all people. Participation is the organizing element of a network.

Nevertheless, a network is *highly* organized according to its committed action that is its focus. A network empowers people to work together in action in a powerful and intimate relationship with other people. A network does not necessarily have

---

279

"members" since its natural relationship is one of people expressing themselves together in action. A network is thus a resource that replenishes and empowers us as individuals—and as a whole.

The worldwide network of humanity is open to everyone, and includes everyone. It also includes our partnerships with one another in empowering people. Most of all, a network has the potential to bring forth a breakthrough in the possibilities for humankind. And, it will do so if you have a powerful and intimate relationship with the people around the world—those who know you profoundly and who are committed to your success.

On Agreement[1]

"You don't get to vote on the way it is. You already did."

The World of Agreement

Society by Agreement

We live in a world of agreements that determine that we should wear clothes in public, that we greet each other upon initial contact, that we obey laws that are enacted to protect us, and just about everything that defines our mutual society. These agreements are so imbedded in our society that we hardly ever think about them. Although there are no obvious reasons for the existence of many of these agreements, they are still a part of our culture. If you were to ask *why* certain agreements exist, then you would discover that there is no plausible answer.

Almost every generation in our society draws attention to the discrepancies between the world of direct experience and that of the "agreement reality" that has been solidified in the society. But, agreements are so powerful that almost everyone eventually participates in the agreement reality that is shared by everyone else. Also, it is very difficult to distinguish between experiential reality and agreement reality.

Personal and Institutional Agreements

When people interact with each other, they create agreements, some of which disappear quickly after the interaction is over while others last a very long time. For example, agreements against incest have persisted through time and have been made solid through our institutions. Agreements like this one become a part of the foundation of our lives, a part of the social reality that is unquestioned. Agreements like this one serve to define the limits of our social relationships.

When we make an agreement with someone else, every benefit of that agreement has a cost associated with it, and the gain and cost can be equal—or unequal. But what about those agreements that were made by others before we even existed? Although we didn't directly agree to these agreements, we still maintain them through our mutual actions. Our society simply cannot function together in groups without institutionalized agreements. These agreements protect us from inadvertent evils that they were designed to guard against. Of course, not all institutionalized agreements that are in force are necessarily beneficial to all of us.

Institutionalized agreements persist to provide benefits, either to a few or to the many. Some may be disadvantageous to the many, while a few may be of no benefit to anyone—although they will persist anyway. Thus, some agreements are perpetuated whether we get any value out of them or not. These may have been perfectly reasonable agreements at the time that they were made, but they may no longer be appropriate or functional anymore. A few may become institutionalized agreements by habit or custom even when they have no apparent reason or function at the outset, such as the wearing of ties by men.

The Basis of Agreements

Institutionalized agreements serve to provide a degree of predictability and security to counter the chaos and uncertainty that is inherent in a group existence. Group participation in institutionalized agreements enhances the feelings of belonging and identity. But, comfort and security are not the only reasons why institutionalized agreements persist. There are vested interests who profit from economic agreements, there are those who exercise power by virtue of political agreements, and there are those who exert pressure as a result of military agreements.

For an institution to function, people must both know and keep its set of agreements. Each institution is structured in such a way as to be the most effective when its set of agreements are internalized—when people take these agreements inside of themselves and make them a part of their personal feelings and sentiments. When these agreements are reified, the internalization becomes the most effective because then people lose sight of them as being agreements. Hereafter, these agreements become representations of reality and the truth.

The Effect of Agreements

Once the institutionalized agreements become reified, then no one will consider changing them. These agreements become the socializing force for the following generations and thus give the institution persistence. But agreements don't work unless we keep them, and so the internalization process acts to shield the original agreements from scrutiny. The internalization process assigns a truth and reality to these agreements in a way that we are run by them because we think that they have a truth and reality of their own. What happens is that we become the *effect* of our agreements rather than their *cause*.

No one has any natural authority over anyone else, and might does not make right. All that exists for our legitimate authority is our agreements. To take charge of our agreements, and to create and perpetuate only those that have value, we must first recognize how agreements function—and how they come into confrontation with each other. Thus, it is imperative that we understand what agreements are, how they are formed, and how they operate in the world. Otherwise, we won't be able to construct institutions that promote group survival and individual satisfaction. And, we will be stuck with all of the agreements that we "unconsciously" made—and which we forgot that we made.

However, there are problems even with "conscious" agreements, especially if they are viewed as being *only* agreements that you may or may not keep. The way of dealing with agreements is to take responsibility for them, and to operate in life based on those agreements. Agreements are an interim arrangement that define how we have structured the world. If we don't want to keep them, then we have to review and revise them to make them more nurturing and satisfying to people. This becomes the process of getting out of a system of agreements and into the experience of alignment.

Agreement and Alignment

Social agreements move the issue of agreement into a bigger context. This situation has to be looked at in the context of distinction between *agreement* and *alignment*. An *agreement* is a structure of relationship that exists among the "*statuses*" that we occupy in our lives. Each of us has a particular way of interacting with others—depending upon our individual "status"—that is organized around our relationships. We also have the experience that lies outside of the statuses that we occupy. The word "*alignment*" is used as the reference for this experience.

We actually experience alignment with each other such as when we meet someone new, when we work with somebody on a project, and when we just do something with someone else. The support and satisfaction that is obtained in these situations enables us to repeat these experiences. However, this is where the problem begins because the original experiences were satisfying as a result of their not being planned—they just occurred spontaneously. To look for the same form again, we tend to make an agreement to recapture those moments.

The difference is that our original experience of alignment was something that was internal—it just naturally came out. When we make an agreement out of it, it becomes external to us, and as such it changes into something that controls us. As an external force, we tend to resist it, the agreement doesn't work, and worse—it now persists. Since the agreement is not working, we will break it, assign blame and look for the reasons why it doesn't work. Then, to solve this problem we will make new agreements to piece together the old agreements—an experience that serves to control us even further. The end result is that we get farther away from owning the relationship and the experience—and from being responsible for having them work. And, the more agreement that we get in this situation, the more complicated and disastrous the results become.

The irony of destroying the experience of alignment by making agreements is that it exemplifies how we get by in life. It drives the satisfaction out of our relationships so that all that we do is resist and break the agreements of those relationships. We wind up being penalized for it because the overwhelming structure of agreements works against us—especially if the structure is backed by power, position, wealth and influence. At these times it becomes very difficult to "choose it to be that way."

Operating in a System of Agreements

With agreements we assign responsibility to others who occupy certain statuses and we make them be accountable for "cleaning things up." When the actions that these people take do not work—when they don't "get it right"—then we start "cleaning it up" ourselves. What happens in the process is that we start getting what we want—with less energy and time being expended, and by not placing blame on someone else. You literally take responsibility for something, even though you may not be the one who was assigned to this task—or even the person who made the "mess."

The major distinction is whether you experience something as agreement or alignment. In agreement you can feel bad about it, hold it as something that you have to do, or you can have it be something that you want to do—as one of your goals. In owning our agreements and in being responsible for them, we move toward a society that nurtures people by moving out of a system of agreements and into a place where we experience people from a context of alignment.

Endnotes

1   From "The Grip of Agreement" by Earl Babbie in the *Graduate Review*, July 1977.

Going Beyond[1]

"If you're not all right the way you are it takes a lot of effort to get better. Realize you're all right the way you are, and you'll get better naturally."

A Choice to be Made

Two Different Paths

In general, we talk about "minor adjustments" instead of the clear challenge: that of transformation. In extricating ourselves from the old issues, we must take actions that are more humane and which assure our dignity. To change our direction of social interaction involves the alteration of your awareness and of your context in which it manifests itself. Doing it with small changes at a time only accelerates the problems which are exponentially growing. Staying the course on our present path will only result in lowered expectations, self-imposed limits, and less satisfaction in life.

On the other hand, you can take the path that offers you adventures in consciousness, a greater depth of human intimacy, and a force that moves toward the reorganization of our society. It can be euphoric—as well as threatening and terrifying—to strive for the adventures of the body, mind and spirit, the aspects of living that we have somehow been "hypnotized" to forget. The idea of transformation lies just beneath the surface—in the "silent majority." The words may not exist to express it, but all of us know that it is something that is lacking in our lives. Certainly, we know that we can do better than this.

What Has to Happen

This doesn't mean that we have to evolve to a "higher form of life." It does entail being more sensitive, strong, empathetic and intelligent—as much as we can be. We also have to be active, get in touch with nature, relate to other people, tune our own bodies and sharpen our minds. It means avoiding things that are not good for us, such as drugs, and living in a way where our success is not measured by how well we compete against others.

Transformation is not going to be easy for there is no "magic pill" that you can take. You can only do this by dedication and discipline—not from a point of view as tyranny, but as a freely-chosen path in which you live your existence. Rather than sitting around and contemplating about this, it is a matter of being an entrepreneur and an adventurer. It is a shift from the world of competition, acquisition and aggression to one in which sympathy and collaboration are the key elements. Instead of dominating nature, we must blend in with nature so that our standard of living is modest, elegant and beautiful. It is living in a world where a more equitable distribution of resources exists, and one in which we have true social justice for everyone.

The Process of Transformation

The larger vision comes out of an organizing principle that clears up the purpose in life, and which frees our energies for the adventures that lie ahead. The evolution of consciousness, of being and of society, will begin to fulfill some of the awesome potential of the human race. It is both an "inward" and an "outward" process that involves social action and personal change.

Transformation is a process with goals along the way—goals that may not be attainable immediately, but which serve to challenge and inspire us nonetheless. If we settle for a world where we are relegated to a life of prejudice, unequal opportunity, crime, mass unemployment, distrust, poverty and ill will, then all that we will wind up with is more chaos. We will have more prisons, more police forces and more military might in a society where enforcement of laws and rehabilitation of offenders are the prime driving elements of it.

Working for transformation means acting with a new sense of community and responsibility—towards a society where people don't have to go to war, where they don't have to commit crimes to survive, and where programs are instituted for the achievement of human potential. It entails having a wide scope and commitment to deal with the unexplored capacities of body, mind and spirit. While we have promising options, we don't have the boldness or vision to carry them out.

The Dangers to Watch Out For

Unexamined visions, however, can lead to trouble, especially if they are demagogic in nature. *It is crucial to avoid gurus who state that that their way is the only way.* Self-appointed messiahs will invade your privacy and will curtail your right to freedom. Following someone like that will only lead to losing interest, disillusionment and a return to cynicism and doubt—the human elements that will work against transformation. What is needed is intelligence, compassion, balance and humor. Humor is especially important because it will enable you to laugh at yourself—in particular, during those times when you are being self-righteous and pontificating.

Risk and fear, however, are still there in anything that involves significant change. Resorting to our need for security will make us adhere to maintaining a "holding pattern" in our lives—even if it is detrimental and creates a feeling of helplessness in us, almost as if the problems are really too big for us. Only by taking responsibility and putting yourself at risk can you get

289

past these feelings of inadequacy. Nothing is really risk-free in the world—in spite of everyone striving for comfort, convenience and material goods. Even the acquisition of personal weapons to protect property and lives—the so-called security factor—only makes us more afraid of the world. As such, all that happens is more anxiety, demoralization, danger and uncertainty.

The health arena is another area where personal responsibility and intelligent risk-taking are major factors in one's well being. Relying on the existing medical system can be full of problems as far as adequate medical care is concerned because the underlying assumption is that the medical establishment is responsible for the health of an individual. However, even though modern medicine is fantastic, and doctors can be marvelous, the prevention of disease and the maintenance of wellness is still the patient's responsibility. Health is something more because what causes most sickness is one's personal lifestyle. Resistance in being well manifests itself as wanting that drug, craving that cigarette and needing that drink. In fact, the abuse of tobacco, alcohol and drugs accounts for over one-half of the hospital beds in the United States[2].

The Ultimate State of Being

In our culture we are not happy until we go through a period of great apparent damage and wreckage before we emerge as health-conscious individuals. When you finally become responsible in the creation of your own health, then that is the ultimate step. This is a process in which you must ask yourself, "Are you willing to give up being sick?" It is a state of being in which you will not settle for anything but robust health. And what has to happen is a balance of *thanatos*[3]—a breaking down—with that of *eros*[4]—a joining. Every second millions of blood cells in your body are being destroyed, and millions more are being created. The breakdown of old forms is necessary for good health, so when you don't exercise, you don't break down enough of them and the old ones stay around—and as a result you won't feel good.

In the same manner, when you look at the situation of the world, there are humane alternatives to the crises of energy, the problems of the economy, the destruction of air, land and water by pollution, and the despair and misery caused by repressive political regimes. Every one of these issues is capable of being transformed within the culture by concentrating on *context* instead of *content*. The particular method or technique that is used to bring about transformation is unimportant. What is relative is what we can do to make this transformation occur.

Endnotes

1   From "Beyond Getting Better" by George Leonard in the *Graduate Review*, March 1977.

2   There is also a matter of accepting death. Over eighty percent of the costs of health care are associated with extending the lifespan—by technological means—for an average of *two weeks* for people who are terminally ill.

3   From the Greek word meaning "death," and similar to the Sanskrit word *adhvanIt* meaning "it vanished."

4   The sum of life-preserving instincts and sublimated impulses that gratify basic needs and protect the body and mind.

The Universal Experience[1]

> "We are all here for one another and every experience that everyone is having is relevant. It all counts. The Universe is so extraordinarily well designed that it needs all of these experiences."[2]

The Functioning of Humanity

The Beginnings of Discovery

Every human being is born naked, helpless, ignorant and with no experience of what to do. We innately have drives of hunger and thirst, curiosity, the need to breathe, and eventually the urge to reproduce. We proceed by trial and error by using a brain that coordinates the information from our senses. The memory records these events and recalls these as special cases. The mind then discovers the relationships that exist between these special cases by observing and categorizing the information into patterns, including mystical beliefs.

Some of us develop a mathematical capability by which we translate the conceptions from mystical beliefs to demonstrable realities. The calculations provide the means to do extraordinary discoveries through further measurements—facts that lead to the awareness of generalized principles, such as the law of gravity. It is in this manner that a few human beings discover synergy—the behavior of whole systems that is unpredictable by observing the behavior of any of the parts in a separate fashion.

In general we are not taught to look at wholes. Instead we are trained to be specialists—to look at the parts, and in a finite fashion. But, generalized principles are only discovered by looking at wholes in an eternal fashion. The finite mode explains how the Universe began, and how it will end—the time and space aspects of it. The eternal mode discovers the infinite of existence—the all-encompassing design. This pure abstraction can be expressed mathematically, and as such we can then make scientific instruments that allow us to understand the generalized principles.

Where the Problem Lies

Unfortunately, the power structure is in control of our human affairs. Even those who are lucky enough to find a place where nature is beautiful, are continually being threatened by the invasion of those who are not so lucky. This lethal inadequacy of life support creates politics and its associated ideologies to deal with the matter—a situation that fosters unfair and illogical systems. Out of these systems, diametrically opposed theories arise which only lead to the survival of the fittest—through arms, power structures and vast amounts of money. The focus is then placed on how to destroy each other—rather than on how to make humanity work. Thus, the focus is strictly on physical properties whereas *the whole game of life is metaphysical in nature.*

We have developed sufficient awareness and have discovered enough principles to function in a much bigger way. Still, the more that we know, the more that we realize just how much we don't know. The technical aspects of information gathering and problem solving are based in terms of scientific truths rather than on someone's opinion. However, the difficulty with this situation is that *less than one percent of the population of the planet is able to understand what technology is talking about.* Therefore, *ninety-nine percent of humanity does not understand the abstractions of technology*—which is all that the

Universe is. And, since humanity at large does not understand these discoveries in technology—the laws that govern it—then it is incapable of apprehending and employing these principles for humanity's advantage. The result is an exploitation of humanity by big business and governments for the production of weapons and the conducting of wars.

Since we have a humanity where the great majority of its members are so ignorant that they are unable to deal with this lethal inadequacy, the only way to cope with this great dilemma is through the understanding of synergy. Grasping the eternal laws of the Universe means simply to apprehend that *the maximum gain of advantage is gotten from the minimum amount of energy input.* Humanity's function is to apply these eternal laws to *physical* problem solving. But, it involves using another model rather than just playing the pure *mystery* games that technologists are using currently.

Technology is not some mysterious process in which only brilliant people can make important contributions. It is possible for even children to understand the concepts of technology in the fields of mathematics, physics, chemistry and engineering. The great realization is that *technology is the process of putting the data of experience into some kind of order.* All great scientists discover laws and principles on their ability to base what they know on their personal experience, and *not on the way that they—or anyone else—believes that a system operates.* They demand *experimental evidence* because they know that *the process of discovery is available to anyone who is willing to be committed to telling the truth about their experience.*

What Can Happen

So what happens when human beings learn the means to handle the problems of the world? This marks the beginning of a process to use the earth's natural energy and to create a new relationship with the earth. By understanding the true wealth of abundant resources that are available to provide an enormous life support in the biosphere, human beings can then discover that *our mental faculties are everything—and that our physical muscle is nothing.*

When conditions open up, the acceleration of technology takes place. *It is only in wartime that the slowdowns occur.* The goal should be one of having complete changes in the state of the art of technology—and to have corresponding changes in the awareness of human beings. The wisdom is to see that these principles operate within ourselves, for all of the faculties are always inside of everyone. It is through encouragement that people dare to think and to go with the truth.

Almost all of us are born geniuses—a quality of being which is soon extinguished by parents, schools and society. Still, if you do your own thinking, and you learn entirely through trial and error, then the mistakes that you make are the ones that will allow you to get where you are going. This is the only way that you can see *what is.* It is under these conditions *how all of the gains of humanity have come about.* But, in our society the making of mistakes is not tolerated, and the threats are always there to convey this thought. Instead, the established system teaches you to learn by rote and by memorization. However, if you don't make mistakes, then you probably don't learn a thing.

The Crisis

While life is a game, you still have to look at it in a comprehensive and integrated way whereby it is tested through its own integrity in the Universe. What we know is that the Universe is always regenerating, it is everywhere transforming, and is at all times everywhere and everywhen. The current evolution can be termed *"Earth's critical moment"* for if *muscle* (the power structure) is still in control, then we may not make it through all of this.

———

Today we are confronted with less misinformation and with more reliable information with each successive generation. However, all of the customs, languages, laws, accounting systems and axioms are still derived from the old, divided and ignorant systems of thought. The specialized knowledge that humanity perseveres is derived from the ancient armed conqueror illiterates. Their systems, which are in place today, have separated human beings in order to make it easier to subjugate them and to proliferate strife.

The challenge to humanity is one of being in harmony with each other and with nature, and to strive for building rather than destroying. In this matter the integrity of the individual is what counts. Will you be thoughtful, will you realize what kind of planet you really want, and will you be willing to share this with others? *An individual's highest potential may only be realized in terms of full interaction with all of humanity's potential.* It is your own will and discretion that determines whether you are a *standby* or an *active* function of the Universe.

But what does it take for a person to realize this? The reality is that *most people go through their lives and never realize what is so.* So how does a person get to realize *enlightenment?* Although evolution is always working in that something is happening to us all the time, it is a system that can undergo extremes that are not always conducive to our well being. However, what must be remembered is that each of us is still a custodian of a vital resource—the diverse inventory of human experience. Whatever you do will be by virtue of dealing with this asset—your experience. *You do this by having to learn how to think—for yourself.*

At present, you are being challenged by the evolutionary process in terms of survival in the game of life. To graduate into the bigger reality of our existence, each of us will have to be a part of the absolute frontier. *This frontier will be whether we are going to survive on our planet or not.* And even though human beings have been around for over three million years, *every minute counts now* for we are in our "final examination."

Endnotes

1 From "Bringing the Universe Home" by Buckminster Fuller in the *Graduate Review*, December 1976.
2 As quoted from Buckminster Fuller.

Creating the Context
of Responsibility

"Once we as a human family recognize the special capacity of context to direct and empower our efforts and
have mastered the technology for creating context, we
will have learned how to empower ourselves—as a
human family—to create a future on this planet which
appropriately reflects our aspirations and magnificence
as human beings."

Creating the Context

The Central Issue

Creating the context[1] of responsibility is one of being able to
transform the quality of your life in such a way that it allows
you to be accountable in the world. It involves expanding your
relationship to include "all of it"—to expand your sense of joy
and aliveness, and to share it with the rest of the world in a
truly meaningful way. It incorporates observation, communication, participation, learning, experience and being the *source*
of things for yourself.

The creation of context of responsibility is the incredible transformation from personality to being—the "space" where you
can experience the aliveness that is literally like "being born
again." The basic questions in establishing this context are as
follows:

- How much are you willing to be responsible for in your life?
- Are you going to be responsible for playing the game of life at one hundred percent throughout your *entire* life?
- Are you willing to make a commitment to that?

That is the central issue: whether to take responsibility or not. The only choice that you have is whether to be conscious of your commitment, or to continue in the lie that there is nothing that you can do to change things. It is all a matter of aligning yourself with what is already going on—and with who you are.

Endnotes

1   Some useful definitions for context are as follows:
   - The unquestioned assumptions through which all of our experience is filtered
   - The ground of being from which we derive the content of our reality
   - That which determines the way that we put things together in our minds

The Context of Transformation

"Every day it becomes more difficult to pretend that we can stand alone and unmoved while millions are affected."

What is Possible

The Human Dilemma

The problems of the world are not something that are impersonal or that exist "out there"—they exist in each of us, in all that is incomplete and unfulfilled in our own lives. Quite literally we have disowned the whole world since millions of human beings die each year, and millions more who remain alive are undernourished, maimed or ravaged by hunger, war and disease. Our combined human failure in the world is reflected in the undeniable testament of the sorrowful cries of children that goes on every day. No matter how hard and how far away we try to place those wails and woes, we cannot escape the reality of what is going on. Temporarily, we can succeed in "escaping," but only at the cost of some portion of our aliveness. When that happens, it diminishes our ability to marvel at the miracle of birth, and to be able to hear and feel the depths of love in someone's voice and emotions.

There are enough resources, land, water and food to feed, clothe and provide shelter for every person who lives on the earth. No reason exists to fight over resources or territories. There are more than enough medicines to cure and plenty of doctors to treat the various diseases that people are afflicted with. There is no shortage of money with which to build hospitals and other health facilities to end the suffering and comfort the dying. The only reason that these problems continue unabated is because we refuse to make the conditions of these problems as our own—to take responsibility for them. All that we seem to do is support doctrines that create their own opposition and solutions and which only wind up producing their own new problems.

What is Needed

The time has come to take a new approach to the problems of famine, plagues and violence that affect the destiny of all humanity and which increasingly reverberate around the globe. The urgent global messages that are now beating at our consciences offer an external evidence that we require a new awakening to realize the deeper connection that we all have with the world. *We are the world and the world is also in us.* Each of us is a context in which we hold all that ever was, all that is, and all that can be. In this light, *each of us has the power to create our own world—our own heaven or our own hell.*

We are at a point where the timeline of history and the advances in technology are meeting to prepare the way for transformation. We must begin this transformation by taking responsibility for the problems that exist in the world. Although it is a relatively simple thing to do, nothing could be more profound than a change in the context of things. In that new context all that happens takes on a new and different life. For rather than being a private and passive matter, true responsibility always involves actions in the world that are different in the following ways:
* no single doctrine

- no right or wrong
- no credit for success
- flexibility and effectiveness

Furthermore, to follow through on a path of action, it is imperative that we do the following towards the intended goal:

- the contribution of time and money
- influencing public policies
- working with organizations
- support of those who are involved
- offering of skills and knowledge

The possibilities are endless wherever and whatever the path which we choose takes us on the journey to the ending of these problems. If we move with the power of personal responsibility—each of us in our own way—then the combined end result *is* the end of these problems. It may take hundreds, thousands or millions of us to achieve something—but only if we act as wholes in alignment with each other, and not as parts in a movement.

But, there is no need to wait because a moment exists for each of us in which the context can suddenly shift. In this moment, what seemed impossible before now becomes quite possible. It is an instant in—and out—of time when we take responsibility for the world and for what it could be. In that instant, the end of these problems begins.

The Power of Context[1]

"Our paradigms—the models through which we look at our relationships—all come from a ground of being of unworkability. You need intention to create a transformed context for your relationships. In such a transformed context, what you do in your relationship works, and what you do also works."

Creating a World That Works

What We Face

The most important interaction that we can have with each other, and what most people really want to have happen because of it, is to have the world work. We want our lives to matter, to make a real difference, and to be of genuine consequence. Deep down inside we know that there is no satisfaction in merely going through the motions—even if these motions are pleasant and make us successful. We still want to know if we have had some impact, we want to contribute to the quality of life, and we want the world to work.

As you look around you, when you see what you can do, you are confronted by the fact that starvation, war, pollution, disease and strife—be it political, economic, social or religious in nature—kill millions of human beings every year. These problems are not your individual burden nor do they call for a sacrifice on your part. But, the existence of these problems, and the unparalleled failure to deal with them, enables us to see that the unworkability is located in the very condition in which all of us live our lives. Thus, we are striving to make our lives work in the same condition that results in starvation, wars and epidemics. These and other associated problems dramatize a world that simply does not work. These problems have persisted throughout our human history, and they have accounted for countless deaths, misery and suffering—probably more than all natural disasters combined have produced throughout time. And, the ones who have suffered the most by these ordeals are the children.

Because the impact on our lives is so great, the existence of these problems is actually an opportunity—one of getting beyond defending what we have, beyond the futility of self-interest, and beyond the hopelessness of making gestures that only seem to invalidate us. In experiencing the truth underlying these problems, one discovers the principles to end these problems—and to make the world work. This is not a solution, reason, opinion, justification, explanation or point of view about these problems. Instead, it is an examination of these problems from the aspect of two specific questions:

- What are the laws that govern and determine the persistence of these problems?
- What are the principles for the end of these problems?

The Examination of the Problems

Fundamental laws and principles cannot be deduced and one does not arrive at these as a function of what is already known— the facts. To illuminate these problems, these laws and principles must be such that they create a new "space" in which knowing can occur. It is not a matter of instituting new programs or about thinking of some more good ideas. *It is about revealing the fundamental principles for the end of these problems.*

In the examination of these problems, the first step is to examine the system with which the problems are going to be examined. The nature and the effect of the perceptions and understanding of these problems depends upon the quality of the findings—and how these are influenced by the examiners. On a personal level, you have to get some insight into yourself—not at what you think or feel, or about your opinions and points of view—but at the "ground of being"—the place that gives rise to your actions, thoughts and feelings. Specifically, you must inquire deeply regarding the unexamined assumptions and beliefs that serve to limit and to shape your individual responses to these problems. You must pierce into your own system of beliefs in order to make the observations about them.

In the examination of beliefs, the first component that emerges is that of *scarcity*. It isn't that human beings think that *things* are scarce, but rather that they think *from* a condition of scarcity. For if we think in this manner, then everything must be doled out carefully, like the payroll, and then only to those who are deserving of this help. Further, if we assume that everything of value in life is scarce—time, money, love—then we will act to protect things—regardless of how much we actually have—because they are scarce. The ultimate example of this is the creation of nuclear weapons to protect property, the extreme case being neutron bombs that kill people but which leave buildings intact.

Examining further, the second component that emerges is that of *inevitability*. If you believe that things are inevitable, then you will always hold in your mind that these problems of the world can never be ended. All that can happen—at best—is a toleration of the major problems of hunger, wars and diseases— much like we tolerate the situations of "death and taxes."

A third component that emerges in the examination of these problems is that of *no solutions*. Hardly anyone exists who would tolerate these problems if he or she thought that a solution existed for them. But, because each of us "knows" that there is no solution to any of these major problems, then what happens is that we put up with these problems instead of doing something about them. However, *these problems exist because of the failure to perceive the conditions that cause them to persist.*

Scarcity, inevitability and no solutions are three filters that color your perception of the world. As long as you hold on to these beliefs, *then it is impossible to be clear about the conditions that cause these problems to persist.* And, it isn't about applying solutions that are *better*, about knowing *more* about the problems at hand, or about doing something *different* than what others have already tried or done. There definitely are solutions, but they do not act to solve the problems because they are mostly the result of taking a position on the matter. The difficulty with taking a position is that it manifests an opposing position which then causes more effort to be invested in the original position. And, when you do so, the opposing position also becomes reinforced.

Moving Away from Our Positions

In the examination of our beliefs, we will uncover the behavior of *gestures* which arise out of the hopelessness and frustration that are associated with problems of this magnitude. If you have accepted the existence of these filters through which each of us perceives these major problems of the world, then you will have moved away from being stuck in these positions. You can then clearly observe these problems and see the opportunity that exists to solve them—not by information, expertise or learning—but by taking responsibility for them.

Observing the mess that surrounds most issues is to look clearly at the confusion, controversy, and conflict that prevent us from seeing the underlying conditions that make these problems persist. All of the existing positions and opinions only serve to create other positions—and opposition—which then get translated into "solutions." The mass of solutions becomes so large that it creates further confusion, conflict and controversy. This mass of solutions prevents the seeing of the truth of what causes these problems. All that occurs is gesturing about more, better or different solutions. These gestures only serve to cause doubt and mistrust, and they wind up creating opinions about these problems that surround *any* position that is taken on the matter.

Any position that you take will not contribute in any way to the end of these problems. This perception marks the end of hope—and you are thereafter left with just what is so about matters. It is only then—when you are operating without the structure of beliefs—that you can see the true nature of the problems and their source. These problems are a function of the condition in which each of us lives his or her own life—rather than about what each of us *is* doing or *not* doing. The condition in which your humanity exists—the environment for you as a human being—is the *"beingsphere,"* a system of concepts and forces that surrounds you and which makes these problems persist.

The Fundamental Idea

A condition is a position that functions as a fundamental ground of being. *Forces* are processes that arise out of a condition, or set of conditions. It is the forces that cause the problems, forces that emanate from the political, economic and social factors of the society—the prevailing concepts that serve to guide it. The forces are consistent with the existing content, or circumstances, and they circle back to reinforce the content in an endless cycle. This is the reason why things don't work—no matter what you do—because it is all a function of these forces. And while you are able to see the results of these forces, the forces themselves remain unseen although they *persist* and cause problems. Although the truth of this matter does not justify anything, it is a place to come from as you work your way to the source of the problems. From there you will see the validity of what Victor Hugo[2] stated: *"That all of the forces in the world are not so powerful as an idea whose time has come."*

It is a fact that when the time comes for something to end, then it ends—and that's it. When the time comes, it happens by whatever means are available at the moment. At times it may take a cataclysm, at other times it may take a calamity, it may even happen through a revolution, and sometimes it occurs through a transformation. Progress and solutions are not what makes things happen; it is when the time comes in which the "space" for creative solutions enables those solutions to work.

But what is it that causes an idea's time to come? Knowing the answer to that is knowing how to have an impact in the world—and then to commit yourself to that. The answer to that question is not a descriptive or explanatory statement, nor is it one born out of theory or concept. The answer is a principle—an abstraction—that comes as a flash of insight, and which transcends the ordinary intellect. To obtain an abstraction only requires a high degree of openness, commitment and intention.

The answer to a question like this represents the creation of a fundamental principle. As such, it is the source of parts—as a whole—rather than the product of parts. Thus, when an idea's time comes, the state of existence is transformed from that of *content* to that of *context*. As content, an idea expresses itself as a position, and it exists only in relation to other positions. The relationship for an idea in content is in the conceptual realm of agreement or disagreement. It is a limiting entity whose boundaries are established between a thing and something else. Therefore, an idea out of content is dependent for its existence on something else that is outside of itself, and hence is not self-sufficient.

When an idea is transformed from existence as a position to that of existence as a "space," then it becomes an idea whose time has come. As such, it requires nothing else to exist, and hence is self-sufficient. It also allows for other ideas to exist in this context. The context is not dependent on anything outside of itself, it is whole, and it allows for the generation of content.

The context is created by the self—out of nothing. This means that you stop identifying yourself as a position and you begin to experience yourself as the "space" for your life. You then experience responsibility for the content in your life, and you will align yourself with others to include all other ideas, positions and notions as part of your context—including those who are skeptics and cynics, as well as those who may oppose you.

Within the context, opposing positions serve to contribute to the establishment of the context. Thus, the very same actions which are part of a problem's persistence are transformed to become actions that increase the awareness of the problem, and which actually contribute to the ending of the problem. The context generates process, and the process in turn serves *to change the content so that it becomes aligned with the purpose of the context.* Then, instead of being a threat to a particular goal, the content begins to contribute to the achievement of that goal.

What Context Achieves

A context generates process that transcends and transforms the existing forces. The forces are aligned to provide a condition of workability in which every expression—including pessimism—and every action becomes a manifestation of the intended goal. The idea is transformed so that apparently opposing ideas begin to validate and to give expression to the main idea. People become aligned within the context so that any of several solutions may work to implement the original idea. Everything that is done becomes a commitment to do what is effective.

Within a context in which the set of forces are realigned, what was done before that didn't work, now begins to work—even if it is the *same* thing that was being done before. The existing context serves to process all of the decisions and discussions by which we arrive at what we do. Things that were stuck and were not moving now begin to work to manifest the goal. It is because the creation of the context brings forth a new climate which makes things workable.

A context is more real and has a power greater than the facts regarding the persistence of the world's problems because it will create the circumstances for these problems to end. Each time that someone dies as a consequence of the world's problems, the individual death is further evidence of the persistence of these problems. When a context is created to end these problems, then further deaths that result from these problems occur within that context. At this point, the same deaths that had been a manifestation of the persistence of these problems become a contribution—in terms of the increased awareness—that serves to end these problems. Within a context, when something happens it is transformed to take on a different meaning which then leads to a different result—because it *shifts* the meaning of the event.

The Generating Principles

The primary question in all of this becomes a matter of what can each of us do as individuals? What is it possible for each of us to achieve that even large corporations or governments haven't been able to do? Underneath our facades is the experience of an innate and natural responsibility for the world in which we live in. What you have to do is experience yourself as the "space" for that experience. In this manner you will create a context in which you will provide your *own* answer to the question.

In the creation of a context, there are four *generating* principles that are crucial in bringing it forth:
- responsibility
- alignment
- creation
- transformation

310

The first principle is about *getting in touch with your "self" so that you will experience a natural and spontaneous sense of responsibility*. The second principle is something in which you are the *whole—about becoming the source for taking responsibility to create a context*. The third principle is about *creating a context—from nothing—so that you have mastery of it all*. The fourth principle is *about experiencing a transformation that affects the quality of your own life by dissolving the limitations*.

These four generating principles are not centered on personal and selfish interests. They contain the whole picture in which through alignment the spontaneous cooperation of wholes comes together from a common purpose. In that context everything that happens becomes a contribution such that whatever you do will be totally appropriate in the manifestation of the intended goal. While you can't predict what will happen, the condition of unworkability will be transformed in the process to create an opportunity for solutions to occur.

Endnotes

1   From "The End of Starvation: Creating an Idea Whose Time Has Come" by Werner Erhard in the special issue of the *Graduate Review*, January 1978.

2   Victor Hugo was a French romantic novelist and dramatist who was born in 1802. He is best known for his lengthy work entitled *Les Miserables*. Addressing many of the social issues of his day, Hugo wrote this epic tome that traces the path of a character named Jean Valjean as he changes from being a convict (stealing a loaf of bread) to that of becoming a near saint. In spite of his obsession with history, Hugo believed in the spiritual possibilities of human beings, and he chose the story of the poor and the outcast to illustrate his view of the "perfectibility of man." Along the same lines, he also wrote a very famous novel entitled

The Hunchback of Notre Dame, a powerful story that evokes medieval life as it tells of the doomed love of Quasimodo, the grotesque bell-ringer at the Cathedral of Notre Dame, for Esmeralda, the beautiful gypsy. Hugo died in Paris, France in 1885.

PART 3 –

The Effect of est on Our Society

"I want to be clear that I'm not looking for agreement because the truth has its own potency."

An Assessment of est

"I want est to totally disappear into the fabric of society."

An American Phenomena

est and Our Culture

The est training and other associated mind-exploration phenomena that have transpired over the last few decades is strictly an American experience. Because of our freedom to explore anything and everything under the sun—and to be gullible at times—many groups have sprung forward to provide the environment and to satisfy the need for our quest to know ourselves. While the practices of these organizations have sometimes bordered on deceit—or at least, persuasion without integrity—the basic intent has always been to help others in the hope of creating a better society for all of us. For all of their shortcomings and questionable practices, they still cannot be faulted for we are all responsible for their existence. After all, if none of us had participated in these events, not one of these people or their offerings would have ever seen the light of day.

It is hard to measure the long-lasting effect of any of these trainings because our American culture has a way of incorporating everything that happens and making it part of the mosaic that defines us as human beings in this society. The est training did spread to Europe, Australia and Latin America in its heyday, and several books were published about est that either promoted the value of the est training—or denigrated its leader,

315

Werner Erhard. In its present form and format—as The Forum—it continues as a means of empowering human beings so that they can impact society in some way. It is still marketed as a transformational gathering in which participants can experience a way of seeing themselves clearly. However, its approach is not as confrontational like the est training was, and it seems to be geared more toward helping people achieve mastery over their lives through a process of profound inquiry into everyday life.

The Effects of est on American Society

It is difficult to assess the lasting effects of the est phenomenon on American society. On a personal level the lasting value of the est phenomenon is akin to the same value that one gains by pursuing some activity—whether it be a spiritual, mental or physical one. It was simply a matter of getting out of it as much as we put into it. And yet, because of its relatively brief but significant prominence on the American scene there seems to be some alteration in the fabric of consciousness that was produced as a result of the est trainings. This is especially true in the movie industry—a medium of profound influence—as a result of all of the actors that participated in the movement.

The World Hunger Project that Werner Erhard began in 1977 was supposed to have solved the problem of world hunger in 20 years. As we all know 1997 came and went without any real significant change in the world with respect to world hunger— or world peace—other than it did become a more prominent topic in people's awareness and conversations, and maybe this was the intended affect of the whole exercise. In 1979, Erhard became involved in auto racing as a means of promoting attention to the world hunger project although it may be suspect that it was more of an activity that he wanted to do rather than an altruistic endeavor to help humanity. In a project that he termed "Breakthrough Racing," Erhard drove a specially manufactured Formula Super Vee racing car (car type Argo JM-4) in competition in the amateur United States Road Racing Championship and the professional Gold Cup series. His heart was in the right place but his means to achieve it became very questionable as time went on. Still, the surrounding controversy, drama and media attention did highlight the nature of the world hunger problem, and again maybe that was the intended effect.

The association with President James Carter of the United States in conjunction with the world hunger project was one result of the push to enlist high-level assistance for the cause. Of course, President Carter was already an established humanitarian and est simply tapped into his generous spirit to endorse the aims of the project. Since that time President Carter has been very active in his participation with Habitat for Humanity (an organization that builds homes for low-income people), the Carter Center in Atlanta, Georgia (an organization that works for world peace and human rights), and with many diplomatic missions of goodwill and peace. Maybe est was just fortunate that a man of his stature and genuine spirituality was in the White House when the big push for "enlightenment and the transformation of American society" was in its heyday.

Werner Erhard's stated goal was to have the est training and its transformational context become a part of the fabric of the human culture. In this manner he felt that its value would be self-evident and that the validity of the est training would be assured. Even after all of these years it is still difficult to assess what impact the est training has had on our society. According to Buckminster Fuller, it takes fifty years before the results of an experiment become evident on a widespread scale. If this is so, then we should start seeing if the "est experiment" manifests itself in the year 2021—fifty years after its introduction by Werner Erhard in 1971.

Personal Effect of the est Training

For about a month after the training I (Robert) was in a euphoric state. My eyes were shining brightly, I thought that I knew everything, and life was just a joyous journey every day. I saw things in a different light, and I saw the "ground of being" of everyone around me. Before the training both of us had started reading *The Awakening of Intelligence* by Jiddu Krishnamurti, but neither of us got past a couple of pages into that book. After the training the words in that book made so much sense that we both were captured by that book until we finished it (to this day Espy still reads Krishnamurti's works almost every day). We also began to be involved in the post training seminars—to the point that we became "seminar junkies."

We even tried an introductory session of Scientology, and enrolled in the "Actualizations" training (the series started by former est trainer, Stewart Emery). Eventually, we did a "wilderness" training in the San Jacinto Mountains near Idylwild, California with Werner Erhard himself and a trainer, Landon Carter, leading the first "6-day training for adults." During these six days we got to know Werner Erhard in a more intimate and intense setting, including an exercise in which all participants were clothed only in bathing suits. Later, Espy enrolled in the School of Oriental Studies located in Los Angeles, California where she was exposed to Buddhist doctrine and other eastern philosophies. Further participation in est events gave us an opportunity to see and listen to a variety of personalities and to more of Werner Erhard's pontifications about life and its precepts. I (Robert) even "assisted" at the local est center in Santa Monica, California for a while. By early 1980, we had dropped out from any further involvement with the est organization.

Since the time when we were both immersed in the est seminar series, we have enjoyed life to an incredible degree (although we were already doing this since the time of our marriage in October 1969). We have both grown together and have gotten a deeper understanding of life than we would have otherwise if we had not taken the est training. We "generate aliveness," and "get value" out of doing things—no matter how insignificant the activity may be—and we have a lot of fun wherever we go and whatever we do. Our goals did not change much as a result of the training although we do find that these are easier to accomplish. "Stuff" still "comes up" for us, problems and events occur, and we have to deal with the same things as we did before. Yet, as we participate in life, we find that somehow things are different—especially in times of crises. There is an awareness that seems to operate from a very magical place that we both created for ourselves in 1975.

You can say what you want about the person known as Werner Erhard and all of his shenanigans and drama that he was caught up in, especially the mess of his family life—both before and after his "enlightenment." But, we must thank him sincerely for the tremendous gift of expanded awareness that he transmitted through his seminars. *Werner Erhard represents the teacher who appeared when we were both ready to learn.* We also extend our thanks to Ron Bynum, Landon Carter and Ron Browning, three of the trainers who belonged to the est organization. From our perspective, they were the most sincere in how they treated us as a couple. In addition, we got a lot of insights from the other members of the est training staff, including Randy McNamara, Ted Long, Hal Isen and Jerry Joiner.

The est training was thought of as a frightening cult of "mind benders" when it was introduced into England, and was ridiculed by media headlines such as "Why 200 People Will Pay to Be Insulted" (the reference to being called "turkeys" and "assholes"). In spite of all the negative press that has happened throughout the years (including a *60 Minutes* hatchet job on Werner Erhard by CBS[1] and a hard-hitting book about his exploits[2]), we can say that the est training has been of great value during the last 27 years since we first participated in the est series. The validity of what we experienced from est still holds true for us to this day although we have expanded into many other areas since that time.

Somehow through the undertaking of all of the processes that Werner Erhard devised for his seminars both of us experienced a shift in our thinking and a transformation of our way of being. Our personalities stayed intact—as did our vocational interests—and yet something happened to us that made our perception and experience quite different from the way that they were before we took the est training. We both can clearly state that "the purpose of the est training has been to clear up the questions, misunderstandings and problems about things that have been bothering us in our lives through the process of experience of life itself." Our lives have been wonderful, full of enrichment, with many travels and remarkable experiences. The est training was definitely a significant marker event in our lives—although as individuals we are in no sense defined by it. Our mutual realization is that "enlightenment" is a lifetime adventure.

End Notes

1 *60 Minutes and the Assassination of Werner Erhard* by Jane Self, 1992.

2 *Outrageous Betrayal: The Dark Journey of Werner Erhard from est to Exile* by Steven Presman, 1993.

A Lasting Association

"Precisely because the impact of starvation on our lives is so great, its existence is actually an opportunity. In experiencing the truth underlying hunger, one comes to realize that the ordinarily unnoticed laws that determine the persistence of hunger on this planet are precisely the laws that keep the world from working. One comes to realize that the principles of the end of hunger and starvation within 20 years are those very principles necessary to make our world work."

The Hunger Project

The Origin

The Hunger Project was started by Werner Erhard in 1977 as a stand against hunger and poverty. Its aim was to highlight the tragedy of thousands of people who die every day from chronic hunger, and to make the world aware of the plight of those who live in such a state of poverty that their minimal nutritional requirements cannot be met. Joan Holmes was named Executive Director of the Hunger Project by Werner Erhard who stated a goal of eliminating hunger within 20 years (by 1997). Erhard maintained that hunger in the world persisted because governments, corporations and people were not organized in a way to ensure that everyone had enough to eat. He also surmised that the problem was not a result of insufficient technology, agricultural production, distribution facilities or lack of other resources. Rather, hunger and its associated conditions of disease and poverty persisted in the world because of the cynical attitude in human beings that this problem was inevitable.

Instead of providing food or the means of growing food, the project's purpose was one of creating a "space," or a context through which the end of hunger and starvation on the planet would come to an end within two decades. The intent was to create a lot of publicity, and to blitz the media with massive periodic events, Most of the money collected for the Hunger Project goes for administration—to pay the salaries of the few employees, travel expenses to make presentations, and printing costs of the literature that is distributed to enroll people in the project. The purpose of the literature is to teach others about the conditions of hunger in the world, and is not about initiating any direct actions to distribute food. Contributions are solicited by having people sign cards with promises of sending cash, checks or credit card donations to the organization.

Current Status

Holmes, who extended the project deadline to the year 2000, has led this organization for almost a quarter of a century because of the insistence that merely giving away food will not solve the problem of hunger in the world. Despite the despair and apathy that is involved with the knowledge of human starvation, Holmes has persisted in her leadership to help create a shift in the paradigm that allows the condition of helplessness to rob people of their true dignity. Instead of adding to the mass consciousness of persistence of seeing starving people as passive and dependent on "foreign" aid, what is needed is the creation of a new context whereby hungry people can become the masters of their own destiny in feeding themselves.

A criticism of the Hunger Project seems to be that it often acts as a vehicle to attract new participants to the training, formerly est and now the Forum. Another criticism that is leveled at the Hunger Project is that the solution to malnourishment will require more than a paradigm shift or mere words. In fact, it will need massive agricultural help, cross-cultural techniques to educate people on nutrition and growing technologies, changes in land use (and in some areas, land reform), and fundamental changes in the economics and politics of societies. Nevertheless, an increased awareness of the problem of hunger in the world has been produced by the work of the Hunger Project through the commitment of Joan Holmes and others in taking a stand for the future of the planet. If they succeed in altering the political, economic and social structures that prevent hungry people from being adequately fed, then they will have succeeded far beyond the original purpose of the Hunger Project. For if this comes about, then the realization will be there for everyone to see that it is possible to create a context that will dissolve other limitations that we have imposed on ourselves—such as the inevitability of war.

The Forum:
est in its Present Form

"Understanding is the booby prize in life."

Landmark Education Corporation

The New Organization

The est training is still around although in its present incarnation it is called "The Forum." The original est training was retired at the end of 1984, and in its place, Erhard created a training called "The Forum" to continue with the series of self-development seminars[1]. The purpose of the Forum was to provide an opportunity for participants to master the ability to create an inquiry that allows access to being in the world[2]. The new training format would have as its expressed intent an expression of a deeper and broader self that would produce a looking outward into an infinite number of possibilities from wherever one began[3]. In 1991, Erhard sold the est corporation to his employees, who then formed the Landmark Education Corporation, naming Harry Rosenberg, Werner Erhard's brother, as the chief executive, and Joan Rosenberg, Werner Erhard's sister, as one of the Directors. The Landmark Education Corporation, which is chartered in California, has over 100 offices worldwide, including Forum centers in the United States, Canada, India, Israel, Great Britain, Australia and Japan. The modified training is packaged as a 3 1/2-day seminar as the

324

starting point with advanced classes that combined cover the span of one year.

The Landmark Corporation and its programs have prospered in spite of the fact that the company has not been able to avoid the controversy left behind by the Erhard legacy. Because Erhard and his work have been the subject of much scrutiny in the media, the stories about him have plagued the successor organization—even though some of these stories have contained falsehoods, misconceptions and misrepresentations. Although the Landmark Education Corporation has taken steps to distance itself from the "creator," Werner Erhard, the unmistakable fact remains that he is at the root of the entire vocabulary, format, processes and delivery of the training materials. The Landmark Education Corporation has made substantial revenues, claiming over 100,000 participants per year. It does have a licensed contractual agreement with Werner Erhard that will enable him to obtain a sizable amount of money by 2009, the figure being equal to one-half of the net pre-tax profits made by the Landmark Education Corporation over the period between 1991 and 2009. At this time Erhard—who will be 74 by then—will also regain full ownership of the "body of knowledge," the copyrighted technology that constitutes the training in all of its aspects.

All Forum participants are encouraged to bring guests to keep the series of trainings in business. The Forum graduates are led through a similar methodology of reinforcement to sign them up for more advanced seminars, to encourage them to become Landmark volunteers, and of course, to bring more guests. This is the crucial and driving recruitment aspect that keeps the marketing strategy which is absolutely necessary for Landmark's survival—just as it was for the est program. Although the Forum literature claims that the training is not about therapy, all participants must sign disclaimer forms that acknowledge that they are in good physical and mental health. Allowances are made for people who are in therapy to attend—as long as they have the permission of their therapists to do so. However, for the most part, these people are discouraged from taking the training to avoid the possibility of lawsuits and adverse publicity in case of mental breakdowns or other post traumatic stress as a result of the mental and physical ordeal.

The Forum Training[4]

The Forum is still somewhat expensive and requires a certain amount of endurance (sometimes 15-hour days)—even though it is not as confining or as confrontational as est used to be since more breaks are allowed and sleep deprivation is not employed. The Forum training is conducted over a three-day weekend with a succeeding evening for graduates to participate in the closing ceremonies and "testimonials." The Forum is presented as a game called transformation and insists on attributes of good sportsmanship, open-mindedness, commitment and participation. Much of the technology is still the same as in est: drawing diagrams on a blackboard, explaining a series of concepts, and establishment of the fundamental principle: that "our rackets,"—our ongoing complaints, manipulations, beliefs, and "stuckness" –are what are "killing our lives." Thus, to avoid "losing in life", and to avoid being limited by a personal "winning formula[5]," it is necessary to transcend these hidden agendas. A racket always has an associated deceit and a "payoff" that justifies the ongoing deceit—and the "racket" persists and is dramatized consistently every time that the "payoff" is achieved through it.

The promise of the Forum is that you can get anything out of the Forum that you are willing to stand for having gotten. The Forum training consists of working on goals that have been specified by each participant beforehand. These goals can be anything and can range from personal development to work-oriented issues, or to relationship problems. The environment in which the Forum training is conducted is still one of an austere, orderly and neutral large-room environment—usually an hotel ballroom that has the barest of furnishings (mostly hardback chairs that are symmetrically arranged and a lecture platform). No food or drinks are available inside except for water. A Forum training leader and the staff of his or her assistants handle all of the issues, questions, problems, concerns and everything else that "comes up" for the trainees. No notes are allowed (since the material is copyrighted), no talking among participants is allowed (except for "sharing") and very little written communication is used other than printing on a plain chalkboard. As with the est training, the structure is designed to break through the resistance of each trainee to alter each individual consciousness in a significant manner. The intent is to wear down the defenses of the personality, and to eventually reach a state where "the mind is let go to reach another level of awareness."

From outward appearances, the format of the Forum training—just like in est—can make it appear as a sort of brainwashing or mind control. However, the techniques that are used are done so with the intent of making the trainee more open and thus more suggestible to the inputs. The processes have as their stated purpose to overcome the self-imposed limitations of the self, to mentally challenge beliefs and held assumptions about life, and to stimulate so as to provide a wider perception of the world and of personal abilities. Thus, the main strategy is to create an isolated but effective learning environment that is not distracted by time, things or events. All rules that are set forth and which are accepted as "agreements" by the trainees are also designed to enhance the teaching of the materials that are presented during the training by the leader. These include rules about the wearing of visible name tags to identify each trainee, not taking any drugs or medications during the entire training (including alcohol), and agreeing to practice confidentiality for whatever is shared during the sessions.

The primary interaction in the Forum is the same as it was in est, namely between the training leader and each participant. The Forum leader acts as the instigator of all conversations. This interaction—which is controlled by this central personality—is what provides the impetus of the entire experience, with the training leader both confronting and challenging each participant who decides to "share." Since everything in life is a conversation in which we create our lives, our problems, and our possibilities, the Forum lays emphasis on the identification of these past conversations in order to create new possibilities with declarations of new statements as to who we are. The crux of the training still revolves around taking responsibility for all actions—something that will enable you to survive and that will serve to empower you in a world that always has risk and uncertainty facing you. The promise is to provide a change in your relationships, in your personal effectiveness and in your striving for excellence in your personal quest of achievement.

The training is conducted in a manner that will help each participant to distinguish between reality and illusion, between the past and the future, and from ideas versus experience. The training is also geared towards separating the facts and events that happen from their interpretations, explanations and meanings that we assign to them as a consequence of our emotional investment in these events. In short, it is about making a distinction between what is real and what we have made up in our minds. All of this is accomplished through the conversations that are instigated, provoked or responded to by the Forum leader's remarks on a particular issue, topic, behavior or "share" by one or more of the participants.

The language structure of the Forum is the same as it was for est with slight alterations as to the purpose of the training. The training still emphasizes responsibility for being the cause of your life—and the distinction between what happens in your life versus your interpretation of the events. The meaninglessness and emptiness of life is also presented to emphasize freedom of choice—that the real meanings of life's events are those that are created by the meanings that are assigned by you. In this view all problems can be made to disappear because they are real only in the sense of the conversation that creates them. The old interpretations consist of "rackets," or ways of being, which have become "formulas for success," or ways of coping and compensating such as being a victim, sufferer, aggressor, procrastinator, and so forth. What keeps these rackets in place are "payoffs,"[6] or reasons such as righteousness, domination, invalidation and being judgmental.

By taking a stand—or creating a different future for oneself—it is possible to create a "breakthrough," or new way of being to alter your experience of old patterns. This is what creates the freedom for you: the removal of all anxiety and guilt from the elimination of the burdens that are associated with these past events and experiences. The effect is to enhance the love in one's life, to have more vitality and an increased feeling of health, and to enjoy a new and different level of satisfaction in life. In doing so, the self-expression becomes prominent so that you become more authentic with others in your life. This is then termed as achieving a "paradigm shift" in one's life, the shift being from action occurring as a series of activities to that of action occurring as a series of conversations.

The strategies, processes and techniques that are used in the Forum are much gentler and kinder than those which were used in est—although confrontation is still used to wear down the resistance of the trainees. The only process from est that has been kept in its original form is the "fear process." In this process each trainee has the chance to experience the fact that life is dangerous and to discover the feelings about what is personally terrifying, scary, fearful or frightening. The intent of the fear process is to get the trainees to get past these imaginary or real emotions of being fearful through a release of the feelings that are associated with these fears. The emotional catharsis that is experienced during the fear process is supposed to alleviate all of the bad emotions that are associated with these fears, and in some cases completely cure them forever.

In brief, the main concepts of the Forum training revolve around distinctions, these being the "winning formula," one's "racket," events and things being "empty and meaningless," and the difference between what happened and the interpretation as to why it happened. The aim of the Forum is to alter people's conversations about events as content that is contained in a context of responsibility. In this regard what is pointed out is that except for the meaning that you put into it, everything in your life is "empty and meaningless"—but that it is "empty and meaningless" to say that it is "empty and meaningless." This is not meant to create an atmosphere of hopelessness and despair, or a climate of impending doom and gloom—or to abandon your responsibilities in life by focusing on nihilism and iconoclasm. Rather, it is meant to point out that one cannot live out of a feeling that bad or evil things might happen in the future because then the aliveness and joy in life disappear with this attitude. It is instead to work these issues of everyday life within the framework of relationships and to use the experience of events to transform who you are being in the world as a function of practice. The practice is one of a replacement of reacting to events from past knowledge with acting from the future by moving forward as a reinvention[7] of yourself through your declared conversation. This practice defines your threshold of capacity in making a declaration for the future that alters your way of being as a consequence of making promises (giving your word) to fulfill that declared future.

Assessment of the Forum

The purpose of the Forum training—just like in est—is aimed at enabling transformation to occur rather than to convey information. Thus, the Forum, like est, is not a religion, nor is it an academic course, and it certainly cannot be classified as a belief system. Rather, it is an experience in which a designed attack on the mind is presented in order to press beyond one's established point of view. This transformation of the individual, according to the Forum (and previously est) is what will enable the individual to change his or her relationships in life. In the process, the desired aim is that in turn the combined effects of transformed individuals will cause similar changes in organizations which will then affect our collective institutions. In this manner, it is deemed possible that our society will change in terms of how the various components are administered by these transformed individuals. Thus, we could have great changes in law, medicine, education, politics and economics which in turn would greatly alter our whole society. In its greatest extension and effect, the radical shift in society would then produce a complete transfiguration of humankind to achieve everlasting peace and good will in the world.

While altering the public conversation as is done in the Forum may produce some effects, the reality is that the truth about human beings has its own track in life. Admittedly, we are at a point where we should realize that our current ways of being are not conducive to long term survival of the human species— along with the rest of all living things on the planet. Since the Forum is a training that is designed to dramatize the problems that human beings carry around with them as a result of past experiences and behaviors, there is still always the chance that some participants may not benefit from the training. A tendency for a few persons to "snap" under the stress that is created during the training still exists, and in more extreme cases, unbalanced individuals may choose to completely abandon the weakened psychological defenses that were keeping them stable, thus unleashing the demons of psychotic behavior for them.

The Forum, like est, is probably a very valuable experience—if it is kept in perspective. The subliminal procedures that are employed to convey information at the subconscious level, and the affirmations of life that are presented during the intense periods of the training are all geared to produce psychological change. Whether the setting of being with complete strangers in an intimate environment produces lasting change or not, the overall effect does create an alteration in the minds of the participants because of the steady flow of inputs that are presented. Of course, many relationships either disintegrate or improve dramatically afterward, careers are dropped or pointed in a different direction, and outlooks on the future become different. Much of this is a result that is produced from the temporary "ecstasy and euphoria," the intense re-experiencing of the past, and the letting go of the problems that were deeply ingrained in one's consciousness during the three days of being enclosed in a controlled environment. Since the conversation is altered, there may be difficulties in the communication with others who have either not taken the Forum training or who have not been exposed to similar experiences. There may also be overzealous feelings as a result of the training that produce proselytizing by graduates to encourage others to participate in the Forum. Those who are really ensnared by the experience of the training may even become "volunteers," an important aspect of keeping the Forum alive as a viable organization.

According to Werner Erhard, the est training—which is at the root of the Forum training—was an experience that gave people the opportunity (the "space") to learn from themselves. Although the climatic point of the est training consisted in telling everyone that they were robots acting from the machinery of the mind performing meaningless actions, the intent of the whole experience was to "blow the mind away" to reach a state where the spiritual realm resides. This essence, or "ground zero" of one's being is where one can see the "movie" or script of one's life from a different perspective. It is this perception that allows the truth about everything to emerge—but only if the mind is receptive to what is discovered.

If the effect of the Forum is the same as what was produced in est, then the benefits far outweigh any of the negative results that sometimes occur. Ultimately, the shifts in thinking by transformed individuals can create a revolution where we can all live in a world where we are all engaged in the practice of making the impossible happen. On the other hand, if all that is produced is a replacement of previous beliefs with new ones, then not much will be altered in society as a whole. And, as Werner Erhard once stated, " I have a worst scenario (for humanity)—that we will go on like this forever."

The Bosnia Peace Project

As with est and its Hunger Project, the Forum also has a frontburner project called The Bosnia Peace Project (BPP). The aim of the BPP is to bring candidates from Bosnia who will then undergo the Forum training. When enough graduates exist from Bosnia, the intent is to create a Landmark Education center in Bosnia so that local trainings can be conducted there, possibly in the city of Sarajevo. This project was started in 1997 and continues to this day with less than two dozen graduates from Bosnia so far. Given the amount of time that has passed, this represents a very small beginning. But, if enough people participate, then this could parallel the Hunger Project by creating an opportunity for peace to occur in a region that has been plagued by conflict for centuries.

Endnotes

1 Werner Erhard was undoubtedly influenced by the work of Martin Heidegger in the shift from est to that of the Forum. Heidegger was a German existentialist who was born in Baden, Germany on September 26, 1889. Heidegger's quest into the nature of being started when he was presented with a book entitled *On the Manifold Meaning of Being According to Aristotle*, a work written by Franz Brentano in 1862. This work that was based on Aristotle's *Metaphysics* began Heidegger's journey into the field of philosophy. Educated for the priesthood in his early years, Heidegger studied Roman Catholic theology at the University of Freiburg where he was a student of the founder of the field of phenomenology, Edmund Husserl. Later, as a professor of philosophy, he turned to a deeper contemplation of existence, and in 1927, he wrote his classic work entitled *Being and Time* in which he formulated a new understanding of what it is to be. He rejected the idea that man's relation to the world is one of subject to object, with the self being conscious of objects. He thought that most human activity was a matter of selfless absorption—rather that it being guided by conscious awareness. Thus, he concluded that people should have an understanding of themselves in the world that would let them respond automatically to situations rather than to be guided by abstract principles constituting some set of ethical behaviors. Since there are no abstract principles according to Heidegger, then a "void" is created which must then be filled by nonrational commitment. This commitment to destiny is what associated Heidegger with the Nazis of Adolph Hitler's Germany. For when you are being the future of your organization, you are a "clearing" in the world of dense and conflicting interpretations through which an invented future can crystallize. In time, others around you will relate to you as this

———

invented future—rather than as a personality. Heidegger's view is that the linguistic distinctions that we make define the world and become our reality—and that the essence of every human being resides in this *"whatness."* Thus, language by virtue of its vocabulary and from the way of speaking it—the distinctions that are drawn—is what creates the world that we inhabit. Hence, the only way that people derive their identities is from stories that they tell about themselves to others. Heidegger's conception of all human existence is thus one of active participation in the world—which despite its inherent limitations—is the only way in which a being can be truly authentic. Martin Heidegger died in Freiburg, Germany on May 26, 1976.

2   The shift from est to the Forum was also possibly influenced by Werner Erhard's interest in the research work of Humberto R. Maturana and Francisco J. Varela, two university professors from Chile who were involved in the field of cognitive biology. Maturana studied at the University of Santaigo in Chile, at the University of Oxford in London, England, and at the University of Harvard at Cambridge, Massachusetts where he received his doctorate degree in 1958. In the 1960's he conducted research at MIT in Boston, Massachusetts where he developed a new perspective on the interplay between cognition and neurophysiology. While doing research in the Biological Computer laboratory at the University of Illinois in Chicago, Illinois, he published his classic article entitled "Biology of Cognition." In this paper he questioned the prevailing notions of cognition and redefined phenomenology in terms of the system of the living organism itself. He returned to Santiago, Chile in 1970 to teach at the University of Chile. Varela, who was born in Chile on September 7, 1946, studied at the University of Chile where he became a student and colleague of Maturana. Varela later studied at the University of Harvard where he received his doctorate degree in

1970. He returned to Chile to study with Maturana until he was forced to flee from his country in 1973 when President Salvador Allende was overthrown by General Augusto Pinochet in a military coup. Varela spent his later years studying consciousness and served in the faculty of the Naropa Institute in Boulder, Colorado. Varela took Maturana's ideas on cognition and living systems and incorporated them into a formalism called autopoiesis—the minimal form of autonomy that is necessary for characterizing biological life. Varela continued to explore issues and concepts associated with cognition, his central work being the *Principles of Biological Autonomy* that was published in 1979. In 1991, his classic book entitled the *Embodied Mind* became a leading text on cognitive science in its unique approach to the study of the phenomenon of mind. Varela died in Paris, France on May 28, 2001. The essential premise of the revolutionary work of Maturana and Varela (*Autopoiesis and Cognition,* 1980) is that living systems have an essential circularity through which they derive their form and structure. The basic circularities are two in number: (1) that everything that is said is said by an observer, and (2) that all knowing is doing, and conversely, all doing is knowing. Thus, the mind reflecting on the world is itself dependent on its structure—and on the knowledge of that structure—a fundamental circularity of cognition. The linguistic behavior that happens in this cognitive domain orients the living system through interactions that are explained in terms of relations—rather than as component properties. The observer explicitly or implicitly accepts the characteristics of the phenomena described by the explanations as a result of these relations—instead of by the properties of the components or the characteristics of the processes.

3   A third influence for Werner Erhard in the shift from est to the Forum was the work of Michel Foucault (*Madness and Civilization, Power/Knowledge, The Order of Things* and

---

The History of Sexuality). Paul-Michel Foucault was born in Poitiers, France in 1926. He was educated at the Ecole Normale Superieure at Paris, France where he studied philosophy, psychology and psychopathology. He embarked on a career as a surrealist writer and philosopher and became a professor at the College de France. His aim was to test cultural assumptions against historical contexts. Traditionally, each person is thought to have an identity that represents a fixed and true character that defines that particular person. This inner essence—those qualities that are beneath the surface—determine who that person really "is." Also, some people have different levels of power through which they are able to achieve what they want in their relationships with others, and with society as a whole. Foucault rejected this view and stated that people do not have a real identity within themselves. Instead he claimed that it was a shifting and temporary discourse that was communicated to others in the interactions with them through which this identity was constructed—but not as a fixed thing within that person's self. The primary characteristics of these discursive formations are as follows: 1) that the statements of individuals are different in form and are dispersed through time, 2) the statements are distinguished by their form and type of connection, 3) the discourse serves to establish groups of statements, and 4) their interconnection and forms in which statements are presented accounted for the identity and persistence of themes. He also stated that people do not possess power. He saw power as an action in which individuals engage in—as an exercise and a fluid relation that could be deployed, and one that also generated accompanying resistance. Thus, he saw that both power and discourses worked to constrain people. In addition, by studying hospitals and prisons, he noticed that the problem of visibility of bodies, individuals and things was one of the most constant and directing principles within the context of a system of centralized observation. The result of this context produced an inspecting gaze through which each individual ended up in the process of interiorization—and thus one wound up exercising a surveillance over oneself—and against oneself. Hence, this situation—freedom of conscience—entailed more dangers than any authority could ever bring to that individual. For Foucault, it was not ideas that ruled the world—but rather because the world has ideas—that the world was not ruled by leaders and teachers who professed to tell the world what it must think. Foucault stated that it was events that manifested this force and which produced the struggles—for or against—that were carried on around these ideas. Throughout his lifelong work Foucault regarded philosophy as an interrogative practice—the discursive practices that revealed knowledge—rather than as a search for essentials. He also viewed philosophy in the context of social and political history as an attempt to do an archeology of history to show the historical validity of truth claims. He did borrow from the ideas of Friedrich Nietzsche in terms of this genealogical approach, and from the ideas of Karl Marx in his analyses of ideology. But, Foucault had no underlying belief in a deep truth or structure from which one could analyze either discourse or society itself. For him there was no ultimate "answer" that was waiting to be uncovered as an explanation of reality. All that exists—according to Foucault—are the discursive practices of knowledge which are dependent upon the objects that are studied and which must be understood in their social and political context: what he called the ontology of the present, and where ontology is defined as the "being of beings." Foucault died in 1984.

4   Taken from *The Children of est*, *Being There*, *The Last Word on Power*, and *Masterful Coaching* (see Bibliography).

5   A winning formula is defined as a lifelong and unconscious strategy that has been developed since childhood as a means

---

of achieving success. It is a set of behaviors that are acquired by what you focus your attention to, by what actions you implicitly and habitually take (your automatic responses), and by what you desire the outcomes in life to be like. The strategy defines your reality, your way of being and your way of thinking—and is also the source of your limitations. Your winning formula is the hidden conversation that is at the heart of who you are in the world. Every time that you exercise your winning strategy and produce a possible result, you compensate for what is not possible to an equal degree—and in the process you expand the scope of what is not possible. But, the truth is that your winning strategy will never completely work, that your life will never be complete, and that you cannot control the outcome of your life. All that you can do is to keep the cycle going in a survival game that ultimately prevents you from making the impossible happen. Eventually all that will happen is that you get stuck in trying to recreate your past (by wishing it had been different) instead of inventing a new future that is not based on your past. As such, the strategy shapes your actions so that in the process it determines for you what is possible—and more importantly, what is impossible to achieve. Since your winning formula is a direct manifestation of who you are—rather than of what you do—it will force you to act in ways that are consistent with this personal strategy. As a result, you will be impeded from taking actions that go beyond this winning formula—even when the circumstances of a situation demand it—because you will inherently believe that some things are not possible. Only by becoming aware of your personal winning strategy will you be able to go beyond its limitations.

6 The nature of a "payoff" is that it maintains the unwanted condition ("racket") in place through three different justifications: 1) you get to be right about the situation, 2) you

get to dominate—or to avoid being dominated, and 3) you get to explain and justify staying the way that you are. However, the cost of "running this racket" is in terms of your health and vitality, your happiness and enjoyment of living, inability to express or receive love from others, and the constrainment of full self-expression in the world. The key then is to identify the "racket," and not to dramatize it ("act it out") so that it will begin to dissolve itself through its exposure.

7   Re-inventing yourself involves a shift from acting through your interpretations of events as if they were the truth and using it to prove something, and instead moving forward through the requests and promises that you have stated for yourself. A request is a commitment to generate something so as to deliver on that commitment. A promise is a stated action to bring forth a future commitment and to actualize that possibility into reality. The responses from others to both your requests and promises can be acceptances, declinations or counteroffers.

A Final Note

"The fact is, until people are transformed, until they transcend their minds, they are simply puppets, perhaps anguished, hurting, strongly feeling puppets, but ones nonetheless limited to a fixed repertoire of responses. And that is what karma is all about."

A Series of Pied Pipers in America

From the Beginning

Since the pre-Revolutionary days this country has been subjected to a variety of consciousness-raising movements. Theodore J. Frelinghuysen, a minister of the Dutch Reformed Church, began a spiritual revival called "The Great Awakening" in the 1720's. However, the Great Awakening as an evangelistic movement was actually launched by Jonathan Edwards of Massachusetts in 1734 who vividly described the onset of the awakening as a divine and supernatural light from heaven. Associated with ecstasies by its participants, the passions created religious conversions by the effects of the fervent sermons that were geared towards trusting the heart and feelings rather than thinking and reasoning. The converts appeared to be overcome with a sense of the divine and looked at this state as being the natural order of things, with feelings that included those of love, joy and compassion—behaviors that were viewed with distrust by the clergy of the established religions.

A visiting reverend and advocate of this revivalist movement from England, George Whitfield, was said to have been able to address as many as 25,000 persons at a time with his booming voice (in a time of no microphones!). Although his life was cut short by illness, he was a magnificent orator whose fame stood out like a bright and shining light. With preachers like Edwards and Whitfield, the revivalist movement[1]—in its prime—swept over the American colonies from Maine to Georgia until about 1745 and converted about one-third of the population in America[2].

The Second Stage

The Second Great Awakening began in the 1790's in the western frontier, and was highlighted in 1801 by the Cane Ridge Revival: a six-day meeting that was attended by over 20,000 people. This revivalist movement was dominated by Charles G. Finney, a lawyer turned minister, and by Asahel Nettleton, a revivalist preacher. Finney's persuasiveness was so powerful that sometimes his preaching resulted in an entire town being converted. His approach centered on social reform—especially with respect to slavery—and many of the later reform movements can be directly traced back to him. Nettleton was equally as powerful and he preached without much rest at revivals, and even performing visits to homes to convert smaller groups. He continued with this schedule until 1822 when he contracted typhus fever. After a two-year bout with this illness, he no longer performed the strenuous activity as before although his preaching still remained very powerful. Nearly one-fifth of the American population was converted as a result of the Second Great Awakening.

Seances became the rage in the late 1840's as Spiritualism spread in America, especially as a result of the spirit interpretations of two sisters from Hydesville, New York, Margaret and Katherine Fox. Daniel Dunglas Home was one of these early influential mediums in America although he spent his later years in Europe. Mesmerism (from the work of a Viennese physician, Franz Anton Mesmer) also became popular as a means for detecting and healing illnesses through therapeutic trances induced by hypnosis.

The Third Period

The Third Great Awakening in America got its impetus during the period between 1857 and 1864, a movement that began with the Prayer Meeting Revival. The revival continued even during the war with both union and confederate soldiers being converted by the thousands. The revivalism began in New York by a missionary named Jeremiah Lanphier. The revivalist movement then spread to the rest of New England, then to the South and then back again to the North. However, it remained in a quiescent state until the 1890's when it flourished again. The Third Great Awakening then continued as a mass movement in its many divided forms into the early 1900's, with preachers like Billy Sunday and Walter Rauschenbusch leading the great revival.

After the Civil War and the quiescence of the Third Great Awakening, Americans again turned inward in the 1870's to find a more relevant expression of their spirituality. One of the first doctrines to emerge was that of Christian Science, a movement that was started by Mary Baker Eddy who wrote about her experiences in a book entitled *Science and Health* in 1875. This same year saw two of the most influential mystics, Helena Blavatsky[3] and Henry Olcott[4], start on their teachings of Tibetan Buddhism that subsequently evolved into the Theosophical Society. The Theosophical Society was formed to promote the goals of universal brotherhood, to encourage the study of consciousness and the world, and to investigate the higher powers of human beings.

The year 1875 also brought the beginnings of Mormonism, a religion based and founded on the *Book of Mormon* by Joseph

Smith, a farm laborer from New England. Subsequently, Smith and his entourage moved to Mississippi, and then to Utah where his congregation flourished in Salt Lake City. In the 1890's, William Quan Judge, one of the founding members of the Theosophical Society, spread his version of Theosophy in America. This effort was continued after Judge's death by Katherine Tingley who established a "Utopian community" at Point Loma near San Diego, California.

The Fourth Era

The 1900's began with revivalists like Billy Sunday, a preacher who had a magnetic influence on people, and with Walter Rauschenbusch, a clergyman and theology professor who led the Social Gospel movement in the United States. Also prevalent were Pentecostal revival movements with their accompanying prophecies, "speaking in tongues," occurrence of miracles, and receipt of words of knowledge from the "Holy Spirit."

The impact of World War I temporarily halted the spiritual movement, but after the war, Annie Besant, an English lady and aristocrat, and one of the primary leaders of the Theosophical Society in India, introduced Jiddu Krishnamurti into the United States in the 1920's. She declared him to be the World Teacher—and the latest and best reappearance of the Christ Spirit in the world. Krishnamurti eventually broke away from the Theosophists in 1929, and went about independently giving talks all over the world until his death in 1986, including many at Ojai, California where he established his primary residence. Krishnamurti never wanted anything—except to set human beings unconditionally free.

The Great Depression and then World War II again took the limelight in America during the 1930's and 1940's. In spite of the war and the accompanying economic impact, people still continued to explore inwardly. One of the most prominent and popular influences was that of Edgar Cayce[5]. For many years Cayce underwent deep sleep trances during which he responded to questions with an uncanny accuracy. He used his psychic awareness during these trances to diagnose illnesses and to prescribe cures. He covered the spectrum from diets to relationships, and his "readings" also touched on the exploration of personal spirituality. Another significant personage was Swami Prabhavananda who established a Ramakrishna Order in Los Angeles, California in 1938. This order was based on the doctrines of Vedanta drawn from the Indian sacred texts of the *Vedas* which are the foundation of the Hindu religion. The Swami enjoyed his greatest popularity during the 1940's.

The 1950's and 1960's were dominated by Scientology with thousands of people attending L. Ron Hubbard's lectures. Many of these enrolled in subsequent "auditing" programs and participated in advanced courses that were designed to result in the goal of a person becoming a "clear." The promise by Hubbard was that if enough people participated in Scientology, and that if a sufficient number of these became "clears," then the overall result would be a world that would function without pain, guilt, or fear by its inhabitants. Thus, the aim of Scientology was to have a civilization without insanity by the discovery of self since Hubbard considered the basic sickness in the world to be the ignorance of the self.

The 1970's were sparked by New Age thinking and the Humanistic movement based upon the works of Abraham Maslow and Carl Rogers. Group trainings such as Mind Dynamics, est, Lifespring and Actualizations rose to the forefront during this decade. Other prominent self-awareness programs included those provided by the Esalen Institute in Big Sur, California, and by Transcendental Meditation. Werner Erhard was the leading figure during this decade as he emerged from a salesman to world stage prominence by virtue of his dramatic presentations.

Neuro-linguistic programming (NLP) was also started in the 1970's by John Grinder, a linguist, and Richard Bandler, a mathematician[6]. Sometimes referred to as software for the brain, NLP has as its emphasis the teaching of a variety of communication and persuasion skills plus the use of self-hypnosis to motivate and change oneself. It relies heavily on Sigmund Freud's theories of the unconscious and their effect on conscious thought and action, on Virginia Satir's Family System Therapy, and on Gestalt Therapy as practiced by Fritz Perls. It uses the process of hypnosis as developed by Milton Erickson, borrows from the linguistic works of Noam Chomsky, and has been greatly influenced by Gregory Bateson, an anthropologist who based his works on communication theory and cybernetics. In its simplest form, NLP can be viewed as the structure of subjective experience (how verbal and non-verbal communications affect the brain) that consists of three premises:

* knowing what you want, that is, having a very clear and concise idea of your outcome for any given situation that you are interested in
* being constantly alert and having all of your senses wide open to notice the results that you are obtaining from the process of pursuing your desired outcome
* being flexible enough to keep changing the strategies of what you are doing until the result that you want is obtained

During the decade of the 1980's, a shift towards New Age religions and fundamentalism also began to take place. Among the most prevalent was the Church Universal and Triumphant that was started by Elizabeth Claire Prophet in 1981. This was really an incarnation of the Summit Lighthouse that had been founded by Mark Prophet, Elizabeth's husband who passed away in 1973. The Church Universal established itself in Montana on a 33,000-acre ranch to offer a community for those

---

346

wishing to escape the "evils" of city life. While most of the inhabitants live the simple life by working on the land, Elizabeth Prophet lives a very luxurious life style with lavish clothes, jewelry and automobiles.

Another very controversial group was initiated by Bhagwan Shree Rajneesh, a charismatic guru and former university professor from India, who established a commune in Antelope, Oregon in 1981 based on esoteric and eclectic Eastern mysticism doctrines of individual devotion and free love. In its heyday, Rajneesh attracted hundreds of followers who seemed to be in a spell cast by his powerful mind. After a series of encounters with the local inhabitants of Oregon and nearby Washington, the self-proclaimed guru who owned 90 Rolls Royce automobiles, was evicted by the United States Justice Department back to Poona, India in 1985. The Bhagwan died in 1991.

In the 1990's, the personal power books (*Awakening The Giant Within, Unlimited Power*) and audio tapes (*Personal Power I and II*) by Anthony Robbins became the rave of America. Tony Robbins is probably the most successful practitioner of NLP techniques, and he has coached thousands of people—including former President William Clinton. Robbins started his own business of motivational seminars after he transformed himself from a "failure" to a very successful entrepreneur. Through the use of techniques such as positive affirmations of life, motivational coaching, "reprogramming" of the brain, and through changing the metaphors for behavior and speech, he has shown others how to achieve their maximum potential and to be congruent in their purposes—and with it, to achieve great success. Robbins has included firewalking[7] sessions in his advanced classes, a technique that he has popularized in the western world. In his latest ventures, Robbins has expanded his work into achieving financial power with courses in Wealth Mastery[8]. At the present time he is acclaimed as probably the

nation's foremost authority on the psychology of peak performance and on using motivational coaching for personal,
professional and organizational turnaround.

As we head into the beginnings of the new millennium, the
current "pop star" of awareness is a reclusive named U.G.
Krishnamurti[9]. He is a "spiritual anarchist" who debunks everyone and everything in the world. His only frame of reference
seems to be to function as a "natural man," free of all societal
and cultural encumbrances that are all based on thought. He
proposes that true happiness lies for each of us as forms of
physiological, unique and individual creations of Nature. But,
if one adheres to his extreme iconoclastic and nihilistic premise,
then the result may be that one is left in a state of complete and
total oblivion. Although he claims to have no message for humanity, and that he has really nothing to say, his words from
recorded conversations have resulted in ten short books so far,
with three of the prominent ones being *Mystique of Enlightenment*, *Thought is Your Enemy* and *Mind is a Myth*.

The Current State

After all of this search for the meaning of life and the place of
human beings in it, where are we now in terms of our spirituality and being? After the evolution of thought of human beings
over the past millennia, what point have we come to collec-
tively as to our existence? Most philosophies don't even touch
on what real freedom is about, and all religions are an enslave-
ment of some sort or another. Almost everything that we have
done in attempts to free ourselves from beliefs, traditions, ritu-
als and ceremonies have not worked, or at least have not
produced any real or viable effects in our collective society. In
this country which—in spite of its failures in human rights,
especially in its treatment of American Indians—offers the greatest of all freedoms that exists on the planet, we still have not
yet achieved a critical mass in terms of "transformation."

As for me (Robert), I will go on searching for anything that provides illumination into the nature of things. As for Espy, she holds that the "Messiah" already came and went and that hardly anyone paid any attention (She is referring to the renowned World Teacher, Jiddu Krishnamurti). She states that if anyone can speak for human beings and explain their behaviors, it is Krishnamurti. His works[10] are the epitome of religious thought, are grounded in clear and concise language, do not involve mysteries, symbolism, dogma or ceremonies, and are removed from all of the traditional trappings that are associated with organized religions. It is her perception that no one even comes close to the clarity of Krishnamurti's teachings.

Endnotes

1   This revivalist movement resulted in the formation of two splinter groups: the Old Lights who subsequently developed into the modern day Unitarians, and the New Lights who evolved into the present day Calvinists.

2   Because of its spiritual as well as political influence, the Great Awakening probably contributed to the revolutionary fervor and the subsequent emancipation of America.

3   Madame Blavatsky was born in Russia in 1831 and came to the United States in 1873. A book by Blavatsky entitled *Isis Unveiled* was published in 1875, a year that saw the creation of Theosophy by Henry Olcott.

4   Henry Olcott was a Freemason who was born in New Jersey in 1832. He was a Union Army officer who attained the rank of Colonel. He was also a member of a three-man board that was appointed to look into the assassination of President Abraham Lincoln in 1865.

5   Edgar Cayce was born on March 18, 1877, on a farm near Hopkinsville, Kentucky. At the age of 6, he began to see visions. At age 13, he experienced a vision of an apparition of a beautiful woman that dramatically altered his life.

He acquired a photographic memory of the content of his schoolbooks—merely by sleeping on them. He later worked in a bookstore, and then as a traveling salesman. He lost his voice for a year due to laryngitis, and was forced to take a photographer's assistant job. During this year, a traveling showman called "Hart, the Laugh King" hypnotized Cayce in an attempt to help him with his chronic laryngitis, but Cayce was still only able to talk in soft whispers—although he was able to speak normally during his "sleep" states. In 1901, Al Layne, a self-educated hypnotist and osteopath, cured Cayce by asking him to explain the problem during one of his trances. Cayce correctly described the problem and prescribed the cure, and miraculously regained his normal voice during waking hours. He also correctly identified Layne's chronic stomach problem, along with the cure. Cayce then continued to do readings for others—some of them remotely, being identified only by name and location. He kept his job as a photographer, married Gertrude Evans in 1903, and established a studio at Bowling Green, Kentucky. He pinpointed a medical problem and cure for Dr. Wesley Ketchum who then promoted Cayce's abilities. When Cayce's second son died after only two months, he fell into a deep depression because he blamed himself for not giving a "reading" in time to save him. But, he came out of it when he gave a correct reading for his wife who was suffering from a severe case of tuberculosis. He then moved to Selma, Alabama to avoid the notoriety and publicity, but upon curing his first son—who had suffered an extensive flash burn injury to the eyes—his fame spread instantly. In 1923, his readings touched on reincarnation and on past lives. In 1925, Cayce and his family moved to Virginia Beach, Virginia, and in 1927, he formed the Association for National Investigators. In 1931, he founded the Association for Research and Enlightenment to investigate and disseminate the information obtained from his readings. Until his death in 1945, he gave over 14,000 readings that covered approximately 10,000 topics He saw psychic visions, developed the ability to see auras, talked about "soul mates," and explored extrasensory perception as he continued to help individuals in improving their relationships and in overcoming life-threatening illnesses. Some of his visions describe future apocalyptic events for the earth and humanity—including World War III—and some of these dwell on past civilizations such as those of Egypt and Atlantis. Growing weak by the strain of doing so many readings, he fell ill in 1944, and died on January 3, 1945 at the age of 67. He never claimed to have any special abilities, and only advised that people focus on their principles to incorporate into their religious life the oneness of all life, including a compassion and tolerance for others.

6   In the early 1980's, the original works of NLP by Grinder and Bandler (*The Structure of Magic, I, The Structure of Magic, II,* and *Frogs Into Princes*) were published. The fundamental logic behind these works was based on George Spencer Brown's book entitled *Laws of Form* that was written in 1969. Much later, Bandler and Grinder fell out of favor with each other and wound up in court—apparently not being able to communicate with each other according to their own model.

7   Firewalking was first introduced into North America by Tolly Burkan. It is a technique of turning fear into power by overcoming these fears through the process of walking on hot coals with one's bare feet without burning the soles.

8   Anthony Robbins was sued in Seattle, Washington—unsuccessfully—by Wade Cook, an originator of many of the techniques and strategies for achieving financial independence. In the suit that was dismissed, Cook claimed that Robbins got the original material for his wealth mastery courses from him.

351

9   Uppaluri Gopala Krishnamurti was born on July 9, 1918, in Masulipatam, India to Brahmin parents. His mother died shortly thereafter, and he was then raised by his grandfather who was a Theosophist. Since his grandfather lived in Madras, India he was exposed to the Theosophical Society in Adyar, India—especially to all of the high-ranking members, including Jiddu Krishnamurti. U.G. enjoyed wealth and a variety of consciousness experiences during his formative years, interacting with many gurus, swamis, mahatmas and all other types of religious persons. He was also exposed to ashrams, retreats and other philosophical places of learning through his grandfather who took him on spiritual pilgrimages all over India. He even studied Yoga under Swami Sivananda in the Himalayas. But, U.G. began to question the whole religious tradition and by the age of 21, he had broken away from practically everything—including his Brahmin tradition. Nevertheless, he was persuaded to visit Ramana Maharshi, one of the great sages of India. Because of this encounter, U.G. changed his direction in life—especially since he now questioned the whole abstract framework of the religious life, including enlightenment. When his grandfather died, U.G. left the University of Madras without graduating. For years he drifted, marrying a beautiful Brahmin woman in 1943, fathering four children in 17 years of marriage, and eventually moving to the United States. He spent all of his inherited fortune, abandoned his family, lost his entire interest in "being somebody," wandered to London, Paris and then Geneva, and was reduced to a subsistence level of existence. Desperate to return to India, he met Valentine de Kerven who was working as a translator at the Indian Consulate office in Geneva, Switzerland who sympathized with him and offered him her residence in Europe in 1963. Since 1957 he had begun to experience recurring and very painful headaches that caused him to experience very powerful

occult phenomena. Finally, on his 49th birthday, while attending a Jiddu Krishnamurti talk in Saanen, Switzerland, U.G. experienced what he called his "calamity." Everything disappeared for him, he lost his quest for enlightenment, and he underwent an extreme physiological change that he described as the "Big Bang" at the level of the cells and chromosomes. He was separated from his thought structure of the past, he experienced a tremendous molecular transformation that altered his eyes and vision, glandular functioning, temperature levels, as well as heartbeat and pulse. He lost his ability to communicate (he has since regained this power), all events in his life became unrelated and he was free from the accumulated knowledge of the world culture. Since that time he has continued to experience physiological changes that have altered his sensitivity to the point where he is affected by everything—including moonlight. He claims to be free of all psychological and spiritual wants, he functions at the primeval level of survival (food, clothing and shelter) and procreation (sex), and he states that what happened to him cannot be used as a model because it is a process that cannot be duplicated. He rejects the whole idea of transformation and claims that no awareness exists through which anyone can change themselves—and that the only freedom that everyone is interested in can only come about at the point of death. He lives in what he calls "a natural state of being," and thus he rejects all spirituality as an invention of the mind. He states that this natural state was achieved through a biological mutation—not a psychological transformation.

10 See, for example, *The Collected Works of J. Krishnamurti*, Volumes I-XVII, Randall/Hunt Publishing Company, 1991.

APPENDIX